THE PROFANE VIRTUES

ALSO BY PETER QUENNELL

Biography

BYRON IN ITALY   BYRON: The Years of Fame

CAROLINE OF ENGLAND: An Augustan Portrait

Fiction

THE PHOENIX-KIND

PETER QUENNELL

THE PROFANE VIRTUES

Four Studies of the
Eighteenth Century

NEW YORK

THE VIKING PRESS

1945

COPYRIGHT 1945 BY PETER QUENNELL

PUBLISHED BY THE VIKING PRESS IN JUNE 1945
PUBLISHED ON THE SAME DAY IN THE DOMINION OF CANADA BY
THE MACMILLAN COMPANY OF CANADA LIMITED

SECOND PRINTING AUGUST 1945

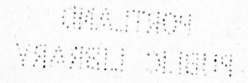

Published in England under the title *Four Portraits*

PRINTED IN U.S.A. BY THE VAIL-BALLOU PRESS

To
ANN O'NEILL

Foreword

———◆———

Among books consulted during the preparation of these portraits, I owe a special debt to the eighteen volumes of the *Private Papers of James Boswell from Malahide Castle,* edited by the late Geoffrey Scott and Professor Pottle of Yale, and privately printed in New York more than a decade ago; the *Letters of James Boswell,* edited by C. B. Tinker; G. M. Young's excellent short life of Gibbon; Gibbon's *Journal,* edited by D. M. Low, and his *Private Letters,* edited by R. E. Prothero; W. L. Cross's admirable biography, *The Life and Times of Laurence Sterne;* and two recent studies of Wilkes, *That Devil Wilkes* by Raymond Postgate and *A Life of John Wilkes* by O. A. Sherrard. I wish also to express my gratitude to Mr. Cyril Connolly for permission to reprint certain passages that have appeared under his editorship in the pages of *Horizon;* to Mr. Leslie Hore-Belisha, who has allowed me to photograph a bust of Laurence Sterne in his collection; and to Sir Edward Marsh, who, with exemplary patience, has helped me correct the proofs.

P. Q.

CONTENTS

ILLUSTRATIONS

JAMES BOSWELL IN 1793
After a drawing by George Dance

JAMES BOSWELL

IN 1763 the war of colonial aggrandisement, waged between France and England since 1756, jolted to an abrupt and (many Englishmen considered) a somewhat ignominious close. England had conquered widely and plundered largely. After the series of humiliating reverses that in every century have been needed to rouse our war-spirit, Pitt with superb self-confidence had assumed direction of affairs; and under his control British fleets and armies had taken Quebec, seized Pondicherry and laid hold of some of France's most lucrative West Indian possessions. It was Pitt who had won the war, but now the old King, second of the Hanoverian line, was dead; and, to open the reign of his grandson George III, an inexperienced but high-minded and obstinate young man who had been reared in strict seclusion by an ambitious German mother, a new minister, Lord Bute, determined to patch up the peace. He accomplished his end by sacrificing—quite unnecessarily, it was believed—a number of important acquisitions. Great Britain would lose her grasp of the Goree slave trade and forgo the sugar, rum and spices of Guadaloupe and Martinique. The City of London, with consequences which must afterwards be described, was moved to indignation; and the City represented a centre of middle-class opposition, resentful of the Court and mistrustful of its ministers, around which many different forces were ready to coalesce. The Peace of Paris was declared to be both unjustifiable and incomprehensible—it resembled the peace of God, said John Wilkes, since it passed all understanding. But, if the peace was unpopular in the City, for a time at least it was welcomed throughout the country. Wars of that age did not fall with a particularly heavy impact upon the civilian population; patriotic animosities were not yet widespread; the learned and fashionable in France and

England continued to correspond. But a European conflict meant expense at home, press-gangs for the very poor, tedious service with the militia for the wealthier classes; and, though the ban on travel was not absolute, it imposed restrictions extremely irksome to liberal and inquiring natures.

The year 1763, then, was one of planning and renewed activity. It was one of those moments, not uncommon in the history of a period, when several gifted human beings happen at the same time to reach a decisive stage, from which their subsequent courses wind away in various directions. A young Englishman left the militia, determined to travel abroad; a young Scotsman had reached London, resolved that he would make his name; a consumptive Yorkshire parson, having won the first rounds in a battle against death, was half-way through the composition of a fantastic masterpiece, which was to introduce a new fashion in style and sentiment; a rakish country gentleman, seizing the opportunity presented by the incompetence of the government and the autocratic intransigeance of their royal master, declared war upon the Court party and thus, almost in spite of himself— for he was neither completely disinterested nor conspicuously upright—fought in the cause of the subject's liberties a fierce and victorious battle. Gibbon, Boswell, Sterne, Wilkes are names that evoke, if not the whole of the eighteenth-century achievement, some important aspects of its fertile and abounding genius. Unlike in many respects, they were alike in their vitality and their versatility, their devotion both to the pleasures of the world and to the satisfactions of the intellect. They lived with gusto; they died regretfully. We place them at once in the architectural setting that belonged to them by right—against sober classical house-fronts or behind the large windows of spaciously proportioned rooms, among equipment as sensible in its grace as it is solid in its structure.

Theirs was an age conscious of its own enlightenment. Already the beginning of the century seemed barbarous and far away. Not only had the period developed a social conscience—tentative attacks were being made upon a dozen public abuses, the filth of the prisons, the plight of debtors, the condition of the poor; but its manners had been purified and its taste refined. During the 'thirties, a diarist had observed that the farm-carts which came up to London frequently travelled home again bearing a cargo of play-books and romances; and since that time the appetite of English readers had grown more and more exacting. Yes, the period, not inaccurately, might be described as an Augustan age; but with the urbanity of its civilisation went an appalling physical harshness. The hand holding a calf-bound volume had been twisted and knobbed by gout; the face under the candle-light was scarred by small-pox. Child after child died before it had left its cradle; women struggled resignedly from one child-birth to the next; the young and hopeful dropped off overnight, a prey to mysterious disorders that the contemporary physician could neither diagnose nor remedy. But these tragedies brought their compensation. Since the accidents of birth and the maladies of childhood then accounted for a large proportion of human off-spring,[1] few men and women reached maturity who did not possess deep reserves of physical and nervous strength. In the debility of such a man as Horace Walpole there was, he himself admitted, something Herculean; and it is, no doubt, this element of intense vitality, hidden beneath the surface, which gives to so many eighteenth-century portraits their vigorous and personal quality. Seldom have human characters been so boldly and frankly displayed; and of the group of Englishmen whose ac-tivities we are observing in the year 1763, each possessed a facial mask modelled on his temperament, shaped by his ruling passion and by the varying experiences through which that passion led him. Across the gulf of almost two hundred years, they continue to command our scrutiny—Sterne's cadaverous simper, Wilkes's crooked grin, half-friendly and half-fiendish, Gibbon's plump impassivity, the sharp nose, pawky smile and restlessly good-humoured features of a self-despising yet self-delighted Boswell.

---

[1] "The death of a new-born child before that of its parents may seem an un-natural but it is strictly a probable event; since of any given number the greater part are extinguished before their ninth year. . . ."—Gibbon: *Autobiography*.

Of the four, it is Gibbon's face that seems to reveal the least, and Boswell's that strikes an observer as the most defenceless. On numerous occasions they met, but seldom with friendly feelings; Gibbon had something about him of the foreign *petit maître,* deliberate in utterance and large in gesture, while Boswell's affectations were so transparent, his vanity was so open and so unguarded, yet the effect of his irrepressible good humour always so disarming, that his friends laughed at him and liked him on one and the same impulse, and learned to like him all the more because they respected him so little. Each was a man bound to an exacting destiny; but whereas Gibbon's destiny moved to a plan—the moment of exaltation among the ruins of the Capitol, when the great master-design suddenly flashed in upon him, came as the reward and consummation of many laborious years—it was the nature of Boswell's genius to work through accident. He was to follow a variety of false trails; even the authentic clue, when he had taken it up, again and again seemed to slip between his fingers; and there were interminable desperate wanderings before he achieved his end. In 1763 his progress was just beginning; as he sat in the back parlour of a London bookseller's shop drinking tea with the proprietor, Tom Davies, and his wife, through the glass door he saw advance a majestic ungainly figure, a huge elderly man in dark ill-fitting clothes, with wrinkled black worsted stockings and a scrubby unpowdered wig. Among the other purposes that Boswell had brought from Scotland was a determination to acquire the friendship of Samuel Johnson (towards whose "inflated Rotundity and tumified Latinity of Diction" he still adopted, nevertheless, a somewhat critical standpoint), and he had begged Davies to present him as soon as the chance occurred. Now Johnson's vast awkward body rolled into the outer shop; and, as Davies announced his arrival with mock-heroic emphasis, Boswell breathlessly prepared himself for the perils of a first encounter.

Almost at once he was felled to the ground by a particularly ferocious snub. But to understand both the temerity that had urged Boswell to take any risk rather than remain ignobly silent, and the elasticity that enabled him, though at the time, as he admits himself, he had been "much mortified," to recover from the blow, it is essential to look back again along the road to Edinburgh and, beyond Edinburgh, to the modest magnificence of the House of Auchinleck. Here, in a mansion "of hewn stone, very stately and durable," which had been built by his father, the successful and famous advocate, not far from the ruins of the ancient castle, James Boswell entered the world in 1740. All his life he was to find in his lineage a source of romantic pleasure; for not only could he claim through his mother, born Euphemia Erskine, a latter-day yet highly gratifying connection with the Earls of Mar and Dundonald, but he had also a remote link with the progeny of Robert Bruce and was directly descended from a certain Thomas Boswell, the first of that name to enjoy the Auchinleck estates, who had fallen with the monarch from whom he had received them on the field of Flodden. Of his origins Boswell often discoursed, and always with complacency. It was something to be the elder son of an old and distinguished line, to have been brought up in the poetic Ayrshire landscape, on the banks of the river Lugar which flowed across the park through a deep and rocky cleft, within sight of the broken battlements of a mediæval stronghold. To these prospects, while he was still a boy, he "appropriated some of the finest passages" of Greek and Latin verse, as he rambled book in hand among crags and pine trees. But, overshadowing Auchinleck, loomed the personality of his father: Lord Auchinleck was the foe of every romantic impulse.

In the parentage of exceptionally gifted men there can be distinguished very often a clash of temperaments; it is as if in the child of an oddly assorted union were embodied some restless longing or unsatisfied aspiration. And Mrs. Boswell, or Lady Auchinleck as her son preferred she should be styled,[1] to judge by the deep affection with which he always regarded her, and his wild grief, years later, when he learned that she had died, was

---

[1] Lord Auchinleck's title, assumed on his elevation to the Bench, was not hereditary. It conferred no rights on his wife or his descendants.

presumably a more affectionate and attractive character than the self-opinionated, grimly sententious law-lord. In her, perhaps, had lain dormant the seeds of the melancholy, poetry and irresponsibility that were to colour Boswell's life. Certainly, Lord Auchinleck's share in the composition of his eldest son is not easy to determine; nor, so long as he survived, did he cease to observe his offspring with a mixture of mild contempt and puzzled exasperation. Himself, he was as grave and steady as James was volatile. For him Scotland provided sufficient scope; when he spoke it was with a rough-edged Lowland accent; he was secure in his possessions and proud of the position he occupied, while James continually hankered after new excitements and dreamed of distant horizons and alien cities, forming all the time fresh projects to baffle and annoy his elders. Not that he was undutiful or emotionally unresponsive; he respected and feared his father, would have liked to love him, and fell in readily enough with the various educational schemes, designed to produce a second successful lawyer, that Lord Auchinleck at one moment or another propounded for his benefit. Thus, after preliminary schooling at Mr. Mundell's academy, James Boswell was entered at the University of Edinburgh, where he began the study of law, and then at Glasgow University, where he studied moral philosophy and rhetoric under Dr. Adam Smith. Undoubtedly he thirsted for knowledge, but in an erratic and irregular fashion. Lord Auchinleck was a scholar, his son a dabbler, with a mind that hovered as delightedly over serious and trifling subjects. Passionate, impetuous, moody and sentimental, he aspired by turn to every virtue and was most vehement in his cultivation of those very moral qualities he was least capable of achieving.

Meanwhile he aspired—that was the important point. And already, during his attendance at Edinburgh University, in Robert Hunter's Greek class, he had discovered the perfect recipient for all his aspirations. William Johnson Temple was both a faithful friend and a remarkably useful foil. Grave, depressed and sober, what had Temple done, to draw down upon himself the fervent protestations of regard and the almost unceasing flow of confidences, enthusiastic, unconventional and many of them (at least from the point of view of the quiet country clergyman into whom Temple afterwards developed) exceedingly improper, with which for the next thirty-seven years Boswell would continue to overwhelm him? But *was* he overwhelmed? May it not have been some essential humourlessness in Temple's character that secured him his position? One supposes that, unlike other acquaintances, he never failed to take Boswell's problems seriously or to be properly impressed by the magnitude of the adventures into which his friend was just about to plunge. Boswell's first recorded letter, written in July 1758, at the age of seventeen years and nine months, exactly sets the tone of their future intercourse. It is at once an appeal for affection and a demand for admiration. Here is the writer, a dutiful son, about to set forth with Lord Auchinleck upon the Northern Circuit, accompanied by "my worthy Mæcenas Sir David Dalrymple," but promising himself to enjoy in Temple's society "all the elegance of friendship" as soon as he returns; and here too is the man of the world and the romantic lover, caught up in a visionary passion for a certain "Miss W——t," "extremely pretty . . . posest of every amiable qualification" and a fortune, moreover, of thirty thousand pounds. "Heaven knows [he subjoins quickly] that sordid motive is farthest from my thoughts." "Miss W——t," nevertheless, was "just such a young lady as I could wish for the partner of my soul," polished but affable in her behaviour, correct in her moral principles and religious opinions, a good singer, a graceful dancer and a clever performer on several different instruments. Really, Temple must not be surprised if his "grave, sedate, philosophick friend, who used to carry it so high, and talk with such a composed indifference of the beauteous sex . . . if this same fellow should all at once, *subito furore abreptus,* commence Don Quixote for his adorable Dulcinea." On the other hand, he admitted easily, it was quite possible he might do nothing of the sort. If she refused him, as seemed not unlikely—in spite of an invitation to drink tea and a request that he would come again "when convenient"—he would "bear it

æquo animo and retire into the calm regions of Philosophy."
Beneath Boswell's capacity for enthusiasm and gift of self-
exposure lurked already certain cool touches of sobering
common sense.

Finally, there emerges the disciple, the born admirer. Though
apparently so self-sufficient, glossy with conceit like some young
and well-groomed animal, even at this period Boswell was discovering that deep dependence, emotional and intellectual,
upon other human beings—a substitute, it may be, for the
emotions he had failed to focus upon his father—which in the
end was to shape his genius and secure his immortality. David
Hume being then in Edinburgh, what more natural than that
Boswell should immediately proceed to pay him his respects?
Neither Hume's seniority—he was forty-seven years old—nor his
celebrity—his great philosophical treatise was far behind him,
and the first volume of the famous *History* had appeared, among
tumultuous acclamation, in 1754—deterred Boswell from this
bold attempt to improve and enlarge his mind. The best-
humoured of philosophers, ponderous, heavy-lidded, apathetic,
Hume seems to have received his talkative admirer with courtesy
and understanding. Boswell, at least, professed himself extremely
satisfied with the results of their encounter; Mr. Hume, he
reported to Temple, was "a most discreet, affable man as ever I
met with, and has really a great deal of learning, and a choice
collection of books. He is indeed an extraordinary man, few
such people are to be met with nowadays. We talk a great deal of
genius, fine language, improving our style, &c., but I am afraid,
sollid learning is much wore out. Mr. Hume, I think, is a very
proper person for a young man to cultivate an acquaintance
with. . . ."

Luckily, perhaps, for his future development, Boswell's dreams
of felicity were not at this time—nor, indeed, were they ever to
become—strictly philosophic. He aspired to knowledge with
fervour, yet passionately loved the world; and the world of Edinburgh, during the period of Boswell's adolescence, included not
only such famous figures as Hume and venerated mentors as Sir

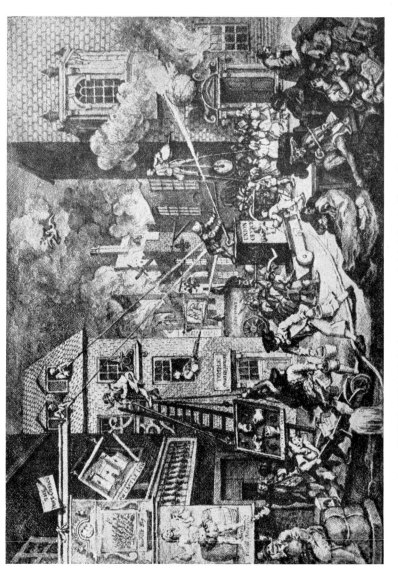

"THE TIMES." A caricature of 1762 by William Hogarth

David Dalrymple (with whom on the Northern Circuit he had the pleasure of bowling in a post-chaise through the length and breadth of Scotland) but "pretty young gentlemen" like his friends Erskine, Hamilton and Hepburn, and James Love (his intermediary in the abortive affair with Miss W——t), poet, dramatist, comedian, theatrical manager and professor of elocution to Edinburgh young ladies, who played Falstaff at Drury Lane and succeeded in borrowing from Boswell a considerable sum of money. Meanwhile, though Edinburgh had its satisfactions, he had begun to think of London. Just as his self-esteem was tempered by a vein of extreme diffidence, arising from the conviction that he was unworthy of his father, and from the mingled fear and respect with which Lord Auchinleck inspired him, so his pride as a man of property and "ancient Scottish laird" was qualified by the visions he had already formed of life beyond the border. In his own view a man of uncommon talents, he was painfully aware that his father was not of the same opinion; and, whereas according to native standards a person of wealth and breeding, he was still haunted by reminders of his provincial background, which clung to him as long and obstinately as traces of his Scottish accent. Beneath his superficial ebullience, he was troubled and ill at ease. Very young men are seldom completely happy: their immediate anxieties are too numerous; the impressions they receive are too violent and too bewildering; they are ringed round by the mystery of an enormous threatening future; but another element increased the difficulty of Boswell's progress. Always waiting to leap out on him and reduce him to subjection lurked an inexplicable, dreadful malady, the disease of hypochondria.

Whence it arose, how it might be contended against, experience never taught him. Called *acedia* by mediæval mystics, *accidie* by French writers of the nineteenth century, "spleen" in the vocabulary of Augustan England, this malady, like a pestilential volcanic vapour, seems to rise through some dark crevice in the human consciousness, some unsuspected fault in our mental stratification, which exhales a stupefying breath of regions below the surface. On Boswell the effects of his distemper were curious and unmistakable. From being the most cheerful of young men, fond of the sound of his own voice, devoted to talk and travel and wine and company, he would decline by rapid stages—though not before his subconscious mind had delivered a preliminary warning—to a condition of apathetic wretchedness in which every sort of obscure anxiety, every form of unanalysable yet inescapable torment, preyed upon his mind. No one, perhaps, should attempt to describe this condition who has not himself endured it—the general impression of personal unreality and individual insignificance that envelops the cowering defenceless ego; the paralysis of the will that cripples all our faculties; the physical lassitude that dims our enjoyment of each separate sense. Such disorders usually make their first attack during early adolescence; and, though Boswell has left no record of when he began to suffer, his equilibrium was already precarious as he approached maturity. But on the credit side were youth, health and an extraordinary greed for life. He did nothing by halves; anything he undertook he usually overdid; and it was with a wild flurry of application that he now threw himself into a course of University lectures, covering subjects as diverse as Scottish jurisprudence and classical antiquities, which lasted from nine in the morning till two in the afternoon. The rest of the day and the whole of the evening were passed in solitary study. Except on Saturdays, he informed Temple, he did not walk out.

His efforts were crowned by matriculation at the University of Glasgow in 1759. It was during the winter months that he received his degree; and as soon as spring arrived, by way of reward, no doubt, for the diligence he had shown in his cultivation of the law, Boswell received his father's permission to visit London. He set forth with the highest hopes and returned with the sharpest regrets. "The wide speculative scene of English ambition" was everything he had imagined, and even more intoxicating. From the society of women of pleasure to the company of men of learning, there was no sort of diversion that London could not provide; and Boswell ran excitedly through the whole scale of its amusements. Escorted by Samuel Derrick, an unsuccessful actor, afterwards Master of Ceremonies at Bath in succession to Richard Nash, he visited the play-houses, where his behaviour in the pit was rowdy and unrestrained, and romped and drank in the stews and coffee-houses of Covent Garden. Lord Eglinton extended his patronage and took him down to Newmarket; and the Duke of York having condescended to smile at his naïve exuberance, Boswell obtained leave to dedicate to him some foolish facetious verses in which he published to the world at large an account of his adventures. It is conceivable, from what we know of Boswell in later life, that the derision of the English Jockey Club, headed by a supercilious Royal Highness, wounded him more deeply than he would have been prepared to admit, and that *The Cub at Newmarket* was an attempt to rationalise his sense of humiliation. But no such temporary reverses could detract from the mood of elated retrospect in which he travelled home to Scotland. At last he had found himself. The immense spectacle of London filled his imagination, its wealth, its noise, its gaiety, its incessantly passing crowds, and, behind them always, the idea of some unknown good waiting to be discovered. He had made the most of his chances of meeting "the great, the gay, and the ingenious"; and there is a possibility that among his other frequentations, he may at this time have obtained entrance to the lodgings of Laurence Sterne, then in London enjoying the advantages of a famous and successful novelist, "five-deep" in dinner parties and importuned by callers.[1] It is stimulating, at all events, to picture their conjunction—Boswell, youthfully corpulent, sanguine and self-assured; Sterne, against the elegant background of his Pall Mall rooms, with his white face, sunken glittering eyes and wasted and shrunken frame, his fund of sentimental quirks and sepulchral improprieties. If Boswell was impressed or appalled, he did not record his feelings.

[1] A strong case for supposing that they may have met, and that Sterne, obliged to listen to *The Cub at Newmarket*, patted Boswell on the shoulder and called him a second Prior, has been made out by Professor Pottle in an article published in *Blackwood's Magazine*, March, 1925.

Temple received no portrait of the author of *Tristram Shandy*. He was treated, however, to an exposition at some length of Boswell's emotions on his return to Edinburgh, with the tumult of Fleet Street still resounding in his ears. Even the satisfaction of being recognised and saluted as "Mr. Boswell of Auchinleck" could not outweigh the disadvantages of life in a provincial city.

Was it to be expected, he demanded of Temple, that he could be content at home? "Yoke a Newmarket courser to a dung-cart, and . . . he'll either caper and kick most confoundedly, or be as stupid and restive as an old battered post-horse. Not one in a hundred can understand this. You do." Temple would also understand the feelings of wild exasperation with which the change in his manner of life continued to inspire him—"a young fellow whose happiness was allways centred in London, who had at last got there, and had begun to taste its delights—who had got his mind filled with the most gay ideas—getting into the Guards, being about Court, enjoying the happiness of the *beau monde* and the company of men of Genius. . . ." The strictness of his father's house and the heavy homeliness of his local acquaintances, expressed in some such well-meant query as: "Will you hae some jeel?" seemed a brutal and gratuitous affront to his new-found sensibility. In the circumstances, perhaps, his behaviour had not been altogether prudent; but "your insinuation about my being *indelicate in the choice of my female friends* [he told Temple], I must own, surprises me a good deal." It was true that, soon after his return from London, he had resorted to "a house of recreation in this place, and catch'd a Tartar"; but, though the effects were unpleasant, the offence was momentary. Nothing was farther from his present intention than ever to fall again.

Meanwhile literature and conviviality helped to relieve and calm him. During his period of Edinburgh apprenticeship Boswell produced an *Elegy on the Death of an Amiable Young Lady*, an *Ode to Tragedy* (published anonymously but dedicated to himself), a song for the "Soapers Club," a Tuesday-night drinking school at which he figured, with some congratulatory verses on his own good nature and inimitable knack of singing comic songs, and a volume of *Letters between the Honourable Andrew Erskine, and James Boswell, Esq.*, which he embellished with a garrulous and lively self-portrait. A man "of ancient family in the West of Scotland, upon which he values himself not a little," he is fond of seeing the world and "has travelled in post-chaises miles without number," "eats of every good dish, especially apple-pie," drinks old hock, "is rather fat than lean, rather short than tall," "has a good manly countenance" and admits himself to be of an amorous disposition. Literary aptitude, however, he had not yet acquired. All Boswell's *juvenilia* seems equally untalented; the discovery of his real talent, as so often happens, had been made almost accidentally, when James Love, who had borrowed money from him and at Edinburgh would appear to have acted as London Falstaff to Boswell's Scottish Prince Henry, suggested that during his expedition with his father in the autumn of 1758 he should keep an "exact journal" of his adventures on the road. It was to be exact—this was the chief requirement—a day-to-day account of the journeyings, doings and sayings of a man who moved, talked, felt, thought in the same rapid, irresistible, rambling *tempo*. Boswell complied; for the actor-manager he had both respect and affection, and regarded him, indeed, as his "second-best friend"—dear Temple, of course, being first and foremost; but this journal, sent sheet by sheet to Love through the post, does not remain among his archives, and the earliest extant proof of the habit of journal-keeping was begun during the harvest-months of 1762. Briefly entitled *Journal of My Jaunt*, it was prefaced by a careful foreword, describing his hopes and intentions.

Few prefaces are more diffident—or more self-confident. Sometimes, he wrote, his narrative would, no doubt, be "trifling and insipid and sometimes stupidly sententious." And yet, he continued, as through the restraining influence of his essential, if somewhat superficial, humility broke the resistless up-surge of Boswell's optimism, "sometimes I would hope it will not be deficient in good sense, and sometimes please with the brilliancy

of its thoughts and the elegant ease of its language. Now and then
it will surprise with an oddity and peculiar turn of humour or a
vivacious wildness of Fancy. . . . At any rate, I have an immediate satisfaction in writing it." Begun during September,
the *Journal* was concluded after a lapse of almost exactly two
months. In themselves the incidents he relates are sufficiently
humdrum. Launched on a round of visits among guileless
country relatives, Boswell jogs quietly from house to house, and
at almost every resting-place he is remarkably well received. The
country cousins are duly dazzled by the "delicious fluency
of declamation" he exhibits for their benefit. They gather
round him, gaping, laughing, wondering: "As a Cousin [Boswell
notes] I had their Affection; as being very clever, their Admiration; and as Mr. Boswell of Auchinleck, their Respect. A noble
Complication."

Evidently (he now understood) he was one of the "finer souls."
A man of the world too, who cut an impressive figure and was
mistaken for an officer—pardonably, since he meant to purchase
a commission in the Guards—when he attended the performance
of a Punch-and-Judy show. There was an amusing adventure (the
prototype of many subsequent adventures and misadventures)
with the pretty servant at an inn, who first refused his advances
and then—as he discovered later, much to his annoyance—tip-
toed into his room and feared to wake him. But these were trifles.
After all, he was still in Scotland. The curtain, raised a few inches
in 1760, to disclose the glories of Newmarket and the joys of
London, glimpses of Court and *beau monde,* the fascinating
half-world of theatres and bagnios and urban coffee-houses, had
swept down again, leaving him isolated in a region behind the
scenes. Could he but approach the footlights, he was sure of
success and applause. No doubt seems to have existed in the
young man's mind that London would receive him as cordially
as he was received in Edinburgh; nor was this prognostication
entirely incorrect. For Boswell was born to achieve his wishes,
yet beneath the hope realised to find always another ambition
mysteriously unfulfilled. He was the type of man (more common

perhaps than might be at first supposed) who is perpetually in search of the "real life" and the real essential personality that continue to elude him. "When I get into the Guards [he wrote] and am in real life . . ." But it is obvious that, had Boswell achieved his military ambition, in the army he would have been as helplessly at the mercy of his sensations and impressions (in which any sense of his own unchangeable identity was temporarily swallowed up) as Boswell at the bar or Boswell the place-hunter. He loved finery, material and intellectual—fine clothes, he said, had upon him the same exhilarating effect as fine music; but, once he had removed the coat and stripped off the waist-coat, he was often unhappy and ill at ease till he had hurried into some new form of spiritual fancy dress. He lived, of course, intensely and excitedly; but he lived through others. Could he never be himself? But what *was* the self? He was everything and nothing, everywhere and nowhere, listening, agreeing, arguing and (whenever it was procurable) gulping down applause. In movement he existed; but left alone he was visited by a dreadful negation of feeling that reduced him to despair. He was no one. There was no real life. He was a wraith, the shadow of a shadow, the echo of a voice he had heard and memorised!

To this sense of insufficiency, and to his desire to establish the outlines of a personality that he recognised in certain moods as weak and vague and hopeless, we owe the patience with which Boswell kept up his journals. Already in 1762, during what he afterwards described as "the most foolish period of my life, viz., twenty-one to twenty-three," he noted that he had "got into an excellent method of taking down conversations" and was developing an extraordinary gift, compact of shrewdness and of naïvety, for resounding the words and reflecting the intelligence of those he admired and loved. In Boswell's existence, to love and admire were complementary functions. And where should he find a worthy object if not in the London crowds? Towards the end of the year 1762 he obtained his father's leave to set out on the Grand Tour, and the curtain began to go up again on the stage he wanted. His newly engaged body-servant rode behind him. Boswell was habited in "a cocked hat, a brown wig, brown coat made in the court fashion, red vest, corduroy small clothes and long military boots."

The Biographer

Destiny is a conception that the historian and the biographer find it equally difficult either to support or to dismiss. In the shaping of the individual human life so large a part is played by hazard, there are so many blind alleys for every direct road; as compared with any single achievement that we can put on record, how gigantic the wasted expenditure of time and energy! Yet, after protracted aimless wanderings, the winged seed may at length come to rest in the soil that can sustain it, the rare insect reach the unpollinated flower that expects its visitation. There are some clues through the labyrinth of trial and error: some travellers, guided by genius, attain to their appointed end. The difficulties, for instance, that had been set in Boswell's way were numerous and formidable. He was young, foolish and obscure; both his principles and his opinions were still extraordinarily unfocused; he had no definite idea of the man he was or the man he wished to be. Johnson, on May 16, 1763, had signalised their first encounter by a deliberate and shattering snub; for although Boswell was quick and nervous, he was extremely tactless, and in his opening gambit he managed to hit upon a pair of topics both of which with Johnson were uncommonly dangerous ground. Rather illogically for a professed Jacobite and a pensioner of Lord Bute—but then, Johnson was very seldom logical—he was convinced that he despised and detested Scotsmen. Secondly, he resented any reference to the success of his former pupil, David Garrick. The dialogue, as Boswell remembered it, proceeded stormily; for, on being introduced, he had begged Davies to say nothing of the place he came from; and when Davies "roguishly" exclaimed: "from Scotland," " 'Mr.

Johnson,' (said I), 'I do indeed come from Scotland, but I cannot help it' "; to which Johnson made the crushing rejoinder: " 'That, Sir, I find, is what a very great many of your countrymen cannot help.' " "This stroke [continues the famous narrative] stunned me a good deal; and when we had sat down, I felt myself not a little embarrassed and apprehensive of what might come next. He then addressed himself to Davies: 'What do you think of Garrick? He has refused me an order for the play for Miss Williams, because he knows the house will be full, and that an order would be worth three shillings.' Eager to take any opening to get into conversation with him, I ventured to say, 'O, Sir, I cannot think Mr. Garrick would grudge such a trifle to you.' 'Sir (said he, with a stern look), I have known David Garrick longer than you have done; and I know no right you have to talk to me on the subject.' "

Yet, curiously enough, a number of the qualities that might have seemed least to Boswell's credit were also the qualities that enabled him to gain his object. Had he been more genuinely and finely sensitive—if his composition had included a smaller share of egotism—he might have slipped out of Johnson's presence and never appeared again. Luckily his self-love was of an exceedingly resilient sort; and, though Johnson was a bully—often a bully in spite of himself—and as such had been quick to pounce on Boswell's deprecatory, "I cannot help it," like a great many bullies he respected courage. Besides, he was an unusually perceptive critic and possessed two sorts of knowledge that formed a remarkable blend of the instinctive and the intellectual. There was the knowledge that he derived from a lifetime's reading; there was also the intuitive, untaught knowledge that, although it may be confirmed by the study of books and sharpened by observation, is in the last resort a natural gift, an attribute with which some men are born and in which others until the day of their death remain totally deficient. He had the knack of appraising almost at a glance the mechanism on which his fellow human beings were constructed. Thus he saw (we may imagine), and he did not dislike, the strange mixture of the bold and the timid, the

cautiously reflective and the foolishly excitable, that constituted
the basis of Boswell's character. He liked the patience and the
good humour with which his talkative Scottish acquaintance
opposed rebuffs. He appreciated the zest, the relish of experience
for experience' sake, with which he himself, in spite of his constitutional melancholy, was so singularly endowed. And when
Boswell presumed to call on him at his chambers at One Inner-
Temple-Lane and opened big eyes at the uncouth apparition of
the slovenly philosopher in his "little old shrivelled unpowdered
wig," rusty brown suit and "black worsted stockings ill drawn
up," Johnson's heart was touched and his sympathies were set in
motion. Once his heart was touched, he felt a debt of moral
gratitude that all the treasures of his intelligence, all the resources of his understanding, were needed to repay.

At their first parting, on 13th June, Johnson observed: "Come
to me as often as you can," and, on 25th June, after Boswell in
his usual effusive manner had produced a brief sketch of his life:
"Give me your hand; I have taken a liking to you." The first
period of their friendship, however, was comparatively brief.
Early in August Boswell, commanded by his father to study law
at Utrecht, left London bound for the Low Countries, Johnson
accompanying him on the stage-coach as far as Harwich. They
dined, prayed together in the parish church, then walked down
to the place of embarkation. As the land receded, Boswell continued to gaze at Johnson. ". . . I kept my eyes upon him for a
considerable time, while he remained rolling his majestic frame
in his usual manner; and at last I perceived him walk back into
the town, and he disappeared."

The years of travel that followed—from August, 1763, to
February, 1766—might be described as the formative period of
Boswell's development, could that fluid character at any time be
looked on as fully formed. They were at least immensely instructive and highly interesting. There was a moment during his stay
in the Low Countries when he descended once again into the hell
of hypochondria, so that the winter months at Utrecht were a
period he remembered always with terror and detestation; but

it is also on record that he attended parties and assemblies, and enjoyed the protection of the Comtesse de Nassau Beverwerd, who showed him the greatest civility and introduced him to a circle of men and women of fashion, which included "so many beautiful and amiable ladies . . . that a quire of paper [he informed a friend] could not contain their praises tho' written by a man of much cooler fancy and a much smaller handwriting than myself." Besides, he had the consolation of meeting the Zuylen family; and Boswell (who had already admitted that he possessed "the most veering amorous affections that I ever knew anybody have") was soon paying his court to Monsieur de Zuylen's delightful daughter, Isabella Agneta Elizabeth, who preferred to be known by her own invented name of Zélide. At a later time she was to become Madame de Charrière and the mistress, as a middle-aged woman, of Benjamin Constant, but at her earliest meeting with Boswell she was a virgin of twenty-three, unmarried, enthusiastic, extremely headstrong, full of emotions with which he sympathised and wild fancies which he deprecated but confessed that he understood.

It was Boswell's first experience of a really superior woman, and almost his last attempt to treat with love on a high emotional level; for after a time the complications it involved proved a little overwhelming. The passionate vitality, which beams from the fine, clear-cut, charming features shown in La Tour's pastel, dazzled but alarmed him; and, though he certainly found her attractive and was gratified to notice that she returned his interest—added to which, her father and mother were uncommonly well disposed—he was alarmed by her excessive energy and disturbed by the heterodox opinions she was continually throwing out. She was almost an infidel; she believed in free love! Her passion for knowledge resembled a raging appetite; and not only did she spend hours of the day and night analysing her own character, both on paper and in conversation with indefatigable ingenuity, but she would leap from bed early in the morning to study conic sections. "Feelings too strong and lively for her mechanism, excessive activity, which lacks a satisfactory object," she declared in a long and careful literary self-portrait—"these are the source of all her ills. With organs less sensitive, Zélide would have had the soul of a great man. . . ." It was evident she had few of the qualities of a complaisant, devoted wife; Boswell, nevertheless, wrote a proposal of marriage, which he dispatched to Monsieur de Zuylen for his approbation and inspection, appending a characteristic note that he would like to preserve a copy, since "I think I shall always be curious to recollect how I wrote on an affair of this consequence." Perhaps he was relieved that she failed to take him up; and his letter, composed in the summer of 1764 when he had already left Utrecht, bound for Switzerland, Italy and the Courts of Germany, is an odd mixture of tenderness and anxious moral reproof, a love letter and a lecture in the same breath, running on page after page with breathless speed and vehemence, as though he wished to bury the whole problem under a weight of words, yet felt reluctant, in the last resort, completely to let it go. He loved her; he did not love her; he believed she loved him. ". . . I am very certain that if we were married together, it would not be long before we should be both very miserable." And so he wishes her rational happiness and hurriedly takes his leave.

Meanwhile he considered Berlin "a most delightful city." But Berlin was only a starting-point; for two and a half years his inveterate inquisitiveness and natural restlessness were to find the exercise they needed in a succession of foreign scenes. His journals became a rag-bag of excited travel-notes. There is something extremely pleasant in the contemplation through his own eyes of the young Scotsman posting about Europe, thrusting his merits on the attention of the great and famous—whom, after the initial shock had subsided, he usually pleased and amused— and laying simultaneous unsuccessful siege to a variety of bewildered foreign noblewomen. Each country seemed to demand of him a separate personal role. By turns he was philosophic, courtly, amorous and devout; and in the preparation of the parts he felt he was required to play he was continually selecting some new human model whom he strove to resemble or sought to outdo. In his journal he made notes of his successive infatuations. "Be Erskine" (he scribbled). "Be Sir D. Dalrymple." "Be Father." "Be Johnson (You resemble him)." "Be Rock of Gibraltar" even! until, suddenly revolting against these extremities of self-imposed servitude, "I must be Mr. Boswell of Auchinleck and no other" (he wrote firmly and defiantly). "Let me make him as perfect as possible."

The last resolution is as characteristic of Boswell's nature as the mood of extravagant humility by which it had been preceded. In his relationships with men older and more celebrated than himself there was always this strange mingling of impudence and self-abasement; and when, dressed in sea-green and silver or in flowered velvet, he had at last wheedled his way into Voltaire's household, he records complacently that he, an unknown Scotsman of twenty-four, and the most famous and the most feared of European writers, had met, talked and argued on perfectly equal terms. Reverential he may have been, but he was not abashed: "For a certain portion of time [he wrote to his old friend, Temple, in a rapturous letter composed at Ferney itself] there was a fair opposition between Voltaire and Boswell. The daring burst of his Ridicule confounded my understanding. . . ." But Boswell's volubility—they were discussing the immortality of the soul and other religious subjects—eventually made its mark: "He went too far. His aged frame trembled beneath him. He cried, 'O I am very sick. My head turns round,' and he let himself gently fall upon an easy-chair. He recovered. I resumed our Conversation, but changed the tone." Voltaire, however, liked him well enough to gratify him before he left the neighbourhood with a letter in English, written in his own small, beautifully rounded hand, rallying the young man on his solemn, self-important concern with "that pretty thing call'd Soul. I do protest you I know nothing of it. Nor wether it is, nor what it is, nor what it shall be. Young scolars, and priests know all that perfectly. For my part I am but a very ignorant fellow."

Rousseau, a far shyer quarry, was also run to earth. He too found Boswell's company somewhat overpowering and fre-

quently begged that his admirer's visits should not be unduly
long; but, like Voltaire, he consented to talk and listen, and was
made the recipient of the traveller's hopes and projects and of the
hundred-and-one phantasmagoric notions that went whirling
through his head. Boswell's originality seems to have struck a
responsive chord; for disdaining to present the letter of introduction with which he had come equipped, he demanded admission
to Rousseau's society as an honour he deserved. Having gained his
point, he appeared on Rousseau's doorstep arrayed in almost
martial splendour; and the Solitary, "a genteel, black man in the
dress of an Armenian," was confronted by Boswell habited in
scarlet and gold-laced coat and waistcoat, boots and buckskin
breeches. "Above all I wore a great coat of Green Camlet lined
with Foxskin fur, with collar and cuffs of the same fur. I held
under my arm a hat with sollid gold lace, at least with the air of
being sollid." The kind of discussion Boswell loved was soon
initiated. Was Rousseau a Christian? he demanded promptly,
and fixed the suspected infidel "with a searching eye." Rousseau's
countenance was "no less animated. Each stood steady and
watched the other's looks. He struck his breast and replied, '*Oui
—je me pique de l'être.*' " Did he approve of polygamy? Boswell
himself had much to say in its favour; but Rousseau demurred at
the heterodox suggestion that Boswell might reasonably be permitted to enjoy a plurality of virgins—thirty was the number he
had first had in mind—get them with child as he liked, and afterwards marry them off to respectable peasant husbands. For Boswell, at all events, these were prodigiously exciting hours; nor,
in his impulsive manner, did he stand on ceremony; and "when
M. Rousseau said what touched me more than ordinary, I seized
his hand, I thumped him on the shoulder. I was without restraint." Finally, on 15th December, after a succession of such
meetings, the moment came for Boswell to say good-bye; and
Rousseau saw him depart, perhaps with relief but also (it would
appear) with something like regret. There were embraces and,
on Boswell's side, there was a sprinkling of tears. "He kist me
several times and held me in his arms with elegant cordiality.

. . ." *"Adieu,"* exclaimed Rousseau, *"vous êtes un galant homme!"* *"Vous avez eu beaucoup de bonté pour moi,"* Boswell replied with fervent gratitude, adding characteristically: *"Je le mérite."*

When he paid his respects to Rousseau and Voltaire, Boswell was, of course, following in the footsteps of many previous travellers. His reception had been flattering; but these encounters had not quite the flavour of singularity that his self-esteem demanded. Italy proved delightful, but deficient in great men; and Italian women, though highly seductive, were rather less accommodating than he had at first expected. Why not Corsica then? He had long been anxious to visit the island kingdom; and on 28th September, 1765, leaving behind him "sweet Siena" and an Italian woman of quality with whom he was carrying on a passionate, entertaining but, from the practical point of view, somewhat disappointing and inconclusive correspondence, he reached Leghorn, whence he set sail on 11th October. At this stage the traveller's private papers add very little to the narrative of the published *Tour*. During the voyage he "threw up," amused himself with his flute and was tormented by "muschettoes and other vermin." But the journal stops short when he lands in Corsica and begins again, when having traversed the island and spent a few days in the company of General Paoli, leader of the Corsican insurgents against the French and Genoese—a man after Boswell's own heart, that is to say, such a man as he could never hope to be, resolute, manly, uncomplicated, independent—he left on 20th November and was driven by foul weather to take refuge on the rocky island of Capraja. There he remained for more than a week, a prey to all the vicissitudes of his capricious humour, now peevish, now downcast, now —as the result of a "too hearty dinner"—strolling about "full of wild and curious" fancies. The end of the month found him at Genoa; and from Genoa he at last turned his face in the direction of Great Britain.

His account of his journey home provides several instructive episodes. At his heels he dragged the undisciplined and ill-

conditioned watch-dog with which Paoli had presented him. A
Swiss servant—hardly less troublesome—was his only other companion; and with this servant, named Jacob, he was perpetually
disputing. Boswell's treatment of Jacob was extremely characteristic. Though he prided himself on being a man of birth and
fashion, he could not refrain—such was his native curiosity—
from conduct that towards a servant he felt to be improper. Why
was his valet so insubordinate? The course that he adopted was
to ask the valet himself. And Jacob, when pressed, returned a
candid answer. He could see at once, he replied, that Monsieur
had not received a proper education. *"Il n'a pas les manières d'un
Seigneur. Il a le coeur trop ouvert."* So struck was Boswell by the
justice of this statement that he forgot to be annoyed. Of course,
he replied, it was quite true that he had been two-and-twenty
before he had had his own servant, to which Jacob responded
that in his opinion the son of a gentleman should learn the art of
managing a servant while he was still young. *"Monsieur force un
Domestique de parler d'une manière qu'il ne doit pas, parce que
Monsieur le tourmente en le questionnant. Il voudroit savoir
tout au fond. . . ."* "The fellow [Boswell concludes] talked with
so much good sense, so much truth . . . that upon my word I
admired him; I, however, hoped that a few years more would
temper all that impetuosity and remove all that weakness which
now render me inconstant and capricious."

Arrived in Paris—after conversations with the galley-slaves of
Marseilles and, at Avignon, with the exiled Jacobite gentry—
Boswell made haste to leave cards on Horace Walpole, who
received him in a polite but distant fashion, and visited Wilkes
whose hospitality was far less guarded. Then, as he sat one day in
Wilkes's apartment looking through the newspapers, he read in
the *St. James's Chronicle* of his mother's death. At first he was
completely stunned. He respected and feared Lord Auchinleck,
but he loved his mother; and a wave of regret and sorrow
promptly overwhelmed him. For a time he rallied and hurried
off to the Dutch Ambassador's. But, no sooner was dinner done,
than the poignancy of his grief once again grew insupportable

and "as in a fever" he rushed to a brothel he had already visited. Next day his mood was calm and sentimental. He prayed to his mother's spirit, like a Catholic to his saint, and soothed his melancholy by singing Italian airs. . . . All this is noted in his *Journal* without a shadow of self-consciousness; for, though he was delighted to exhibit his strong and fluent emotions, Boswell had little of the affectation of the contemporary Man of Feeling, and was too honest a self-observer to attempt to magnify their spell. That filial sorrow should drive him headlong into sensual dissipation was a fact that he observed with interest and with some surprise. His thirst for information—that passion to *savoir tout au fond* which Jacob had observed—made him the candid recorder of happenings he did not attempt to justify.

"Mr. Boswell of Auchinleck" had set out from Harwich—it was "Corsica Boswell" who returned to England. The horizons of the Augustan Age were still agreeably limited. Whole reputations might be founded on some solitary achievement—a single published tour or a clever occasional essay; and in the small homogeneous society through which he moved, the adventurer, once his reputation had been established, found a multitude of appreciative acquaintances to recognize and welcome him. How much he owed to Corsica, Boswell himself admitted. It was wonderful, he told Paoli at a later period, what the island had done for him, "how far I got in the world through having been there. I had got upon a rock in Corsica and jumped into the middle of life." Yes, temporarily at least, the feeling of personal unreality by which he had been haunted had almost disappeared. He stood firm. He looked calmly out at the London prospect; and London seemed to have shrunk in size and to have lost something of that peculiar magnetic charm which, during his first visits, had troubled and obsessed him. Even Johnson "for some minutes" seemed "not so immense as before"; while Rousseau, who, having been expelled from Motiers by the Bernese government, had fled to England at Hume's suggestion a few weeks earlier, struck the returned traveller as decayed and elderly. But then, with re-gard to Rousseau, Boswell's ticklish conscience may well have nagged him; for it had been his privilege to act as escort to Thérèse le Vasseur, and on the journey from Paris to London he had seduced, or had been seduced by, the middle-aged virago with whom Rousseau spent his life—an adventure both unedifying and, as it turned out, unnerving and disconcerting, since "Mademoiselle," far from paying the tribute he expected to his youth and vigour, had informed him that she found his attentions extremely clumsy; and Boswell, offered instruction in the art of love-making, had been obliged to rush from the room and drain a bottle of wine secreted against emergencies, before he could summon up sufficient courage to embark on a preliminary lesson.

Luckily, it had never been Boswell's way to exaggerate his setbacks. And, compared with the numerous triumphs of the last two years, even the misery he had endured at Utrecht and the inexplicably cool reception he had found at Turin, the snubs or provocations of Italian countesses and the churlish behaviour of his valet Jacob, finally the partial fiasco with Mademoiselle le Vasseur, were fleeting shadows on a career of glorious self-fulfilment. His enthusiasm and self-confidence were again unlimited; and shortly after his return to England the same wave of energy that had brought him back from Corsica carried him into the presence of one of the greatest British statesmen, to whom Paoli had requested that he would bear a message. For this interview Boswell assumed, not his scarlet-and-gold, his green-and-silver or his flowered velvet suit, but the complete apparatus of a native Corsican chief, with stiletto and pistol, long gaiters and military cap completed by a tuft of cock's feathers. The elder Pitt failed to repress a smile, but was courteous and condescending. Pinned to his chair by an attack of gout, "a tall man in black cloaths, with a white night cap and his foot all wrapped up in flannel, and on a Gout Stool," he gravely questioned Boswell concerning the state of Corsica, but observed that, although for the moment he was out of office, as a Member of the Privy Council he could not properly receive messages from foreign statesmen, no matter how worthy the cause they represented. Boswell spoke of Paoli's high regard for Mr. Pitt's character and dwelt on his disappointment at not receiving a reply to a communication he had previously addressed to him, drawing from Pitt a reply in his noblest rhetorical style: "Sir, I should be sorry that in any corner of the world, however distant or however small, it should be suspected that I could ever be indifferent to the cause of liberty." With this sonorous recollection, and with the knowledge that he had taken a permanent place in Johnson's friendship—had not this venerable friend, at their first meeting, seized him in his arms and hugged him "like a sack"?—Boswell during the late spring made ready to return to Edinburgh.

The mood in which he returned was somewhat apprehensive. Months earlier, beneath an enervating southern sky, at a time when he "did not THINK, but leap'd the ditches of life," he had considered how very pleasant was his existence, so long as he "followed purely the inclination of each moment without any manner of restraint," but had reflected sadly that "this could not last"; for Scotland, across the breadth of Europe, "stared me full in the face." Yet, once confronted, just as London had appeared somewhat less attractive, so Edinburgh loomed less austere and less forbidding. Self-indulgence, strangely enough, seemed positively to have strengthened his powers of application, and into the next seven or eight months he managed to cram such a variety of work and pleasure that, looking back, he was bewildered and delighted by the distance he had travelled. "What strength of mind you have had! . . ." he apostrophised himself admiringly. He had been called to the Scottish bar, he had worked and enjoyed his work, preparing briefs, delivering pleas, arguing and pamphleteering on the subject of a then-famous Scottish lawsuit, till even his father, the dour law-lord, had "ceas'd to treat him like a boy." Simultaneously he had been involved in an exciting escapade, had had his "soul ravaged by passion," been "in torment with jealousy" and "felt like Mark Anthony, quite given up to violent love." His mistress, a certain Mrs. Dodds, otherwise "Circe," "Lais," and "the Moffat woman," had had many previous lovers. She was mercenary, "ill-bred, quite a rompish girl," but "very handsome, very lively and admirably formed for amorous dalliance." Was he right or was he wrong, he demanded of his friend and counsellor, the Reverend William Temple, in what he himself agreed to be one of the oddest letters ever written to a country clergyman. Such a liaison might be perilous; but (he protested vehemently) there were worse alternatives. "Can I do better than keep a dear infidel for my hours of Paphian bliss?"

The bliss he experienced, however, was of an extremely tempestuous sort. There were moments when his feverish imagination presented him with such vivid and horrifying glimpses of her previous admirers "in actual enjoyment" of Mrs. Dodds as to leave him not only distraught but utterly unmanned. Furious, he would curse her for a "lewd minx." Then, suddenly, "her eyes look'd like precious stones," and he collapsed in a transport of love and confidence. Yet, even in the crisis of his passion, he did not cease to reflect dispassionately on the nature of the sentiment, observing "how lightly passions appear to those not immediately affected by them" and musing that "even to yourself will this afterwards seem light." Amid these emotional tempests—disturbing, of course, but not altogether unsatisfying—Boswell continued to revolve for several months until family duties called him home to Auchinleck. There the passion that had preoccupied him gradually dwindled away; and with astonishment he asked himself if it were "really true that a Man of such variety of Genius, who has seen so much, who is in constant friendship with General Paoli . . . was all last winter the slave of a woman without one elegant quality?" Meanwhile, as the image of the rompish girl receded, he began to pay his court to his cousin, Miss Blair, a substantial Lowland heiress, who first encouraged, then eluded him and finally aroused his resentment by permitting the advances of a rich East-India merchant. But Boswell's chagrin was neither serious nor protracted; and, when he left Auchinleck and returned to Edinburgh, Mrs. Dodds (who during the interval had borne him an illegitimate child) once again figures in his private journal, till she drops quietly out of the record, never to re-emerge.

Such was the usual course of Boswell's passions. Varying in their scope from chimerical aspirations for attractive heiresses, or for any young woman who sat next to him at dinner, to lively infatuations for delightful, deceptive creatures of the type of Mrs. Dodds, they boiled up quickly but, after a period of intense excitement, died down as abruptly. His love-affairs were seldom edifying and often commonplace; but never quite commonplace was the effect they produced on Boswell's imagination or the response that they evoked from his peculiar sensibility. Behind the amorist lurked always the literary analyst. To Boswell his sensations and impressions were always new and strange. How odd were the interactions of vice and virtue! How curious to observe that, after some particularly acute crisis of sensual satisfaction, one felt not only a calmer and stronger, but also a more virtuous man! Thus, finding an uncommon degree of contentment in the embraces of an Edinburgh strumpet named Jenny Kinnaird, he "very philosophically reasoned that there was to me so much virtue mixed with licentious love that perhaps I might be privileged. For it made me humane, polite, generous." Yet, though he adored variety, he aspired to constancy. The least consistent and the least circumspect of human beings—a man, indeed, whose chief value consisted in the protean quality of his intelligence and the extreme facility with which he plunged into the lives of others—he had set himself an ideal of complete composure. By disposition exceedingly active, except for those periods when a fit of hypochondria temporarily deprived him of the power to act and enjoy—was action really necessary to human happiness, he would demand of his acquaintances. Dr. Blair considered it might be. Boswell gave enthusiastic support to the contrary opinion: "You said yes, but only as a remedy to distempered minds. The sound and perfect human being can sit under a spreading tree like the Spaniard, playing on his guitar, his mistress by him, and glowing with gratitude to his God. Music, Love, adoration! There is a Soul!"

Meanwhile, his travels abroad had paid him a literary dividend. The *Account of Corsica*, published during February, 1768, created considerable stir even as far afield as Paris, where Madame du Deffand spoke of it appreciatively to Horace Walpole; and on 17th March the author set out for London. He was uneasy, however, "at leaving Mary." To this "pretty, lively little girl," another Jenny Kinnaird, Boswell had recently become much attached. Before he left, he deposited with her as many guineas as she assured him she could live upon till his return; but then, with a touch of romantic inquisitiveness, inspired, it would seem, by one of Cervantes' long short-stories embodied in *Don Quixote*, he persuaded two separate friends "to promise to go to her and offer a high bribe to break her engagement to me, and to write to me what she did." What, in fact, Mary did is not recorded. As Boswell hurried excitedly down the Great North Road, any hopes he had founded on her fidelity appear to have been soon forgotten, and he lost himself in an agreeable reverie concerning his present and past life. Today (he observed) he felt "quite strong." Indecision had vanished, and with it the exaggerated instability, emotional and intellectual, that at one period had tormented him. Then his mind might have been compared to "a lodging house for all ideas who chose to put up there." And the lodgers had been of every description. Some (he continued), gentlemen of the law, had paid him handsomely. Divines of every sort had visited him and troubled his peace of spirit—Presbyterian Ministers, who made him melancholy; Methodists, whose eloquence had moved his feelings; Deists, whose scepticism perpetually alarmed him; Romish clergy, who filled his imagination with solemn splendour and who, though their movable ornaments had since been carried away, "drew some pictures upon my walls with such deep strokes" that traces of their tenancy were still discernible. Moreover, he was obliged to admit, there had been raffish company, "women of the town" and "ladies of abandoned manners. But I am resolved that by degrees there shall be only decent people and innocent gay lodgers." A certain bustle and confusion were still to be expected; but his mind was now "a house where, though the street rooms and the upper floors are open to strangers, yet there is allways a settled family in the back parlour . . . and this family can judge of the ideas which come to lodge."

Neither this resolve, nor his determination to resemble an impassive Spaniard, who glowed with gratitude to the Deity and worshipped a single mistress, was fully reflected in the adventures of the next few weeks. For no sooner had Boswell arrived in London, on 22nd March, taken lodgings in Half Moon Street and unpacked his trunk, than he "sallied forth like a roaring Lion after girls." Next day he witnessed an execution—a type of spectacle that, in common with George Selwyn, he much appreciated—noticed that the first malefactor was deathly pale and watched the second, a prim Quakerish middle-aged man, composedly eat a sweet orange with the rope around his neck while he listened to the prayers of the Newgate ordinary. Johnson, he had learned, was staying in Oxford; and on the 26th, in a crowded stage-coach, along roads that resounded with "Wilkes and Liberty" (a battle-cry that, together with *"No. 45,"* was chalked on the panels of every passing carriage), he drove down to the citadel of High Church Toryism. Like many other apparently tactless men, he had the gift of the right gesture. And nothing could have been better calculated to appeal to Johnson than the eagerness with which Boswell had rushed to meet him. " 'What,' said he, 'did you come here on purpose?' 'Yes, indeed,' said I. This gave him high satisfaction"; with the result that he showed a flattering interest in Boswell's stories and professed surprise at his account of the sums he had already gained by his practice of the law. "He grumbled and laughed and was wonderfully pleased. 'What, Bosy? two hundred pounds! A great deal.' "

Such was the effervescence of Boswell's feelings that it is unusually difficult during the months that followed to chronicle his progress. Even the fact that he paid a heavy penalty for his usual practice of "blending philosophy and raking," and was confined to bed under the care of a surgeon (where he groaned over his criminal folly yet looked forward "with great complacency on the sobriety, the healthfulness, and the worth of my future life") did not check the overflow of exuberant high-spirits. Zélide had begun to write again; and there were moments when he felt that his "charming Dutchwoman" must at any cost of security or propriety be secured as Mrs. Boswell; ". . . . Upon my soul, Temple, I must have her. She is so sensible, so accomplished, and knows me so well and likes me so much, that I do not see how I can be unhappy with her." Besides, his reception in London was extremely flattering; he was now "really the *Great Man*," and Hume, Benjamin Franklin, Johnson, Garrick and many other *literati* all visited him in Half Moon Street and enjoyed his excellent claret. During August he was suddenly transported by a new and absorbing passion. As he contemplated the attractions of Miss Mary Ann Boyd, "*La Belle Irlandoise* . . . just sixteen, formed like a Grecian nymph, with the sweetest countenance, full of sensibility, accomplished, with a Dublin education, always half the year in the north of Ireland, her father a counsellor of law, with an estate of £1000 a year, and above £10,000 in ready money," he congratulated himself on having escaped from "the insensible Miss Blair and the furious Zélide. . . ." At the risk of hopelessly confusing the issue, it must be admitted that, once Boswell had returned to Edinburgh, both Miss Blair and "the Moffat woman" recaptured their previous hold. Nevertheless, during the spring of 1769, he left Scotland for Ireland, apparently still in pursuit of the sixteen-year-old Irish nymph, to dance jigs, dine with the gentry, and raise funds and whip up enthusiasm for the cause of the Corsican patriots. Accompanying him on this expedition, was a cousin, Margaret Montgomerie, a quiet, sympathetic, understanding, tender-hearted young woman whom he had long known and respected and had for some time past chosen as "the constant, yet prudent and delicate *confidante* of all my *égarements du coeur et de l'esprit.*" Visions of felicity with his Irish nymph failed somehow to materialise; but, during the course of his Irish tour, Miss Montgomerie's companionship grew more and more attractive. She pardoned him when he got drunk; she listened gravely to his excited outpourings when he was talkative but sober; when he grew melancholy, as often happened, she supplied just the consolation and support he needed. She was his "my valuable friend," "my own affectionate friend," "allways my friend and comforter." Besides, it was clear that she loved him in her sober and steady fashion—not as Zélide had perhaps loved him in her wayward exacting style, but with a love that remained comfortably clear and even, that would never blaze into romantic fury or subside into disgusted satiety or conventional indifference. He warmed his hands at her affection; presently it became obvious to him that he must be in love himself. Of course, he loved his cousin! If she refused him, he would leave the kingdom and take refuge (he declared) among the wild Indians of America. But Margaret Montgomerie did not refuse him; and, when they returned to England, a "solemn engagement" was registered on August 7, 1769. A meritorious step; and Boswell resolved it should have momentous moral consequences; in spite of which, a day later, he was obliged to record that he had become "outrageously jovial and intoxicated myself terribly and was absurd and played at Brag and was quarrelsom," exactly as he might have done a week or a year before.

Like so many men born without domestic virtues, Boswell was evidently foredoomed to tumble into marriage. The problem had always fascinated him. "Must the proud Boswell [he would inquire] yield to a tender inclination? Must he in the strength and vigour of his youth resign his liberty for life to one Woman?" If his destiny would have it so, let him at least "chuse a healthy, chearful woman of rank and fortune." Margaret Montgomerie was still at the time a passably healthy woman and, if not remarkably cheerful—as her marriage developed, her reasons for being high-spirited grew less and less—there is no doubt that she proved, on the whole, extraordinarily long-suffering; but her rank in life was modest and the fortune that she brought to her husband was not at all impressive. Boswell knew what he had to offer; and during the period of their engagement his feelings seem to have been divided between real gratitude to Miss Montgomerie and a sense of the various benefits, social, financial and physical, that he conferred by agreeing to become her husband. Such a moment of swelling self-esteem overtook him on the occasion of the Shakespeare Jubilee when, as he prepared for the Masquerade, which was to crown Garrick's elaborate but ill-managed celebrations, he gazed into the looking-glass and there saw reflected a sanguine, solid figure, dressed in the Corsican costume which had already diverted Pitt, equipped with musket, dagger and pistols, the newly designed cap bearing a gold-embroidered device: *Viva la Libertà*.[1] His visit to Stratford, whither he had travelled from London, having missed Johnson whom the Thrales had carried off to Brighton, was to be a last glorious fling before he settled down to matrimony. Bands were playing, choruses chanting; fashionable acquaintances were crowded in damp marquees; rain fell, fireworks sputtered, celebrated actors delivered speeches, and there were beautiful actresses, including Mrs. Baddeley of Drury Lane, for Boswell to distinguish by marked, admiring stares. But at the Masquerade it was the armed and feathered Corsican (so he himself afterwards recorded) who monopolised the lime-light. He had arrived, carrying a staff "with a bird finely carved upon it, emblematical of the sweet Bard of Avon"—to some the bird suggested a serpent, to others a kind of duck—and a poem he intended to recite in praise of his Corsican friends. Though "prevented by the crowd" from embarking on a recitation, he was convinced that his manœuvre, both from the patriotic and the personal point of view, had succeeded in its object, and returned to London, well satisfied, before the celebrations at Stratford had drawn to a dripping close. He was anxious to see Johnson, but for the moment perhaps even more anxious to welcome General Paoli. The patriots had at length succumbed to the weight of French aggression; their leader was now in exile; and Boswell, as a personal friend and the authority *par excellence* on the affairs of Corsica, must naturally be among the first Englishmen who arrived to greet him. It was a bold stroke to arrange that he should dine

---

[1] There is no foundation for the story that Boswell appeared wearing a ticket inscribed "Corsica Boswell" fastened to his cap; it is derived from reports of the theatrical representation of the Masquerade afterwards staged by Foote in London.

with Johnson, whose references to the Corsican struggle had sometimes been impatient; but, as often happened, Boswell's temerity secured him a glowing reward. His two revered mentors, personifications of manly courage and of exalted moral wisdom, delighted their admirer by paying a dignified tribute to one another's greatness. The General was superbly courteous, and Johnson informed Boswell that Paoli had "the loftiest port" of any human being he had yet encountered.

During November Boswell reluctantly set out for Scotland; and towards the end of that month he was married to Margaret Montgomerie, on the same day that his father, Lord Auchinleck, married for the second time. Of Mrs. Boswell Johnson was afterwards to write, with somewhat cruel concision, that she had "the mien and manner of a gentlewoman; and such a person and mind as could not be in any place either admired or condemned. She is in a proper degree inferior to her husband; she cannot rival him; nor can he ever be ashamed of her." To her credit, she seems never to have been ashamed of Boswell; but she found his literary friends extremely hard to bear and had "not a spark of feudal enthusiasm"—her attitude towards his pedigree was lamentably matter-of-fact. A limited and unremarkable character, she yet displayed, so far as Boswell was concerned, remarkable devotion and a degree, no less remarkable, of human understanding. Seven children were born to the couple, of whom five grew up; and Boswell, in his erratic way, was an exceedingly affectionate parent. The main chapter of his existence was now fully and fairly begun. That much of its interest was derived from Johnson, and that the magnificent portrait he gave to the world in 1791 provided him with the spiritual justification he had long and vainly sought, are facts generally accepted since his book appeared. But that Johnson was by no means the *whole* of Boswell's life is a point of which recent biographers have been at some pains to remind us. Throughout two decades Boswell was Johnson's devoted follower; but it has been calculated that, during that space of time, there were only eight hundred and seventy days on which their physical circumstances would have allowed a meeting,[1] and on many of those days there is not the smallest evidence that they actually met and talked. At three separate junctures they were separated for a period of over two years. Each had his habits and his round of pleasures, Johnson his intimacy with Mrs. Thrale, that strange and touching *amitié amoureuse* which closed in sudden bitterness when Mrs. Thrale remarried; Boswell, his career as a Scottish advocate, his life as a husband and father, the hundred-and-one remarkable episodes in which his curiosity, his sensuality and his unconquerable restlessness successively involved him. Yet Johnson remained a fixed star in his admirer's universe—the guardian of moral law, the embodiment of conscience, treated by him, nevertheless, as consciences are sometimes treated, with regard and awe, into which a good deal of evasion, not to say duplicity, very often entered. If his venerable friend *could* be persuaded to supply the right excuse for something that Boswell was privately determined to do, the disciple enjoyed the consciousness of being the happiest and best of men. Could he, for example, but induce Johnson to say a word, founded on classical or Biblical texts, for the polygamy that Boswell felt more and more inclined to practise! . . . But Johnson showed an uncommon aptitude for brushing aside the various moral sophistries in which Boswell, at one time or another, endeavoured to engage him; and the younger man went his own way, uncomforted but undeterred.

Just how much one knew of the other we can never exactly tell. In Johnson's life there were dark tracts—abysses of gloom and nervous fear and superstitious horror—that Boswell merely skirted (though Mrs. Thrale had many terrifying glimpses into the depths of Johnson's desperation); while in Boswell's there were large territories of adventure and experience that, so far as Johnson was concerned, he left prudently undescribed. Few associations have been more productive; yet from its history, as from the history of most friendships and almost every love-affair, emerge the essential separateness and solitariness of individual

---

[1] See *James Boswell* by C. E. Vulliamy, 1932.

human beings. Boswell could console Johnson, but he could not help him; Johnson's affection provided Boswell with the support he needed, but the good advice he so often gave was very rarely taken and, had it been taken, we may doubt if it would have conduced to Boswell's ultimate advantage. Suppose that he had stayed at Auchinleck and minded his estate, that he had remained sensibly in Edinburgh and laboured in the Scottish courts—he would have kept out of debt, pleased Mrs. Boswell, brought up his five legitimate children in comfort and security; but he would at the same time have been untrue to that mysterious guiding spirit which, though it ruined his health, impaired his fortune and destroyed his happiness, at last produced the justification he had always been in search of—"my Magnum Opus" or (as he described it prophetically to William Temple) "without exception, the most entertaining book you ever read."

Luckily, the demands of his temperament—expressed as a perpetual hankering for life in London—were too strong to be resisted. From November, 1769, till February, 1772, he stuck more or less contentedly to his work in Edinburgh. Then a lawsuit provided the excuse for making the journey south; he wrote at once to Johnson, receiving in reply a warmly affectionate welcome; and during the early spring Boswell was admitted to the house in Johnson's Court, Fleet Street, heard the great man's weighty footsteps as he ascended the wooden stairs, and saw him appear upon the threshold in "an old purple cloth suit, and a large whitish wig." His greeting was cordial, and he embraced Boswell "with a robust sincerity of friendship," immediately bade him sit down and began to talk at length. Johnson was now sixty-three, still basking in the Indian summer of that long platonic love affair which (as he was afterwards to write in the letter that broke it off) "soothed twenty years of a life radically wretched." Since 1766 he had tasted domestic happiness. During the autumn months of 1765, when Boswell was still gallivanting light-heartedly to and fro among the courts of Europe, Johnson had sunk into the lowest depths of nervous and moral gloom. His own household, distracted by the squabbles that frequently broke out between his various thankless pensioners, Robert Levett, blind, ill-tempered Mrs. Williams and the other pathetic waifs he provided with bed and board, was dreary and uncomfortable, and the obscurity that filled his mind seemed to grow more and more oppressive. Thick and fast, the phantoms continued to crowd in—the horror of death, the dread of damnation, the pangs of a guilty conscience which laboured under some inexplicable but inescapable load. Then Arthur Murphy—"dear Mur"—suggested one day that they should dine at Streatham; he met the stolid good-natured brewer and the brewer's exuberant wife; and henceforward, though the gloom was never completely dissipated, certain rays penetrated the darkness, and with the Thrales he found a refuge from his worst prevailing fears. Gradually, he was calmed, domesticated, civilised. But it was no easy task that Mrs. Thrale had undertaken. His moods were overbearing, his habits unattractive; he was "more beastly in dress and person [observed a fastidious lady] than anything I ever beheld. He feeds nastily and ferociously, and eats quantities most unthankfully." His new devotee had both the wit to discern his genius—and to appreciate some of the complexities that lay beneath it—and sufficient strength of mind to withstand the shock of his outrageous manners. As she once wrote in an imaginary dialogue, "Mrs. Thrale, among her other Qualifications, had prodigious strong nerves—and that's an admirable Quality for a Friend of Dr. Johnson's." At times she could be submissive, but she was hard to browbeat. Besides, she enjoyed talking as much as he did himself and would converse far into the small hours and pour incessant cups of tea from a four-quart tea-pot, thus sparing him the exquisite anguish of his solitary midnight musings. "I love to hear . . . my mistress talk," Johnson exclaimed, "for when she talks, ye gods! how she will talk." A mentor to be looked up to—paternal, omniscient, grave, exacting—he was also a dependent, by whom she was loved and needed. Below the rugged exterior she caught strange glimpses of his amazing sensitiveness. To her and to her alone he had laid bare his heart, and had divulged the "Secret far dearer to him than Life" (which may or may not have had to do with fear he was going, or had already gone, mad); and it was to Hester Thrale, when black depression made him incapable of leaving his room, that he wrote cryptic notes in French, imploring her help and counsel.

Johnson, maybe, had not yet guessed how profound was his dependence. Boswell, certainly, did not divine that he was facing a serious rival. The Thrales were a pleasant family, the hospitable inhabitants of a luxurious country house. He liked and admired Mrs. Thrale; it was not till later that he learned to regard her with furious hatred, as Johnson's traducer and his own inveterate foe. Yet Mrs. Thrale's impressions of the great man's personality were very far from worthless. It is true that, when compiling her memoirs, she expanded, condensed or rearranged the fragments so as to produce a more amusing or a more distinct effect; but Boswell, composing his *Life*, was at least as uninhibited. Only in one respect do they differ immensely: Mrs. Thrale's narrative is coloured by the bitterness and misunderstanding that followed her romantic marriage to Gabriel Mario Piozzi, whereas Boswell's is a work of love from the first to the last line. Many pious memorials make tedious reading; if Boswell's record, for so long a period as he had Johnson beneath his eyes, is always penetrating and vivid, it is because, besides loving, he had the power of seeing, and with the gift of veneration a talent for observation; because he was at the same time an exceedingly passionate and an oddly dispassionate character. Who could hope to improve on the story of his numerous meetings with Johnson during the next decade as he himself has told it? That part of his career must be supplied from the book he wrote —with the reservation that, although he saw much, he did not see all; and that there are aspects of Johnson's temperament which must be supplied from other sources, from the reminiscences of Mrs. Thrale, who had opportunities and personal privileges that Boswell lacked, or from the prim, perspicacious jottings of Miss Fanny Burney. But Boswell's portrait, undoubtedly, is the largest and most impressive, for none other unites so many traits of the physical and spiritual man; Johnson

roaring for a clean shirt to Barber his Negro servant; on Easter
Sunday, in a solemnly devotional mood, turning over the pages
of a Greek New Testament, while his features twitched and
grimaced and his heavy lips emitted a mysterious muttering
sound; or in his various conversational phases, now shedding
broad beams of classical common sense, now thundering, like an
angry and bigoted Jehovah, from his cloud-enfolded Sinai. . . .

Boswell watched, admired, noted and also, sometimes, suffered.
But, invariably, his pride and pleasure exceeded the pain he felt.
His visits to London in 1772 and, again, in 1773, proved unusually rewarding; Johnson talked with magnificent gusto; Boswell listened or interposed with tireless energy; and on April 30,
during his second visit, Johnson proposed him and he was duly
elected as a member of the Literary Club, an assembly which
included Reynolds and Burke and Garrick, Sheridan, Fox,
Gibbon and Dr. Burney, and a sprinkling of such cultured men
of the world as Lord Spencer, Lord Palmerston and Topham
Beauclerk. And that same autumn he achieved his greatest
triumph. There could have been few bolder suggestions than
that Johnson, elderly, infirm and indolent, who, though he professed to love travel, was firmly convinced that he hated Scotsmen, should go as far afield as Edinburgh and thence allow himself to be bear-led around the Hebrides; but the Doctor, whose
curiosity had already been aroused, and on whom Boswell for
some while had been patiently pressing the scheme, suddenly
signified his consent and wrote to announce his departure. In
mid-August, 1773, a note informed Boswell that his venerable
friend had reached Edinburgh and been safely set down "at
Boyd's inn, at the head of the Canongate." Leaving his wife to
brew tea, Boswell hurried to meet him. It was late; the night was
dark; and as they walked arm in arm up the High Street, to Boswell's house in James's Court, "the evening effluvia of Edinburgh," the reek of its open drains and the stench wafted from
the tall ancient houses of the Old Town, smote strongly on their
nostrils. Johnson grumbled a little; but Boswell was too exultant
at his good fortune to be greatly disconcerted, while his pleasure

was increased, as soon as they reached his house, by the ceremonious politeness with which Johnson treated Mrs. Boswell,
and by his evident satisfaction when he observed that his "singular habit" of drinking tea far into the night had been remembered
and provided for. Mrs. Boswell was less elated; she found her
guest uncouth, alarming, troublesome, a formidable projection
of that mysterious London world which drew her husband away
so often, after which (she knew or suspected) even among his wife
and children he very seldom ceased to hanker. Still, she played
her part dutifully; but it was with some uneasiness (Boswell observed) that she bade good-bye to the two oddly matched
travellers who, on Wednesday, August 18, 1773, set out towards
St. Andrews, Johnson in his "very wide brown cloth great coat,
with pockets which might have almost held the two volumes of
his folio dictionary," carrying a heavy stick of solid English oak,
his companion, no doubt, clad in one of the fashionably cut,
brightly coloured garments which, for particularly momentous
occasions, he always much affected; while Boswell's servant,
Joseph Ritter, a Bohemian, "a fine stately fellow above six feet
high," concluded the procession as it emerged from James's
Court.

Till the second week of November it was not to reappear; and
during the interval Boswell enjoyed perhaps one of the most
exhausting, but certainly most interesting and gratifying, experiences of what he himself had always considered an extraordinarily romantic life. Among the luggage Johnson had left
behind him at James's Court, besides the pistols and ammunition
which his *cicerone* had assured him he would not need, was a
volume of a "pretty full and curious diary" (which Mrs. Boswell,
strange woman, greatly to her husband's surprise, failed to have
transcribed or even look into while he was away!); but Boswell
rarely travelled without his private journal, and to this journal
he now entrusted a detailed description of their day-to-day
adventures. Afterwards, with a few omissions and minor alterations, it was to be edited and published. From a literary point of
view, the *Journal of a Tour to the Hebrides* ranks far below the

Life of Johnson, just as it ranks far above the *Account of Corsica.* It is a memorable and delightfully readable book thanks not so much to the writer's style, which is often confused and clumsy, as to the romantic quality of the diarist's mind and to the air of heroic dignity with which he invests his subject. On Johnson he confers an air of magnitude that is both physical and spiritual. Now the old man stalks "like a giant" through the luxuriant thistles and nettles that surround a ruined fortress; now "like a magnificent Triton" sits high on the stern of a boat as the Hebrideans row them along the rugged coast of Scalpa; now, in a storm at sea, reclines "in philosophick tranquility," with his back against a greyhound, or braves an Atlantic gale, the flaps of his hat let down and secured by a handkerchief knotted beneath his chin; now he steams before a peat fire, brandishes a broadsword and a Highland target, or complaisantly allows Boswell to crown his bushy grey wig with a large blue bonnet, thus presenting "the image of a venerable *Senachi*" and seeming "much pleased to assume the appearance of an ancient Caledonian." There are quarrels, of course; Boswell's susceptibilities were affronted and his feelings grievously mangled; on one occasion at least he succumbed to the effects of punch, fell into bed at five in the morning and woke at noon, embarrassed and ashamed, reflecting gloomily that his behaviour overnight had been "very inconsistent with that conduct which I ought to maintain, while the companion of the *Rambler*." But the *Rambler,* unexpectedly, was in a mild, forgiving mood. "What, drunk yet?" he inquired pleasantly as he entered Boswell's bedroom, and, when their host arrived with brandy, encouraged him to take a dram.

Neither of the tourists had much taste for savage undisciplined nature; in this, Johnson was the more honest—the mountain that Boswell called "immense" he was content to describe as "a considerable protuberance"; and it was with some relief, though not without a pleasing consciousness of duty done, that they returned to the Lowlands, to Inveraray—brightened for Boswell, as he passed along the corridors, by a glimpse of "ladies' maids tripping about in neat morning dresses," though overclouded

by the frigid and supercilious behaviour of the Duchess of Argyle
—and to the House of Auchinleck, where Johnson and Lord
Auchinleck, Boswell's father by blood and his father by adop-
tion, became involved in some stormy interchanges over controversial topics. It was disturbing, nevertheless uncommonly exciting, to observe two human beings whom he revered so deeply,
"my honoured father and my respected friend," grappling hand-
to-hand in the pose of "intellectual gladiators." But Lord Auchinleck so far forgot his resentment as to attend Dr. Johnson politely
to the post-chaise; they regained Edinburgh; then, on the morning of December 22, a coach picked Johnson up and the tour was
ended. It left Boswell in an exhilarated, but unusually exhausted,
mood. Far too long his mind had been "at its utmost stretch";
mentally and physically, he was almost worn out; and the strain
continued to be perceptible during the months that followed.
Moreover, he was approaching a serious inward crisis. The next
three years were to find him in a state of moral revolution, which
he could neither explain to himself nor excuse to those about
him. The turmoil of his mind and senses began to exceed all
bounds. He noticed the results concisely; he looked on with a
sort of wondering despair at his own disastrous progress. But he
could not determine the cause, and proved utterly incapable of
checking his downward flight.

He was in the mid-thirties—usually a difficult, and sometimes
a dangerous, period. Always unbalanced, he gradually lost the
small degree of self-restraint—though his faculty of self-analysis
was never weakened—that he had carefully built up during the
earlier years of marriage. His restlessness, his excitability, his
thirst for amusement and passion for experience, grew less and
less controllable. He had moments of explosive happiness; but
the explosion was at once followed by a long interval of
melancholy. There was "a coldness and darkness" in his mind; a
hideous physical languor clogged all his movements, till he was
obliged to admit that only from eating and sleeping could he
derive the slightest satisfaction; he worried over his financial
prospects and was tormented by interminable, unprofitable mus-

ings on the fate of the soul after death and the awful questions
of predestination and human free-will. Then, as suddenly, he was
happy again and young and confident. Snow had fallen overnight; and he "felt a kind of agreeable wintry sensation which
the sight of snow allways gives me"; or a regiment went marching through Edinburgh, and his spirit was uplifted by the sound
of fifes and drums. Any pleasant impression might help to change
his mood—good talk, celebrated friends, a beautifully appointed
room: "external conveniences and elegance [he had already
written] render me not only happy but benevolent." He loved
his fellow human beings, and he loved their company. He liked
cards; he enjoyed wine; but whereas in London he had been
often drunk, in Scotland—thanks to the drinking-habits of his
compatriots and the addition of whisky to claret and burgundy
and port and punch—after a certain hour of the evening he was
very seldom sober. During the summer of 1774, he was frequently
"talkative and vociferous," sometimes "outrageously intoxicated." He would wander out and accost a whore in the alleys of
the Old Town; stumbling home, he would be "fretful and
horridly passionate"; next morning, it was only with the very
greatest effort that he struggled through his causes. He thought
of the noble example set him by the men whom he respected, his
father and Johnson and Paoli, remembered his wife and his
delightful children, and drifted back after a day or two into pre-
cisely the same excess.

Yet he was still equal, when the need occurred, to systematic
application. His career as a Scottish advocate had been only
moderately distinguished; but it was redeemed, at least from the
humanitarian and moral point of view, by his enthusiastic
championship of a number of penniless and unhappy gaolbirds,
in whose salvation (we may hazard) he was seeking to find his
own, and on whose behalf he laboured without the hope of a fee.
Such was John Reid, the sheep-stealer, once acquitted of a theft
of which he had, in fact, been guilty but, during the autumn of
1774, condemned to death for a similar offence of which Boswell
—probably with some reason—believed him to be innocent. Bos-

well defended him with ardour and drew up an elaborate petition which was forwarded to London. The petition miscarried; and poor Reid, in his white grave-clothes and his tall white night-cap, his wife's green cloak thrown over his shoulders, his knees knocking together with fear or cold, trudged reluctantly towards the scaffold. Boswell attended him, consoling, admonishing, noting every detail. He had hatched a plot that Reid's body should be cut down from the gallows, carried into a stable and there resuscitated with the help of a surgeon and a quantity of warm salt. But the project proved impracticable; the innocent felon was well and truly hung; while Boswell was threatened with a challenge by the son of the presiding judge, who declared that his father had been libelled by the defending counsel in a letter to the newspapers—a threat that caused Boswell some miserably anxious moments. He discovered, to his surprise and distress, that he was not a courageous man, and lay awake, with his wife at his side, wretchedly meditating upon extinction.

The shock had been severe; but during the course of the spring, fortunately, he was able to travel south, passed through the town of Grantham "in charming health and spirits"—somewhat disturbed, however, by the presence at the inn of an extremely handsome maid-servant, who revived his old predilection for "Asiatic multiplicity"—saw Johnson, dined with Wilkes, now Lord Mayor of London, presiding magnificently at the Guildhall, called on Lord Pembroke at Wilton (whence he wrote to Johnson complaining that he was "weary and gloomy"), visited Temple in Devonshire and, exposed to the influence of that excellent clergyman, took an oath "under a solemn yew"— one of many such oaths, all equally abortive—that henceforward he would abstain from the consumption of any form of alcohol. He had not counted on the atmosphere of Edinburgh or the effects of hypochondria. Autumn descended; and Boswell's unsteady shape was again to be seen wandering through the lanes of the Old Town and up the slopes of Castle Hill, with various blowsy companions whom a chairman had procured for him or he had himself picked up, Mrs. Boswell occasionally in pursuit,

more often sitting at home, apprehensively watchful till he ha
staggered back to bed. Even now, he wished that the diary of hi
adventures should be as complete as he could make it. "—I hav
a kind of strange feeling [he had recorded] as if I wished nothin
to be secret that concerns myself"; but he had contracted th
habit of using Greek characters to obscure the narration o
particularly scandalous scenes; and he was startled and dismaye
when Mrs. Boswell's knowledge of the Greek alphabet prove
sufficient to enable her to decipher his surreptitious jottings
Later, he would reproach himself with his violent and foolis
conduct, recollecting how at home he had been seized with
longing to break everything in sight, how he had sworn, an
vociferated, flung an egg into the fire and some beer after it, an
marvel at the stoical patience that pardoned and consoled him
He remained the devoted admirer of his wife's exemplary virtues
and the spectator—grieved, perplexed, never entirely unhopeful
always clear-sighted and dispassionate—of his own manifol
shortcomings and superabundant follies.

In agreeable contrast to his early idol, Jean-Jacques Rousseau
he did not seek to attribute his frequent mishaps to some dia
bolical cabal engineered against him by society. No, Boswell'
misadventures were patently Boswell's fault. He had hope or
his side, youth, energy and brilliance. Soon it would be tim
to return to London, where he would enjoy the inestimable
privilege of the company of Dr. Johnson; and, when spring cam
round, he punctually appeared in Fleet Street, learned that John
son was staying with the Thrales at their London house in South
wark and hastened thither, to find Johnson flanked by Mrs.
Thrale, placidly established among breakfast tea-cups. His effect
on Boswell's spirits was almost at once apparent; "in a moment
he was in a full glow of conversation, and I felt myself elevated as
if brought into a different state of being." He was "quite re-
stored," Boswell burst out; to which, "There are many who admire and respect Mr. Johnson; but you and I *love* him," Mrs.
Thrale replied in her sensible, motherly way. Better still, Johnson had planned a "jaunt"—to Oxford, Birmingham and his

native city, Lichfield—of the kind from which both Boswell and
Johnson derived the very liveliest pleasure. "Life has not many
better things than this," remarked Johnson as a post-chaise
whirled them through the country. Their sightseeing was instructive, their conversation endless; and, while Boswell reverted at
some length to his favourite "Asiatic" theories and demanded
why, if the Hebrew patriarchs had been allowed a luxurious
plurality of wives and concubines, James Boswell should not be
permitted the same indulgence—Johnson, however, declined to
rise to the bait—he "expressed a desire to be acquainted with a
lady who had been much talked of, and universally celebrated
for extraordinary address and insinuation."

That lady, we can safely conjecture, was the notorious Mrs.
Rudd. During 1776, two forgers, Daniel and Robert Perreau,
had been hanged at Tyburn. Their accomplice, Margaret Caroline Rudd, was also Daniel Perreau's mistress. At their trial she
had turned King's Evidence; and at her own, where she appeared
decorously habited in a suit of "second mourning," she had conducted her defence with such consummate skill, and so eloquently
expressed her trust in the virtues of a British jury, that she had
been acquitted to the accompaniment of the loudest applause
ever yet heard in a London court of law. There could be no
doubt that she was clever, and she was said to be attractive.
"Many a time [Boswell wrote to his wife, in a letter which, perhaps wisely, he afterwards decided against posting] you heard me
rave with a strange force of imagination about the celebrated
Mrs. Rudd." On his return from the Midlands, he learned that
she was even then in London and had taken rooms in Westminster. It was an opportunity far too good to miss. Late one
evening he knocked at her front door and, though Mrs. Rudd
was not at home, elected to wait in a "decent enough" upstairs
room, only lighted by a pair of tallow candles. His account of the
meeting that followed forms one of the most unexpected, characteristic and entertaining chapters of Boswell's "curious archives." The observation is minute, the touches of self-revelation,
part deliberate, part inadvertent, are numerous and vivid. Panic

fears assailed him in the small ill-lighted room. True, the books he saw lying there seemed sober and harmless enough— pamphlets on the trial, Pope, an edifying novel; but his "fearful suppositions" could not be held in check, and he thought of murderers and bullies and, worse, that the ghosts of the Perreaus might suddenly rise from the floor. There entered "a little woman, delicately made, not at all a beauty, but with a very pleasing appearance and much younger than I imagined . . . she was drest in black clothes, with a white cloak and hat." At once she embarked on the story Boswell had come to hear, speaking "with wonderful ease and delicacy" and an air of conscious innocence that was "quite amazing." She added that she was in poor health; she explained that she loved to read. Meanwhile, Boswell watched her closely; Mrs. Rudd, we can assume, watched him more closely still; and before long he had struck out on an intimate impulsive line. "I said she was reckoned quite a sorceress, possessed of enchantment." But Mrs. Rudd merely smiled and answered that her enchantment was certainly a thing of the past. "I begged her pardon, and, with exquisite flattery, said, 'My dear Mrs. Rudd, Don't talk so. Every thing you have said to me till now has been truth and candour"; he was sure that she could enchant, but begged that he himself might not be too much enchanted. Presently, he had "seised her silken hand"; by a graceful transition, he dropped a kiss there; and Mrs. Rudd suffered him to do so without prudery or effrontery, but with the "complaisance, or complyance" peculiar to a woman of fashion. Her very voice was soft and mellifluous; she was modest and self-assured; she did not seek to dazzle but "cheered . . . with a mild light." Altogether, an astonishing and moving evening, with Mrs. Rudd, in her black dress, looking up quietly under her eyelashes at the noisy excitable visitor, Boswell now much at his ease, stirring the fire, snuffing the candles and stealing covert glances at an unusually pretty foot, glad to observe that he "felt no confusion" when his eyes met hers. They parted with a kiss; and the adventure was presently sealed by Dr. Johnson's approbation— he envied Boswell, he declared, his acquaintance with Mrs. Rudd.

He could not guess that, years later, she would play the part in his friend's life of a second "Moffat woman" and help to satisfy for some restless months Boswell's luxurious whim.

Amusing in itself, the episode has also a certain symbolic value. Problems of good and evil, of belief and unbelief, of salvation and damnation, often formed the troubled background of Boswell's private thoughts. In an incoherent fashion, he was a deeply religious man; but his emotions and convictions refused to take shape, and new evidence was perpetually disturbing some old-established *credo*. His naïvety demanded a completely consistent world. The good man should be at peace. But had he not heard Johnson himself speak with terror of damnation, witnessed his abiding fear of death and watched him start back from human bones "with a striking appearance of horrour"? Mrs. Rudd was a criminal who had narrowly escaped the scaffold; yet her conscience seemed to be clear, her spirit calm and easy. On another plane, there was the awkward problem presented by David Hume. For Hume was an unbeliever, arch-advocate of scepticism and foe of Christianity; but, scepticism apart, he had led an exemplary life. Back in Edinburgh, during the summer months of 1776, Boswell was informed that Hume lay dying. An unbeliever faced death! Boswell could not refrain from closer contemplation of so strange and dramatic, and (he devoutly hoped) so comforting and edifying, a moral drama. Surely, there must be a change in sight? Yet, although he found the philosopher propped up in his drawing-room, no longer plump and round-faced but "lean, ghastly, and quite of an earthy appearance," and though Hume admitted that he knew that death was close, he was "placid and even cheerful," while his animadversions on religious subjects were as odd and bold as ever. He was unchanged, unafraid; there was none of the solemnity about their meeting that Boswell had expected, and "Death for the time did not seem dismal." Instead Hume talked, joked and declared that "when he heard a man was religious, he concluded he was a rascal," admitting nevertheless, with his customary sense of justice, that he had known "some instances of very good men being religious."

The doctrine of survival he dismissed as "a most unreasonable fancy." Boswell had no rejoinder prepared; "a sort of wild, strange, hurrying recollection" of his mother's early lessons and Dr. Johnson's excellent precepts went racing through his mind; he was "like a man in sudden danger" confusedly groping for defensive weapons. The infidel continued to talk and joke, Boswell to expostulate and utter muddled protests. But Hume quietly brushed them aside; he remained most "indecently and impolitely positive in incredulity"; and Boswell "left with impressions which disturbed me for some time."

To an element of genuine moral perplexity, as well as a strain of natural levity, must be attributed many of the misfortunes of Boswell's middle-age. He had honestly longed to reform; but his weakness and his strength were so closely bound together that only by indulging his folly could he hope to exploit his genius; the propulsive force of his destiny was far too strong and subtle. He must go on and on, gathering experiences, accumulating memories, piling up regrets, and in the process must break resolution after virtuous resolution. Thus, the oath under the solemn yew had very soon collapsed; but it was quickly followed by a promise given to General Paoli in London during the spring of 1776, that "I shall not taste fermented liquor for a year. . . . I have kept this promise [he told Temple] now about three weeks. I was really growing a drunkard." The ensuing period, however, was "sadly dissipated"; yet it was during this period, on his various jaunts to London and on a visit to the great man's old friend, Dr. Taylor of Ashbourne, that he put together probably his finest collection of Johnsonian portrait-sketches. Boswell's account of Johnson's life between 1776 and 1784 equals in bulk his published narrative of the whole of the previous epoch; nor does his gift of literary generalship, as revealed, for example, in the rash but successful plan of persuading Dilly to invite Johnson to meet and dine with Wilkes, seem any less masterly in the later than in the earlier pages. At the same time, he reverted to journalism and nursed political projects; and from 1777 onwards there began to appear in the *London Magazine* a series of papers,

igned by "The Hypochondriack" which endeavoured to give
ome account of Boswell's moral malady. Though from a literary
)oint of view the result was not impressive, this attempt to drag
)ut into daylight the phantoms of the darkness would appear, at
east temporarily, to have achieved the end in view. During 1781,
(ohnson was obliged to write him a sternly reproving letter, pro-
/oked by a gloomy and perplexed effusion on the subject of
iberty and necessity, in which he took him to task for what he
:alled, not without reason, the "hypocrisy of misery," bade him
·efrain from tormenting himself and vexing others and added,
nore gently, that "I love every part about you but your affecta-
.ion of distress." Yet, at the end of 1782, Boswell was able to in-
·orm the readers of the *London Magazine* that the Hypochon-
lriack had been free for so long from his "direful malady . . .
·hat I almost begin to forget that I was ever afflicted with it." One
)f the factors that had most unsettled his youth was his relation-
;hip with a dour, unsympathetic father; and in the August of
1782 his father died. Lord Auchinleck's death (Johnson observed
·uccinctly) "had every circumstance that could enable you to
)ear it." As the new Laird of Auchinleck, he felt his "feudal en-
:husiasm" mount into a lively blaze. He had a comfortable rent-
·oll; his attitude towards his tenants was kindly and paternal.
But, even at Auchinleck, there was still the attraction of the
;outh-bound London road.

While the disciple's spirits improved, the master's were declin-
ing. Mr. Thrale, that silent, gluttonous but dignified and authoritative personage, had expired of an apoplectic seizure in
1781; and speculation immediately broke out among her London
friends as to whom his eligible widow might choose to marry.
Would Johnson be at last united to his *"Thralia dulcis"*? Boswell was not behind-hand. At once he produced some facetious
and improper verses. Soame Jenyns dashed off a quatrain. Soon
the journalists took up the cry; and scraps of highly coloured
gossip appeared in many daily papers. Only the Doctor remained
aloof; he trusted his "Dearest Mistress," and he believed that she
trusted him. That Mrs. Thrale, before her husband's death, was

already desperately enamoured of the sweet-tempered, ox-eyed Italian singer, Gabriel Mario Piozzi, and that her emotions, long repressed during years of marriage, were preparing to burst forth with explosive violence, was a discovery for which his egotism was totally unprepared. The scandal, when it was at length sprung, convulsed the whole of London. So distraught was the victim—what with the disapproval of her daughters, the antago-nism of her friends and the unaccountable hesitations of her be-wildered and frightened swain—that even Queeney Thrale, taciturn, disapproving girl, confessed that her mother's sanity was threatened. From the intellectual women of her circle poor Mrs. Thrale received neither encouragement nor comfort. ". . . There must be [decided Mrs. Chapone] really some degree of *Insanity* in that case. . . . The 4 daughters renders it a most frightful instance of human wretchedness indeed! it has given great occasion to the Enemy to blaspheme and to triumph over the Bas Bleu Ladies." Yet in the June of 1784, Mrs. Thrale formally announced her second marriage; and Johnson wrote her two letters—a letter of furious and unfair recrimination, followed by a message of regretful tenderness. With character-istic resolution, he attempted to destroy the past, burned all her correspondence, and struggled (he told Fanny Burney) to drive completely from his thoughts the woman he had once regarded as the first of human beings; then settled down into the twilight of uncomforted old age.

He had not far to go. His ailments were multiplying, his strength decreasing. Mrs. Williams had vanished, accompanied by Robert Levett. He was almost alone; yet so intense was his fear of death and so tenacious the grip with which he clung to the pleasures of life—letters, a friend's conversation, the full tide of existence sweeping along Fleet Street—that he fought ob-stinately, step by step, against the advance of disease and age. Boswell dined in his company for the last time on June 30. After dinner a coach took them to the head of Bolt Court; but Boswell refused to enter the house, fearing that his own unequal spirits could not withstand the strain. Through the coach window he

SAMUEL JOHNSON IN OLD AGE

An engraving by Arthur Smith, from a portrait by James Barry

heard the old man's sonorous "Fare you well" and noted the "kind of pathetick briskness" with which he plunged out of sight beneath the archway of the dusky passage. As the year drew to a conclusion, he learned that Johnson had died, still desperate but religiously resigned, on December 13.

For his disciple the loss was complex. To wish to be loved is the commonest of human failings. Less common is an ability to repay affection with affection. But both traits were present in Boswell's character; and though it is true that he clamoured for love and noisily demanded notice, his response to friendship was always immediate, and the return he made so profuse as to be sometimes overwhelming. He was an enthusiast—that was his strength and, ultimately, his downfall. With the curious sensitiveness for which even his admirers did not often give him credit, Johnson, on one occasion, seeing his friend particularly despondent, told Boswell that he had recently heard him described as "a man whom everybody likes." And was there more, he demanded, that life could give? For Boswell, at least, there could be no greater happiness. With Johnson, and in Johnson's circle, he had achieved perhaps the highest form of human satisfaction—he had arrived, that is to say, at an almost complete balance between his talents and his opportunities; he was perfectly situated to do what he was qualified to do best. Thus it came about that Johnson's death was a catastrophe from which he never quite recovered. Henceforward, however lively his friendships or however tumultuous his enthusiasms, there was always a residue of romantic enthusiasm, human affection, intellectual veneration, for which he could not find employment. He might not take the excellent advice that "Ursa Major" offered him and might persevere, obstinately and cheerfully, in exactly the opposite course; but Johnson could absorb—such was his majestic egotism—every particle of interest his companion could supply. Johnson gone, Boswell was embarrassed by his own interior wealth which he longed to invest worthily yet squandered casually, without a plan or a ruling passion to guide his spending. Life which, during the long periods of his association with Johnson, had worn the romantic colouring of hope and self-esteem—the latter being for Boswell the equivalent of self-respect—seemed progressively darker, stranger and more chaotic as he advanced through middle age.

Suddenly he felt the resurgent symptoms of his old and dreaded disease. For a time he imagined that the threat had been beaten off. Now hypochondria again declared itself, and a nameless, formless depression descended on his spirit. But, in Boswell's case, the disease was not accompanied by any cessation of activity. Rather, in the search for relief, he grew busier, more talkative, spasmodically and superficially more ebullient. He was still—or still believed himself to be—the man whom everybody liked; but no longer was he quite sure of the position he occupied. It became more and more difficult to remember next morning what he had said at dinner; the hours that followed had usually melted into a vague alarming haze; and the little that he remembered seemed often best forgotten. Yet his love of activity, his thirst for movement, did not diminish. Ambition glowed in the bosom of the indefatigable diner-out. A year after Johnson's death, in 1785, against the advice of his friends and notwithstanding the pleas of Mrs. Boswell, whose health was then giving him grounds for serious anxiety, he threw up his Scottish practice and determined that he would be called to the Bar in London. The plan did not succeed. Neither on circuit nor in Westminster Hall did his assiduity bring him in a single brief. Next, he aspired to Parliament. Lord Lonsdale, the owner of no less than nine pocket boroughs, should nominate him to a safe Tory seat. Lord Lonsdale must be courted; and, when Boswell courted, he courted with abandon. The methods he adopted were seldom discreet or dignified. The magnate, it is true, consented after some pestering to take him on, appointed him to the Recordership of Carlisle, employed him in one somewhat discreditable transaction and destined him for others. With regard to Boswell's candidature he proved considerably less obliging; and presently it came to his henchman's ears that Lord Lonsdale, in his abrupt and brutal manner, had remarked that, were he to put him up, Boswell

would undoubtedly "get drunk and make a foolish speech."
Boswell was bitterly offended—all the more offended because he
may have admitted that this cruel forecast had a certain inherent
probability. Even so, he did not revolt. He submitted to the
affront as he had submitted to the practical jokes at Lowther,
where Lonsdale's friends had stolen his wig and he had been
"obliged to go all day in my nightcap," till he could drive into
Carlisle and get another fitted. And when his patron commanded
his presence at the Carlisle elections, though he protested that his
attendance was quite unnecessary, and explained at vast length
the extreme inconvenience to which he would be subjected if he
were obliged to leave London, with much grumbling and many
secret pangs he prepared to set forth.

The journey was postponed; it was postponed again. Lord
Lonsdale was capricious, Boswell sulky. Tempers were tried; the
situation on both sides grew more and more explosive; then
Lonsdale burst forth into a downright rage, blurted out that he
supposed Boswell thought he meant to bring him into Parliament but he had never had any such intention, and "in short
. . . expressed himself in the most degrading manner, in the
presence of a low man from Carlisle and one of his menial
servants." Exposed to "such unexpected, insulting behaviour,"
and deprived at a blow of all the hopes of fortune and preferment
he had been so carefully nursing, Boswell "almost sank," yet
rallied sufficiently to embark for Carlisle in his patron's carriage.
At Barnet, where they paused on the road, there was another
appalling scene. Some unfortunate complaint by Boswell raised
Lord Lonsdale's passion "almost to madness," so that he addressed his fellow-traveller in "shocking" terms. "You have kept
low company all your life," he vociferated. "What are *you*, Sir?"
A gentleman, replied Boswell, and a man of honour; at which
Lonsdale agreed to give him satisfaction, but refused to lend him
pistols, obliging Boswell to wander round Barnet in search of
weapons and a second, until his anger had begun to evaporate
and he crept back dejectedly into Lonsdale's presence, to be
roughly placated and told to forget and forgive. . . .

Our authority for this tragi-comic narrative is not, as might have been supposed, some malicious friend or gossiping acquaintance who happened to be present. It is Boswell himself; for, even at his most dejected, a kind of queer lucidity never quite deserted him; and while his wounds were still smarting and his head still ached, he sat down to his journal to record the humiliating story of his private misadventures. He had got drunk again. That, of course, had happened often enough at happier periods—it had occurred, indeed, under the very eyes of Dr. Johnson; but Boswell's spells of nocturnal sobriety nowadays were growing more and more infrequent. He loved wine, and the glow of companionship that wine promoted. More decisive, perhaps, he was an extraordinarily restless man. At a certain stage of the evening, the restlessness that gnawed at him became intolerable and—with no Johnson to lead him off on a stroll down Fleet Street, concluding virtuously but agreeably over Mrs. Williams' tea-cups—he launched out, flushed and excited, into the hazes of nocturnal London. Sometimes he resisted temptation and regained his own house; but, once he had arrived there, the impulse he had controlled came tumultuously flooding back and he would wheel round and rush out to seize what the occasion offered. There was a dreadful night when, like the drunkard's child in some improving moral story, his schoolboy son, Sandie, had followed him into the street and pleaded with the much-intoxicated Boswell to remain at home. There were other occasions when he had been severely bruised by tipsy tumbling, returned home plastered with mud and found his pocket picked; and that unfortunately was not the sum total of the harm he did himself; from the after-effects of his random amatory adventures he was seldom completely free.

Was ever man more unhappy, he demanded frequently and passionately, in the long miserable outpourings he dispatched to Temple. Mrs. Boswell, affectionate, ill-used, devoted woman, had died of consumption in 1789; and with bitter remorse her husband recollected how "often and often when she was very ill in London have I been indulging in festivity with Sir Joshua

Reynolds, Courtenay, Malone, &c., &c., and have come home late, and disturbed her repose. Nay, when I was last at Auchinleck on purpose to soothe and console her, I repeatedly went from home and both on those occasions, and when neighbours visited me, drank a great deal too much wine." Three years later, he continued to grieve—intermittently it is true—for the companion he had lost. "I get bad rest in the night [he wrote to Temple on April 2, 1791], and then I brood over all my complaints—the *sickly mind* which I have had from my early years—the disappointment of my hopes of success in life—the irrevocable separation between me and that excellent woman who was my cousin, my friend, and my wife—the embarrassment of my affairs —the disadvantage to my children in having so wretched a father —nay, the want of *absolute certainty* of being happy after death, the *sure prospect* of which is *frightful*. No more of this." Yet the old flighty exuberant Boswell had not been extinguished; and the same letter that presents this melancholy chronicle of anxieties and apprehensions includes a reference to the project he had just formed of marrying a Miss Bagnal "who may probably have six or seven hundred a year . . . about seven-and-twenty, lively and gay, a *Ranelagh girl,* but of excellent principles, in so much that she reads prayers to the servants in her father's family, every Sunday evening. 'Let me see such a woman,' cried I; and accordingly, I am to see her. She has refused young and fine gentlemen. 'Bravo,' cried I. 'We see then what her taste is.' Here now, my Temple, I am my fluttering self. . . .'"

The flutterings, the agitations, the recurrent bursts of gaiety and self-esteem, never quite subsided. There were delightful dinner-parties, gratifying encounters, further plots to marry— Miss Bagnal was succeeded by "Miss Milles, daughter of the late Dean of Exeter, a most agreeable woman *d'une certaine age* . . . with a fortune of £10,000." Or he appeared at Court, and "was the *great man* (as we used to say) . . . in a suit of imperial blue lined with rose-coloured silk, and ornamented with rich gold-wrought buttons." The confidence he felt in himself, however, had now largely evaporated; Boswell's existence, after Johnson's death, it is customary to observe, was gloomy, sordid and un-profitable. Boswell's most recent biographer, indeed, has gone to the length of suggesting that, during the latter part of his life, he was actually mad; but no evidence can be produced for this odd hypothesis; and there is little indication of distraction or de-rangement in the uninterrupted lucidity of his private papers. It is certain that he was weak, dissipated and unhappy; but (thanks to his gift of candid exposition) there is a kind of uni-versality about Boswell's weakness, and he becomes, not a great tragic, but undoubtedly a great typical, figure. He stands for every man who has sat up late, while a nervous and ailing wife expected him home; who has made noble resolutions he was conscious he could not keep, in the muddled hope that at least to have made them would prove somehow its own reward; who has groaned over his past life and shuddered at future prospects; who has felt his youth slipping away from him, and admitted that, though age has cost him much, it has taught him little; who has hurried out and got cheerfully drunk, to wake up in a welter of cheerless thoughts and disturbing recollections.

Yet the man who detailed his miseries to Temple in 1791, added casually that his *Life of Johnson* was "at last drawing to a close. I am correcting the last sheet, and have only to write an Advertisement, to make out a list of Errata, and to correct a second sheet of contents. . . ." The work was certainly projected before Johnson's death and probably begun during the early months of 1785, when Boswell, having completed his manuscript of the *Tour to the Hebrides* (published that autumn), wrote to a number of Johnson's acquaintances, soliciting material. Thence-forward, it struggled on by slow and laborious stages. In January, 1789, he informed Temple that he was now "very near the con-clusion of my rough draught"; but there had been many occa-sions, he added in a letter written during November of the same year, when he had thought of giving it up. "You cannot imagine what labour, what perplexity, what vexation I have endured in arranging a prodigious multiplicity of materials, in supplying omissions, in searching for papers, buried in different masses—

and all this besides the exertion of composing and polishing."
Every author knows the agony of such prolonged endeavour, how
often hope is succeeded by desperation, and desperation by disgust, how insistently, now and then, a positive nausea for every
sentence he has composed presses on his spirit. And Boswell's life
at this period was more than usually unsettled. There were his
fruitless efforts to gain a foothold among the advocates of Westminster Hall and, for a time, there were the demands made by
the outrageous Lonsdale who dragged him away from his proofs
to attend to legal jobbery. Sometimes his hand was so unsteady
that it proved extremely difficult to mark on the proof-sheets the
corrections he required. But, through all this, he was sustained
by a belief in the book's potential value and by the complete trust
he continued to put in the plan he had adopted. ". . . Though I
shall be uneasily sensible [he declared to Temple] of its many
deficiencies, it will certainly be to the world a very valuable and
peculiar volume of biography, full of literary and characteristical
anecdotes. . . ." And elsewhere: "I am absolutely certain that
my mode of biography, which gives not only a *history* of Johnson's *visible* progress through the world, and of his publications,
but a *view* of his mind, in his letters and conversations, is the
most perfect that can be conceived, and will be *more* of a *Life*
than any work that has ever yet appeared."

His judgment was, of course, correct. Not only did the *Life of
Johnson,* when it at last emerged on the 16th May, 1791, set a
wholly new standard in the art of modern biography, but it forecast a new, larger and more ambitious method in the treatment
of individual human beings as the raw material of literature.
The clear, hard, definite strokes, with which Walton or Johnson
himself had built up their portraits, pre-supposed a view of
human character as of something largely static, composed of
attributes that could be described in a few words, and of virtues
and failings easy to harmonise in a concerted moral scheme. Here
Boswell's observation of his own character, pursued so patiently
since he first began to keep a journal at the age of eighteen, may
be assumed to have had very great importance in the task he had

undertaken of anatomising Johnson. Human beings were *not* consistent; in the study of his own life, he had remarked that vices and virtues, talents and disabilities, were closely interleaved. No single generalisation could resume a temperament; one must allow for both Johnson's brutality and his kindness, his energy and his sloth, his strength of mind and the vein of weakness that exposed him to the horde of nervous terrors by which he was perpetually surrounded, his enjoyment of life and his pervading melancholy. To delineate so complex a personage, one could not depend on the frank outlines, bold colouring and formalised background, hitherto adopted by contemporary biographers. One must show Johnson so far renouncing his prejudices and principles as to be won over by Wilkes at a London dinner-party; must display him, as a genial eccentric, "buffeting" his books among clouds of dust and feeding his cat on oysters; or in an uproariously convivial mood, with hands "not over-clean" [1] squeezing lemons into a bowl and demanding: "Who's for *poonsh?*"

Over the strange rugged landscape of Johnson's character— fertile valleys hemmed in between frowning mountain-walls of prejudice and superstition, uplands of serene intelligence giving place to wild volcanic regions where obscure and terrible shapes moved through a perpetual gloom—Boswell's scrutiny travels in lively insect-leaps. The prospect seems all the larger because Boswell is so small. Without question he was a conceited, but he was never an arrogant, man; false pride did not stand in his way when he desired to achieve an effect; complete candour was the goal he had nobly set himself. The truth was always worth relation, ran his splendid if vague belief; the truth about human nature is always dignifying, though at a first glance it may seem undignified and even squalid; there is a tragic beauty in the *whole* truth that no degree of decorative evasion can ever supplant or conceal. Thus Boswell, in common with Rousseau, the

---

[1] This detail was later suppressed at the instance of Edmond Malone, the distinguished Shakespearian commentator, who encouraged Boswell to finish his book and in whose "elegant study" he did much of his revision.

JAMES BOSWELL
From a sketch by Sir Thomas Lawrence

"genteel, black man" whom he had met at Motiers, anticipated those heroic attempts at dispassionate self-portrayal which bulk large in the literature of nineteenth-century Europe. He is one of the first English writers to be more interested in himself, as a text for minute critical examination, than in the impression that he made, and to be less concerned with style than with the fascination of his subject. Such an approach has its disadvantages. We may argue that Gibbon's æstheticism tells us as much as—perhaps more than—Boswell's realism; that Gibbon's elegant circumlocution, while he is unfolding his life-story, traces as fine and as authentic a pattern as Boswell's unashamed directness. Both, however, are now an inseparable part of the literary tradition to which we have been born; and of the two it is probably Boswell who has had the greater original influence. By conviction he was a conservative, by disposition a revolutionary; and his attitude towards the material he handled is far ahead of his time. In the *Life,* it is true, his revelation of himself may be sometimes inadvertent; but in the *Journals* (which, if he did not intend them for publication, were certainly destined by their author for the instruction of posterity) he set out with the idea of preparing a full-length self-portrait, in which he would embody, so far as he could, all those elements in his composition that puzzled or delighted him. He did not claim to have conducted his life well; but he could assert at least that, whatever he had done, he had done with wide-open eyes. "You have told me [he wrote to Temple in 1789] that I was the most *thinking* man you ever knew. It is certainly so as to my *own life*. I am continually *conscious,* continually *looking back* or *looking forward* and wondering how I shall feel in situations which I anticipate in fancy. My *journal* will afford materials for a very curious narrative."

Alas, when he achieved victory by the publication of his *magnum opus,* so far as happiness and peace of mind were concerned he had already lost the battle. His book was well timed but came too late to save him; and, though he certainly relished success and responded to the praise of his friends—Jack Wilkes had said it was "a wonderful book," and Boswell, characteristically, wrote to beg that he would put his opinion down in writing that he might "have your *testimonium* in my archives at Auchinleck"—his triumphs could do little to heal the wounds inflicted by experience. Three years after the publication of the *Life,* he was once again as tormented and as despondent as in the days when he was still struggling with his proof-sheets and fighting off Lord Lonsdale. He was well aware, he told his brother, that he could expect "only temporary alleviation of misery; and some gleams of enjoyment. But these it is my *right,* nay, I think my *duty* to have." In other words, he refused to remain at Auchinleck. Prudence suggested that he should reside on his estates, save money and lead the life of a cultured country gentleman. But always London beckoned him, with its noise and company; there was always the hope that some public man might recognise his merit; and as a last effort, he wrote to Dundas in 1794, begging that the Secretary of State would appoint him Commissioner Plenipotentiary to a Liberated Corsica. The appointment went, however, to Sir Gilbert Elliot, for Boswell's reputation as a responsible personage was now beyond repair; and the only result was another failure to add to a lengthening list. Desperately he sought refuge in crowded urban scenes—"as London [he had reflected] is the best place when one is happy, it is equally so when one is the reverse . . ."; but the daily allowance of wine he had for several months adhered to while he was finishing his book—"four good glasses at dinner, and a pint after it"—had gone the way, long ago, of many other salutary resolutions, and the effect of his nocturnal rambles grew more and more demoralising. Worse still, he suffered from the pangs of solitude. A number of old friends had vanished; new acquaintances treated him with less indulgence; "his joke, his song, his sprightly effusions of wit and wisdom [observed the author of a critical but not unkindly obituary notice] were ready, but did not appear to possess upon all occasions their wonted power of enlivening social joy. . . . Convivial society became continually more necessary to him, while his power of enchantment over it continued to decline." Now that the book had left him, and had embarked upon that independent existence which is the lot of masterpieces, assuming new colours and gaining new interest as the decades go by, the man who had produced it began to stumble and falter. James Boswell died after a brief illness at his house in Great Portland Street, in his fifty-fifth year, on May 19, 1795.

EDWARD GIBBON

---◆ ◆---

THE atmosphere of the eighteenth century was less clouded than our own. Its movements seem more precise because they were more leisurely. The voyagings of its characters have an air of symbolic significance, lost in the confused rapidity of modern travel. Boswell reached London for the second time towards the close of November, 1762; a few weeks later, by post-chaise and packet-boat, Edward Gibbon hurried away on the Grand Tour. For him, too, it was a decisive journey. Behind him lay several years spent in the militia, years which, although they had been educative, had not been entertaining. Cheerfully, he had thrown aside the regimentals that suited him so ill—the trappings of the South Hampshire Grenadiers with the motto *Falces conflantur in enses,* suggested by himself—and then, after a brief stay at his father's country house, set about collecting the various letters of introduction he was to take with him to Paris. Both the sedate assiduity with which he laid his plans, and his annoyance when the French Ambassador received him "more as a man of letters than as a man of fashion," are characteristic of the basic quality of Gibbon's character. Like Boswell, he valued himself on his birth and breeding, and was not dissatisfied with what he had already learned of his talents and capabilities; but, whereas Boswell's form of self-love was often self-destructive, it was part of Gibbon's genius to be usually his own best friend. In this happy gift he may have been strengthened by the experiences of childhood; and if his vital spark burned with a smooth and steady glow, diffusing a constant but moderate warmth through all his faculties, that no doubt was because during the first fifteen years of his life again and again it had seemed to be flickering towards extinction.

Naturally he valued and husbanded what he had so nearly lost;

and looking around him, surveying the position he had inherited, the free, prosperous country in which he had been born and the happy, enlightened century of which he was a product, Edward Gibbon considered dispassionately that he had had much to lose. From his family, for example, he derived all the advantages that go with a certain degree of security but none of the disadvantages of downright affluence. They were a credit to him, moreover, this assemblage of country gentlemen and merchants, the Gibbons and the Portens, who, though they had never risen to high rank, had held their possessions and maintained their dignity and independence for several hundred years. Such families are celebrated in the memorials of innumerable English country churches, with their blazons and their quarterings, their modest or pompous epitaphs, their effigies, ruffed or periwigged, placed high on the wall among classical wreaths and pediments, or reclining at full length, in alabaster, beneath the gilded and marbled canopies of Elizabethan tombs. During the period that preceded the Industrial Revolution and the first and second Reform Bills, the landed middle-class, merging on the one hand into the aristocracy, on the other linked by many ties with the world of commerce, constituted the most representative, respectable and also, perhaps, the most influential section of the English social structure; and out of their midst, from the marriage of Judith Porten and Edward Gibbon, a descendant of the squires of Rolvenden in the Weald of Kent, was born Edward Gibbon the younger, at the pleasant Thames-side village of Putney, in April, 1737.

Following him into the world came five brothers and a sister. But as parents Mr. and Mrs. Gibbon, even for that period, proved unusually ill-fated, since all their children, with the exception of the eldest, died in early infancy. Nor did it seem likely that Edward had long to live. A puny, unhealthy child, he suffered for many years from a painful nervous cramp and other infantile disorders both "various and frequent."[1] Mrs. Gibbon,

---

[1] They included, according to one of Gibbon's autobiographical drafts, Memoir C, "feavers and lethargies, a fistula in the eye, a tendency to a consumptive and to

weakened by repeated child-births, concentrated such remaining energies as she possessed in attachment to her husband; the care of Edward fell to his aunt, Mrs. Catherine Porten, who nursed and brooded over him with intense devotion. She was "the true mother [he afterwards declared] of my mind as well as of my health." It was she who confirmed him in his love of reading and introduced him to Pope's translations of the *Iliad* and the *Odyssey,* and the *Arabian Nights' Entertainments,* "the two first books of which I retain a distinct and pleasing idea." The little regular training he received was desultory and intermittent. No sooner had he been placed at a school than illness snatched him away; and after a couple of terms spent at Westminster, where he lived in the boarding-house his aunt had set up on the loss of her father's fortune, he was removed to Bath, then to Winchester, then back again to Putney and the Gibbons' house at Buriton. His mother had died, from the effects of her latest child-birth, in 1747; and Mr. Gibbon, a capricious, inconstant character, prone to sudden decisions and rapid changes of mood, had thereupon abandoned himself to a dramatic excess of grief, given up his parliamentary schemes—he had sat at one moment as a member for Southampton—said good-bye to the social world, of which during his wife's existence he had been an assiduous frequenter, and resolved to return to the placid ranks of the Hampshire landed gentry.

Thus Buriton Manor became Gibbon's background—such a house as only England produces, neither small nor very large, an unself-conscious mixture of different architectural periods, with its imposing Georgian front (raised by Gibbon's grandfather, the successful business man) tacked on to a low rambling Elizabethan structure. There were farm-buildings around it, and near by stood the church. Whale-backed downs and "long hanging woods" completed the pastoral landscape; and in these surroundings life continued in a simple and regular pattern, varied, when

---

a dropsical habit, a contraction of the nerves, with a variety of nameless disorders. And, as if the plagues of nature were not sufficient without the concurrence of accident, I was once bit by a dog most vehemently suspected of madness."

the roads were dry and the moon was full, by excursions in the family coach to neighbouring country seats. Gibbon, during his later years, might deplore the monotony of this existence, but he appreciated its solidity. Certainly he did not rebel against it; impulses of revolt played no part in that serious but equable nature, which already turned from the world of action to the sphere of imagination. Nevertheless, the prospects that confronted him were bleak and overshadowed; and he might well have come to manhood "an illiterate cripple," had he not during mid-adolescence, between the ages of fourteen and sixteen, reached and passed through one of those mysterious climacterics in which the whole constitution of the body seems suddenly to change and its energies to receive a new and surprising impetus. For no reason the physicians could determine, his ailments vanished away. Henceforward, though never robust, he was seldom troubled by illness; and Mr. Gibbon, thinking that the moment had now come to resume his education, placed him at Esher in the house of a certain Reverend Mr. Philip Francis, a clergyman who had translated Horace, but soon proved to have no other qualifications as educationalist or guardian, since he was more often to be found diverting himself in London than at home among his pupils. Mr. Gibbon then took one of the abrupt, thoughtless decisions to which he had always been addicted and, sweeping his son off to Oxford, without preparation and almost without warning, entered him as a Gentleman Commoner at Magdalen College before he had quite arrived at his fifteenth birthday.

The effects of this inconsiderate gesture were certainly far-reaching; but, as has so often happened, the influence of Oxford on Gibbon's development was very largely negative. Out of the fourteen months of frustrated idleness he was to spend at Magdalen, loitering on the threshold of a gate that none of those about him troubled to unlock, came no positive improvement in his knowledge of men or letters. Oxford gave him a casual, if a not unkindly welcome; but in the dreamy maze of University life there was nothing he could grasp, little he could admire; he

arrived at Oxford hungering for knowledge, and went away unsatisfied. Afterwards he was to crystallise his disappointment in
one of the most famous and envenomed passages of his autobiography. As an essay in literary invective, the six or seven long
measured paragraphs, into which Gibbon concentrated his scorn
and detestation of the University, set a standard that the modern
biographer dare not attempt to rival. Here and there, nevertheless, one may append a footnote; for, although both Gibbon's
narrative and the style in which he unfolds it are extraordinarily
revealing, they reveal Gibbon in the flush of his triumphant
middle age. Far behind him was the innocent, awkward Gentleman Commoner of Magdalen; and just as he had declined to
dwell on the nature of his childish illnesses, since they were a
subject too tedious and too "disgusting" for adult contemplation, so the origin of many of his youthful misfortunes is left
largely unexplained. With few friends of his own age to teach
him to enjoy himself, and no encouragement from older members of the University (those "decent easy men," whose "conversation stagnated in a round of college business, Tory politics,
personal anecdotes, and private scandal," whose "dull and deep
potations excused the brisk intemperance of youth") to develop
the random studies he had already begun at home, it is not un-
natural that Gibbon should have been bored and restive, or that,
finding his tutor would always accept excuses, he should have set
out during term-time on "costly and dangerous frolics" as far
afield as Bath in one direction and London in another. It is more
surprising that, from the sunny emptiness of his life at Oxford,
he should have taken refuge in the dark labyrinths of religious
speculation.

Yes, there had been a time (the adult Gibbon was obliged to
admit) when theology had absorbed him. From his childhood he
had liked disputing on points of doctrine—poor Mrs. Porten was
often puzzled to defend the mysteries of a faith in which she had
not yet ceased to believe; and thus it came about that in the mood
of "blind activity" through which he was now passing, Gibbon
began to examine his own faith with a bewildered and critical

eye. How he progressed, and whether it was Bossuet or Parsons, the Elizabeth Jesuit, who completed his conversion, is today of very small importance. In fact, during the course of a solitary excursion to London, he inquired at a Catholic bookseller's in Covent Garden for a priest who could instruct him, was recommended to the Chaplain of the Sardinian Ambassador and by him solemnly received into the Roman Catholic Church, on the 8th of June, 1753. "Youth [he was to write at a later period, tolerantly, it is true, yet perhaps not altogether unregretfully] is sincere and impetuous; . . . a momentary glow of enthusiasm had raised me above all temporal considerations." That it was impossible to ignore such considerations, however, soon became apparent. "An elaborate controversial epistle," approved by his director, had broken the news, not very gently, to Mr. Gibbon at Buriton, who, in his usual impetuous way, at once divulged the whole story to the University authorities. From the point of view of the fellows of Magdalen, sympathetic as they might have shown themselves towards almost any other shortcoming, public apostasy ranked as a crime that admitted of no excuse; and Gibbon's University career was brought to a sudden end. Far worse, after much discussion with various friends and advisers, Mr. Gibbon decided that his son's predicament called for a strenuous remedy. In deep disgrace, during the same month that had witnessed his conversion, Edward Gibbon, at the age of sixteen, was ordered out of England.

The apostate went as he was commanded—he had no alternative; with the result that, at the beginning of July, Monsieur Pavilliard, a learned Calvinist minister of Lausanne, gazed in astonishment at the strange spectacle presented by a very small Englishman, whose diminutive body supported an enormous head, standing before him and eloquently urging the case for Romanism by means of the best arguments that the minister had ever heard put forward. Gibbon was to remain at Lausanne for nearly five years; and, at a very early stage, a measure of respect, bordering on affection, developed between the Swiss master and his curiously gifted pupil. Gibbon put up a stiff fight in defence of his new-found creed; but his spiritual obstinacy (Pavilliard soon distinguished) was accompanied by a strong backing of intellectual honesty. *"Il n'est pas* [wrote Pavilliard to Mr. Gibbon] *ce qu'on appelle chicaneur."* Another young man might have collapsed completely, have been insolent, peevish, insubordinate or withdrawn into sulky silence; Pavilliard's pupil kept his dignity and continued to dispute his ground. He experienced, nevertheless, all the gloom of an exile's life—in a household whose language he had not yet learned to speak, among surroundings which contrasted painfully with the substantial elegance that had encircled him at Buriton and Oxford. Madame Pavilliard proved "ugly, dirty, proud, ill-tempered and covetous." Her table-cloths were soiled; the warmed-up legs of mutton she served her *pensionnaires* were meagre and unappetising; grim stoves took the place of blazing open fires; the room which had been assigned to Gibbon was small and cold and squalid. Moreover, Monsieur Pavilliard had been instructed to allow him at first very little money. Lost to the faith of his childhood and cast off by his father, too poor to make an advantageous appearance in the company of his fellow Englishmen who passed through Switzerland, still half a boy, and in spite of much desultory reading, more than half uneducated, he was a youth as forlorn and solitary as any in Lausanne.

Self-pity, however, even at the age of sixteen, was not among his failings. Thrown back on his own resources, he began for the first time, under Pavilliard's guidance, to drive his way through the classics with systematic application. He read, translated and compared. So long as one read one need never be unhappy, absorbed in the gradual development of some mighty intellectual prospect, seen dimly at first through a fog of ignorance, more and more distinctly discerned as one stumbled slowly forward, till the whole landscape came into range, territory on territory up to the farthest skyline, magnificent with the works of the past, cities and fortresses and roads and aqueducts, multitudinous with the marchings and countermarchings, the migrations, feuds and alliances of unnumbered human beings. It was not so much that he was concerned to escape from the present day—though the splendid images evoked by some Roman historian were certainly a very welcome relief from the impression made by soiled table-cloths and cramped, uncleanly rooms; but the past gave to the present the justification that it needed, suggested a continuity in human affairs that, at a first glance, seemed often strangely lacking, supplied the perspective essential to a clear and dispassionate view. At thirteen, writing to Mrs. Porten in the earliest letter extant among his archives, he had described how, on a country expedition, he had examined "the Remains of an ancient Camp which pleased me vastly"; and the boy who, stepping from the family coach, had surveyed with delight the huge grassy earthworks, the trackways, moats and enclosures of some prehistoric settlement, lost in the lonely undulations of the Wiltshire or Hampshire downs, felt his excitement spring up afresh as he explored the monumental achievements of the Roman poets and historians, and discovered an immense new world of experience which completed and enclosed his own.

Little by little, thanks to the promptings of Monsieur Pavilliard, to the effects of separation from his family, but most of all to the pleasure he had now learned to take in thinking for himself, the "honourable and important part" he had hitherto played, as convert, enthusiast and religious exile, grew less and less attractive. Learning was his true mistress, faith a passing love; years later, he remembered his "solitary transport" when he hit upon a philosophic argument against the mystery of transubstantiation; and on Christmas Day, 1754, after nearly eighteen months of polite discussion, carried through without the smallest hint of acrimony between the pastor and his pupil, he received the sacrament and was readmitted to the arms of the Protestant Church. But he was not (as perhaps he had expected) immediately welcomed home. Till the spring of 1758, he was obliged to remain abroad; and in the meantime his father had re-married —an event which filled him, when he first heard of it, with the gloomiest apprehensions, since it seemed to threaten his own chances of future independence—and he had learned to speak and write in French, but during the process had almost forgotten the use of the English tongue. His letter to his aunt, announcing his re-conversion, was an odd jumble of French phrases literally translated. "I am now a good Protestant . . . [he wrote to Mrs. Porten], I have in all my letters taken notice of the different movements of my mind, entirely Catholic when I came to Lausanne, wavering long time between the two systems, and at last fixed for the Protestant. . . ." M. Pavilliard (he concluded) "appeared extremely glad of it. I am so extremely myself, and do assure you feel a joy pure, and the more so, as I know it to be not only innocent but laudable."

Simultaneously, M. Pavilliard had relaxed his discipline; and the same letter that brought the news of his return to Protestantism included a report of an unexpected and, for Gibbon, a somewhat dreadful mishap. He had lost forty guineas at cards to an English traveller; a further seventy, when he claimed his revenge, had vanished the same way; and the young man, penniless and completely distraught, had been "a great while hesitating [he told his aunt] upon the most violent parties." In the end, he had borrowed a horse and, although he was an exceedingly bad horseman, ridden as far as Geneva, with some vague plan of proceeding to London where he could raise the money. But at Geneva Pavilliard had overtaken him and had brought him back to Lausanne. Mrs. Porten invoked the assistance of Mr. Gibbon who, as a former devotee of the great world, could not consider gambling a particularly serious vice; and he had good-naturedly agreed to settle the debt of honour. It was to be one of the few examples in Gibbon's life of definite imprudence, of the kind of thoughtlessness so often displayed in the careers of other young men, at a time when the desire to live to the full is least under control and most destructive; and, in this form at all events, it would never occur again.

There still awaited him, however, an emotional setback. Gibbon's nature was keen but cool; there was little in his make-up of that muddied and troubled fervour from which are hatched the great majority of so-called romantic passions; in later life, as soon as he felt, he began at once to think and, by taking thought, usually stifled the emotion before it disturbed his repose. Yes, it was difficult, as he reviewed his progress, to see himself as at one time a staunch believer, ready to sacrifice all in the cause of his chosen faith; it was more difficult still, though a pleasing flight of memory, to regain that infinitely remote, if unforgettable, period when he had been deeply and honestly in love, and had had his love returned—with a warmth and energy, indeed, which, even during the heyday of the sentiment, proved not altogether unembarrassing. Slight, solemn, ceremonious, in person only a little over five foot tall, a poor rider and a diligent but indifferent dancer, Gibbon showed few surface-qualities that seemed likely to engage a woman; but Suzanne Curchod had the wit or the sensitiveness to discover his attraction. His physiognomy, which still wore the indecision and the charm of youth, with smoothly rounded cheeks that had not yet begun to swell and droop till they eclipsed the rest of the face, she described in the literary character that she wrote of him as *"spirituelle et singulière."* Herself she was, if not quite a beauty, one of those rare, radiant, delightful and delighted beings, produced now and then by northern European countries, whose candour is expressed by a clear and luminous skin, and whose energy is reflected in their large translucent eyes. Mademoiselle Curchod's eyes were big, her nose intelligently proportioned, her hair a fine blond, her body light and elastic, her carriage spirited but graceful. It may be surmised—a point not without significance when we are discussing their relationship—that Suzanne was the taller of the two, just as it is clear that she was also the more impetuous. Yet there is no doubt that he really loved her. Over the whole brief, innocent, inconclusive episode breathes an air of Alpine freshness, very much in keeping with the background of lake-shore, vineyards, snow-peaks and neat white-walled, green-shuttered houses against which it was enacted. Suzanne Curchod lived at Crassy where her father was the minister. She met Gibbon in the summer of 1757. He was now twenty; Mademoiselle Curchod was two years younger. During June he recorded in his journal that love had triumphed—"I saw Mademoiselle Curchod. *Omnia vincit amor et nos cedamus amori."* At the beginning of August he visited Crassy and passed two days there, which were followed by a visit of nearly a week in the middle of November. Meanwhile he had sworn "an attachment beyond the assaults of time." He gazed and the young woman did not withdraw her gaze; in her looks "I thought I read your tenderness and my happiness." Soon his infatuation was observed, and their companions teased him. ". . . My heart was too full to reply. I pretended business and locked myself in my room."

Gibbon's temperament, however, included an essentially cautious strain. There was the knowledge that he must return to England, and meet his father and his stepmother; and there was the certainty that Mr. Gibbon would receive with horror and amazement the news that his only son purposed to entangle himself in an obscure and alien marriage. The income at his own disposal would, no doubt, be extremely small. Suzanne was the first woman he had loved—perhaps *"la seule femme qui eût pû me rendre heureux";* but reminders of Buriton and England were powerful and omnipresent. He hoped and planned, nevertheless—though not so resolutely as poor Suzanne seemed to consider natural; and when he was at last summoned home in April, 1758, and disguised as a Swiss Officer (such was the latitude that warring armies of that happy period allowed to the travelling civilian) had passed through hostile French territory and embarked at a Dutch port, he left behind him a definite promise to return and claim her. His hopes were quickly crushed; the vision soon evaporated. On landing in England, he had immediately hurried round to his Aunt Kitty's house in College Street, Westminster, where the whole evening was spent "in effusions of joy and confidence." His approach to Mr. Gibbon was far more tentative; he still remembered the awful severity with which his father had been invested five years earlier, and looked forward to meeting him again with a tremor of nervous anguish. But both had changed, and, on each side, the change was favourable. The advance of age had softened and modified

Mr. Gibbon's character; he received his son "as a man and a friend"; an understanding sprang up between them which was never afterwards to be interrupted; henceforward they were fellow men of the world who lived together "on the same terms of easy and equal politeness." With his stepmother, whom he had dreaded meeting, the relationship Gibbon established proved to be no less happy. Middle-aged, possessed of an independent fortune, Dorothea Patton was a sensible, intelligent and charming woman. Second only to dear Aunt Kitty, she was to become the closest and most constant of all his woman friends.

There remained the problem of Mademoiselle Curchod. Hesitantly Gibbon laid bare his heart; and Mr. Gibbon's response was what he had expected and, it may be, already acquiesced in—a vehement and aggrieved refusal to give him his paternal blessing. Through such a marriage his son would be completely lost to England. As it was, he was half a foreigner; and indignantly Mr. Gibbon pulled out a pathetic stop, describing the guilt Edward would incur by thus cutting adrift from his family and his ancestral ties, and the misery he would bring down on those who loved him. The young man demanded two hours for reflection; and two hours were enough. Resignedly he agreed to give up Suzanne: "I sighed as a lover, I obeyed as a son. . . ." The famous phrase rolls out perhaps a little too smoothly. Was the struggle as "painful" as he afterwards persuaded himself? Had the battle not been already lost as soon as he set foot in England, and felt the gaiety and brilliance of London and the placid dignity of Buriton gradually steal in upon him and undermine his spirit? He was an Englishman first and foremost—but, as it turned out, an Englishman without an established place; for the nine months he spent in London during the next two years were, on the whole, a dull, disappointing and uneventful period. In Switzerland, he had sometimes visited M. de Voltaire's private theatre at Monrepos and heard him mouth his way through his own tragedies of *Zaïre, Alzire, Zulime* with prodigious pomp and gusto; and now in London he became an enthusiast for the heroes of the English stage, and applauded David Garrick, then at the zenith of his genius and celebrity. Otherwise his amusements were few. At a later time, he was to observe (as a fact gratifying to the pride of the nation but destructive of the happiness of the individual) "the poor figure a man of two thousand pounds a year makes in London with great Œconomy"; and the income in his possession was a mere three hundred. Besides, his father's old friends, on whom he depended for introductions, had died or proved forgetful. There was the aged Lady Hervey, a relic from the days of Queen Caroline and Frederick Prince of Wales, who received him with the somewhat misty kindness of a decrepit *grande dame*, and David Mallet, who had known and still remembered Mr. Gibbon, and who first presented his son to Lady Hervey's circle. But many were the evenings when he sat quite alone, in the lodgings that cost him a guinea-and-a-half a week, while passing coaches rattled over the Bond Street cobbles. Now and then, looking up from his book—very often one or other of the great modern historians, Robertson and Hume—he would breathe a faint sigh in the direction of Lausanne; and, when spring came, he abandoned "without reluctance . . . the noisy and extensive scene of crowds without company, and dissipation without pleasure." His education had yet far to go; he was still swaddled in a close chrysalis-shroud of innocence and immaturity.

In the meantime, he did not fret unduly against life at Buriton. Mrs. Gibbon was a good hostess and a skilful housekeeper; and in agreeable contrast to the "uncleanly avarice" of Madame Pavilliard was the "daily neatness and luxury of an English table." Footmen and farmhands frequently exchanged their functions; and Mr. Gibbon's favourite team, "a handsome set of bays or greys," usually worked in the fields when they were not harnessed to the carriage. Gibbon derived a detached literary amusement from the completeness of the picture; but his father could never inspire him with a love of farming; he did not shoot, rode as seldom as possible and usually ended his walks at a quiet, convenient bench, where he pulled a book from his pocket and began to read again. For reading was his chief passion, his real existence—the English philosophers and historians, the Roman classics, the works of Homer (in which he had made some progress, though his knowledge of Greek was still imperfect, under Monsieur Pavilliard's direction) or the productions of such continental *savants* as the Neapolitan Giannone. A great part of his quarterly allowance was spent in the purchase of books, and he would not soon forget the joy with which he had "exchanged a bank-note of twenty pounds for the twenty volumes of the *Memoirs of the Academy of Inscriptions.*" The library was a comfortable room. He entered it early in the morning, and left it, unwillingly but obediently, to join the family at the "long and regular" feasts with which they celebrated the hours of breakfast, dinner, tea and supper, or when, after breakfast, his stepmother wished him to attend her in her dressing-room and, after tea, his father expected him to talk and read aloud the newspapers. Now and then, the arrival of some tiresome neighbours broke in upon his solitude. There were occasional dinner-parties, and even visits to race meetings, at which Mr. Gibbon had entered a horse to run in the hunter's plate; and composedly Gibbon admired the beauty of the landscape, the prowess of the thoroughbreds, "and the gay tumult of the numerous spectators."

In these surroundings, under the lulling influence of this tranquil regimen, the recollection of Suzanne was no longer so compulsive. Mrs. Gibbon had intercepted certain letters from Switzerland in which Mademoiselle Curchod made a last effort to regain her hold, and had written back a letter of polite discouragement. The engagement was not definitely broken till 1761; but during the interval any genuine bond had gradually disappeared, while the progress of war in Europe, sweeping up towards and threatening the shores of England, had given a new direction to Gibbon's thoughts and put new and formidable obstacles in the way of a foreign marriage. To meet the danger of invasion, thirty-six battalions of militia were called up during 1759 from twenty-three English counties. In June both Gibbons obtained commissions—neither was of a particularly martial turn, but as country gentlemen it was their duty to set a good

example; and during the following year, somewhat to their surprise and much to the younger Gibbon's exasperation, the South
Hampshire Regiment was called out for active service. Thus began two and a half years of a "wandering life of military servitude." Almost from the outset, the burdens of a military life were
aggravated by the "prolix and passionate contest" that sprang up
between the officers of the South Hampshire Regiment and the
Duke of Bolton, Lord Lieutenant of the county, concerning the
appointment of their colonel, in which the Duke claimed jurisdiction over the North and South Regiments, his opponents
declared that it extended only to the North, and each side dispatched frequent and embittered appeals to the Secretary of State
for War. Gibbon was involved in endless paper-work. Moreover,
according to the whim of the War Office, the South Hampshire
Regiment was always on the move—from Winchester, where
they had first assembled, to the new-built and hospitable town of
Blanford; to Hilsea barracks, "a seat of disease and discord"; to
Cranbrook in the Weald of Kent, where they were set to guard
French prisoners in the ancient, half-ruined castle of Sissing-
hurst; to the chalky hills above Dover, whence they surveyed the
cliffs of France and saw the tall sails of the English fleet beating
up and down the channel; to Winchester again; to the "populous
and disorderly town of Devizes," where life was at its worst and
there were numerous cases of the clap and several courts martial;
back to "beloved Blanford"; and so at last to Southampton, a
fashionable seaside resort, where they remained till the Regiment was eventually disbanded.

"A most disagreeably active life," concluded Gibbon, after
seven or eight months of marching and counter-marching. He
had scarcely taken a book in his hand since he put on his regimentals; the first novelty had soon worn off; and he was "sick
of so hateful a service" and "tired of companions who had neither
the knowledge of scholars nor the manners of gentlemen." But it
was not long before his native pertinacity, in spite of the demands
of his new career, the stupidity of his associates and the convivial
habits imposed upon them all by their "bumperising" command-

ing officer, Sir Thomas Worsley, had begun to reassert itself. A book was produced from his luggage whenever the chance occurred; in his journal, besides recording the various exercises through which he led his company and the devious ramifications of the squabble with the Duke of Bolton, he kept track of the strange and fascinating journeys his mind had travelled. Even under canvas, in cold and stormy weather, when the officers were "crouded from morning to night into the Suttling booth; where reigned such noise and nonsense, as made it impracticable to read or think," he managed to run through the pages of a favourite volume. Mr. Gibbon had grown proud of his son's attainments; and at the end of April, 1761, at his father's request, Gibbon completed and revised for publication a literary thesis on which he had originally embarked at Lausanne, a defence, written in French, of the study of ancient literature against the iconoclastic tendencies of modern French criticism. This laborious juvenile work has now largely lost its interest; but it confirmed him, with his father's blessing, in the career of a literary man. An early copy was presented to the Duke of York, when he visited the Regiment—the same Royal Duke who had deigned to smile at Boswell—by its author who had just returned from a field day and made his bow "somewhat disordered with sweat and dust, in the cap, dress, and acoutrements of a Captain of Grenadiers." Other copies of the essay found their way to Paris, and created a small approving stir among the inhabitants of literary *salons*.

Meanwhile, war in Europe continued its wearisome course; and, reluctantly yet resignedly, the little awkward, serious figure of Captain Gibbon, jogging at the head of his rustic grenadiers, continued to circulate through English country towns. "The Gentlemen of the County [he records] shewed us great hospitality . . . but partly thro' their fault and partly thro' ours that hospitality was often debauch." It was during this period that Gibbon acquired the habit of hard but cheerful drinking. Other vices, however, he did not acquire. The undergraduate who had been too timid or too cautious to explore, "like a manly

Oxonian," the brothel and tavern quarter of Covent Garden, the innocent, delicate lover of Suzanne Curchod, preserved a certain romantic reticence in his dealings with the opposite sex. Women attracted him but still alarmed him. During his peregrinations he set eyes on a number of young women—particularly a Miss Chetwynd of Winchester—whose charm caused him "some uneasiness," to whom he bowed distantly and devotedly, and who made him wish, now and then, that he were a more accomplished dancer; but the emotions that they aroused were rarely beyond his control. He could hold his own, nevertheless, in rakish and worldly company; and when, during the spring of 1762, he found himself sitting upon a General Court Martial with that extremely profligate and loose-spoken officer of the Buckinghamshire Militia, Colonel John Wilkes, he was highly entertained by the extraordinary verve, indecency and pointed intelligence of the Colonel's after-dinner conversation. Of his personal deficiencies Gibbon was well aware. "Wit I have none," he wrote on his birthday, April 27. He was virtuous (he considered) and incapable of a base action, but "proud, violent, and disagreeable in society"; the pre-eminent qualities of his mind were "extensiveness and penetration; but I want both quickness and exactness." ". . . While every one looks on me [he added a few months later] as a prodigy of application, I know myself how strong a propensity I have to indolence." So different is a self-portrait from the impression that is formed of us by our friends or by our readers! Indolence is not a weakness with which we are inclined to credit Gibbon; for, in spite of many evenings of military "bumperising" and some mornings when, he is forced to acknowledge, he could "do nothing . . . but spew," till he scarce wondered "at the Confessor who enjoined getting drunk as a pennance," the thread of ambition he followed was never completely dropped; one project followed another; patiently he still groped ahead towards his unknown goal, the majestic, mysterious, undetermined book that waited to be written.

Was it to be an essay on Sir Walter Raleigh? Or a *History of the Liberty of the Swiss,* prepared, by way of contrast, in conjunction with a Medicean history of the Florentine Republic? Where was he to write it? How find time to begin? Then, on September 1, inspiriting news reached headquarters at Southampton. Peace negotiations had been opened. He was "once again a free man," Gibbon told himself with an impulse of immense relief. He could read uninterruptedly, travel as he pleased. Yet, all things considered, we cannot regret for Gibbon, nor at a later date did Gibbon regret for himself, the busy, exhausting years of his tedious militia service. Few historians who wrote of war could claim to have drilled a company, to have mastered the intricate exercises of a modern regiment, or experienced some of the physical rigours of an active military life. He had returned to England a foreigner. In two and a half years of bloodless campaigning, he had travelled over several hundred miles of the English landscape, become the familiar of English country towns, with their inns and their assembly rooms, their tradesmen and their gentry, and had learned to talk, drink and transact business with a not inconsiderable variety of his fellow human beings. Proud and disagreeable though he imagined himself, Gibbon's recorded behaviour provides no evidence of either of these traits. With his predilection for solitude went a delight in company; and when for the second time he encountered Wilkes, who was visiting Southampton and dined at the officers' mess, he observed that he had "scarcely ever met with a better companion; he has inexhaustible spirits, infinite wit and humour, and a great deal of knowledge." But Wilkes's reckless vitality proved somewhat shocking; and to his eulogium he added that the Colonel—at that time almost completely unknown, apart from his reputation as lecher and *bon viveur*—was "a thorough profligate in principle as in practice . . . his life stained with every vice, and his conversation full of blasphemy and bawdy. . . . He told us himself, that in this time of public dissension he was resolved to make his fortune." Gibbon seems to have been sober enough to be slightly taken aback; but Sir Thomas Worsley and the other officers were much less sensitive; and when Colonel Wilkes had deserted the mess-table, they broke into his room and obliged him, with up-roarious insistence, to drink a bottle of claret in bed.

At length, on December 17, 1762, came "the memorable day of our final separation." Gibbon wasted no false sentiment on the career he was leaving behind. His view of the last two years was rational and philosophic. It was true he had lost time, but he had also learned much; ". . . my principal obligation to the militia was the making me an Englishman and a soldier. After my foreign education, with my reserved temper, I should long have continued a stranger to my native country, had I not been shaken in this various scene of new faces and new friends; had not experience forced me to feel the characters of our leading men, the state of parties, the forms of office, and the operation of our civil and military system." The conclusion of his service was marked by a crescendo of conviviality. On December 17, Gibbon supped with "old Captain Meard" and all his officers, which "made the evening [he confesses] rather a drunken one"; and on the 23rd his own grenadier company was marched over to Alton to be disembodied; "they fired three volleys, lodged the major's colours, delivered up their arms, received their money," sat down to a dinner at Major Gibbon's expense, "and then separated with great cheerfulness and regularity." Gibbon himself proceeded to Buriton, and from Buriton to London, where he celebrated his independence in a late and agreeable gathering, from which "I could but just walk home about four o'clock."

The Historian

GIBBON's return to the Continent was peculiarly well-timed. The war just concluded had left behind it very little bitterness and, for reasons that modern experience makes some-what hard to follow, had added no inconsiderable lustre to our intellectual reputation. The great period of Anglomania was now beginning: "Our opinions, our fashions, even our games, were adopted in France; a ray of national glory illuminated each individual, and every Englishman was supposed to be born a patriot and a philosopher." He himself (Gibbon adds modestly) was assured of a special welcome. Both his name and his essay were known in Paris; and with him he carried letters of friendly recommendation from Walpole, Lady Hervey and the French Ambassador. It seems probable, however, that, as he looked back, he tended to confuse the earlier and a later visit. His Essay was a small thing, and had created a minor stir; the personality of the essayist was neither dominant nor dashing; he was received politely but without enthusiasm. The Duke of Bedford, then English Ambassador, did not proceed beyond the limits of cold official courtesy; Gibbon paid a preliminary call, but was never received again.

Lady Hervey's letter, on the other hand, procured him an entry to the celebrated *salon* of Madame Geoffrin; and there, as at the establishment of the lesser luminary, Madame du Bocage, and, later, through Madame Geoffrin, at the houses of Helvetius and the Baron d'Holbach, he found "a place without invitation" four days in the week and heard "more conversation worth remembering," and saw "more men of letters among the people of fashion," than he had done "in two or three winters in London." Though very often attempted, the portrait of Madame Geoffrin remains, nevertheless, perhaps a trifle hazy. She was rich; she loved learned men; yet by temperament Madame Geoffrin was not at all a bluestocking. She lived in the society of advanced and liberal writers; yet so pronounced was her dislike of excess, that the writer imprudent enough to have himself, for some offence against conservative opinions, committed to the Bastille, soon noticed, when he was released from confinement, that a shade of disapproval underlay the cordiality of Madame Geoffrin's greeting. For she was unswerving in her attachment to rule and measure. *"Voilà qui est bien"* was the set-phrase with which she put a term to any intellectual sally that threatened to become violent. Dignified and charming, with her silvery hair, simple black hood knotted beneath the chin, wide sleeves and exquisitely delicate and spotless linen, she ruled quietly but firmly over the turbulent crowd of writers and painters she had gathered at her table. By descent she belonged not to the aristocracy, of the court, the country or even of the robe, but to an *haute bourgeoisie* that had assimilated the aristocratic virtues. Her husband was a dull and elderly man, who had grown rich in trade. Monsieur Geoffrin had never shone and, when his dim light was at length extinguished, his disappearance seems to have been noticed by few of his wife's admirers. Her celebrated visit to the King of Poland—that semi-royal embassy—had not yet been undertaken; and she remained meanwhile an essentially urban and Parisian personage who adored company, loved the city in which she had been brought up and rarely left its confines. Such an intelligence, acute but limited, was likely to appeal to Gibbon. He shared many of her personal prejudices; her way of life had a grace and detachment that as yet he had failed to achieve.

Hostesses are not notorious for their discovery of unexploited talent; and we have no reason to suppose that Madame Geoffrin, on her side, made very much of Gibbon. Maybe, as a biographer has suggested, he was happier and more at ease in the society of Madame Bontemps, "a very good sort of a woman, agreeable and *sans prétensions*," who had "conceived a real motherly attachment" for the odd engaging young man who had known her son in England. Gibbon suspected for a moment that her feelings were slightly more ambiguous. She spoke to him at length of her private affairs: *"elle avait même quelquefois des Ouvertures que je ne comprends pas trop encore. Elle me parlait des plaisirs des sens . . . et lorsque . . . je m'émancipois un peu, elle me repoussait faiblement et paraissait émue."* It would be tempting to conclude that the excellent and affectionate Madame Bontemps played a decisive rôle in Gibbon's education, but the phrase that follows—*"avec un peu plus de hardiesse j'aurais peut être réussi"*—would seem to show that Gibbon's native caution prevailed over any desire to enlarge his worldly knowledge. Meanwhile, the time had come when he must continue his journey; and, during the month of May, after repeated snubs from the Duke of Bedford, some instructive evenings with the Encyclopædists and many pleasant, if uneventful, hours with Madame Bontemps, he left Paris, passed through Besançon and arrived again in Switzerland. He had said good-bye to Lausanne as an inexperienced youth; he returned, at least in his own opinion, a finished man of the world.

As such, he established himself, not with Monsieur Pavilliard but at a *pension,* both more comfortable and more fashionable, kept by Monsieur de Mesery. As such, too, he found it a relatively simple matter to hold at arm's length Suzanne Curchod, who still hoped that her prudent lover would finally renew his attack. Gibbon had considered the question, but decided otherwise. He was horrified to notice how even the quietest and best-conducted virgin might conceal depths of deliberation beneath an innocent unruffled mask. When he saw that she was prepared to pursue him, he quietly stepped aside. "Playing at love if not busy with it," advertising a string of adorers she encouraged and held off, professing an air of candour, and pretending to weep (though she remained dry-eyed) at Monsieur de Voltaire's tragedies, she struck terror into his naïve heart and provided him with a curious subject for critical observation. The family at Buriton, he knew, would never approve; by his own standards of feminine fitness, Suzanne would never do; and, after a short renewal of their friendship, his attitude towards Mademoiselle Curchod grew positively envenomed. *"Fille dangereuse et artificielle!"* he apostrophised her angrily. Much safer was it to enjoy with his friends Deyverdun and Holroyd (later Lord Sheffield) the mild amusements afforded by the good society of Lausanne, to consort with a company of well-brought-up young people known as the *"Société du Printemps"* (the Swiss girls, Holroyd noted, were "not so reserved as English misses but . . . extremely shy of pawing or handling") and to indulge in tentative but amusing flirtations with a certain Madame Seigneux.

During August he visited Geneva for the purpose of seeing Voltaire perform at Ferney. It proved a strange yet stimulating experience—to watch "Voltaire at seventy, acting a Tartar Conqueror with a hollow broken voice, and making love to a very ugly niece of about fifty." But the play itself, which lasted from eight to half-past eleven, was followed by a "very elegant supper of a hundred Covers" in which the entire audience was asked to join, and supper by dancing which continued till four o'clock. Voltaire's talents as a tragedian appeared no longer so impressive; but the spectacle of such munificence, accompanied by such vitality and such a delight in living, helped to efface the cadaverous oddity of the patriarch's speech and manner. Other evenings passed in a less respectable fashion. There were bouts of masculine "bumperising," followed by dismal mornings passed *"à vomir et à dormir"*; yet, in spite of these occasional excesses, the tenor of his stay at Lausanne was on the whole diligent and dignified; and when, after nearly a year spent beside the Lake of Leman, he set out for Italy in April, 1764, he took with him a considerable equipment of miscellaneous learning. Not only had he renewed his acquaintance with the Latin Poets, but he had devoted much assiduous study to the investigation of medals and antiquities, the topography of Rome and the geography of ancient Italy. The pleasure with which he approached his goal, bobbing across the Mont Cenis in a "light osier chair, in the hands of the dexterous and intrepid chairmen of the Alps," and enjoying simultaneously "a very fine day, a most romantick variety of prospects, and a perfect consciousness that there could not be the smallest danger," was poetic and visionary as well as archæological. In Turin, it is true, he found very little interest; for the society of the place was stiff, and the Court proved old and dull; but Gibbon engaged in a lively conversation about Lausanne with the Piedmontese princesses, and so far forgot his reserve in the royal presence-chamber as to rap on his snuff-box and inhale a pinch of snuff, continuing his discourse in "my usual attitude of my body bent forwards, and my forefinger stretched out." A visit to the Borromean Islands was wet and overclouded.

From Milan he had intended to turn aside to Venice; but reports of "crowds and dearness," and of "shoals of English pouring in from every side," induced him to change his plans and travel straight to Florence, passing on the road through Parma, Modena and Bologna. From Florence, where he dined with Horace Mann and reposed in congenial company during the heat of the summer months, he departed for the south as September drew to an end. "A very agreeable tour," lasting ten days and embracing Lucca, Pisa, Leghorn and Siena, brought him at length to the Milvian Bridge, whence he entered the streets of Rome.

Arrived at his destination, he passed a restless night and rose early. To minimise, rather than exaggerate, his emotions was always Gibbon's instinct: "My temper [he would write] is not very susceptible of enthusiasm, and the enthusiasm which I do not feel I have ever scorned to affect." But the establishment of his fame and the passage of twenty-five years could not efface the impression made by that momentous morning; he could never forget the exquisite excitement with which he started out upon his pilgrimage; there remained always a residue of emotion he could not translate into words. It was with a full heart and "a lofty step" that he explored the ruins of the Forum. Applied to so small and inconspicuous a traveller, the expression "lofty" has a peculiar charm, since it suggests at once the slight absurdity of Gibbon's physical presence, his sense of his own dignity (founded on a firm consciousness of his own integrity) characteristic both of his style and of the man behind the style, and the romantic imagination by which his style was coloured. Yet, however strong the impetus of emotion, there were still the claims of scholarship to exert a restraining influence. He was "almost in a dream," he wrote to tell his father. Books had prepared him for the experience; but "whatever ideas books may have given us" of the greatness of the Roman people, and of the splendour of Rome itself during its long imperial heyday, "fall infinitely short of the picture of its ruins. I am convinced there never, never existed such a nation, and I hope for the happiness of mankind there never will again." The effect was at first chaotic and, somewhat unexpectedly, he proceeded to describe Trajan's column by remarking that the thirty drums of "purest white marble" of which it was composed were "wrought into bas-reliefs with as much taste and delicacy as any chimney piece at Up-park," the new-built residence of a newly rich neighbour, Sir Matthew Featherstonhaugh. But, after "several days of intoxication," of dream-like impressions and wild comparisons, he embarked, under the guidance of a sober Scottish antiquary, Mr. Byers, on a "cool and minute investigation" of the craggy tree-grown ruins, half buried in the rubbish of centuries or embedded in the fabric of mediæval palaces and churches, round which the papal city clustered. More than four months were devoted to this delightful, exhausting task. He emerged towards the end of January, confident that his labour had been repaid, and that he had acquired a solid groundwork to be built upon at leisure.

Meanwhile the period of assiduous sightseeing had brought him somewhat more than knowledge. The eighteenth century was prolific of travellers; other students, no less attentive, had wandered through the Forum; it remained for Gibbon, on the 15th of October, 1764, only a few days after his arrival, while his feelings were yet tumultuous and the months of systematic research were only just beginning, to enjoy one of those flashes of insight, one of those sudden and tremendous glimpses into the nature and possibilities of any given subject, loosely and perplexingly entitled "inspiration," that concentrate all the dispersed elements in the artist's creative impulse. How it descended, what prepared it, we cannot exactly tell. Its origins lay deep in his youth—they might be traced back to the pleasure with which, as a boy of thirteen, he had examined the earthworks of a so-called Roman camp, or perhaps even farther, to his first notions of antiquity, gathered as a sickly nervous child who had learned to read beside the arm-chair of kindly Mrs. Porten. Certainly the experience owed much to Monsieur Pavilliard; the years of military servitude, when the young officer, beneath the flapping canvas of a rain-drenched mess-tent, had taken refuge in a volume of classics from the "noise and nonsense" raised by vulgar companions-in-arms, had strengthened the habit of concentration that such an experience needs. But the determining factor was, of course, Rome itself—the city that has changed so often, survived the assaults of so many vandals, foreign and domestic, yet in the mysterious influence it exercises has changed so little, as if that influence were a property of its very soil and air, as if the splendour of its fountains and colonnades, the stateliness of churches and terraces and triumphal stairways, were indigenous to the place like the beauty of its light and flowers. Gibbon was no doubt insensitive to the charm of mediæval Rome. But spells, the most powerful, are seldom felt distinctly; and that October evening, having ascended the steps of the Capitol and sat down—not, it is permissible to suppose, without some careful looking and dusting—upon a slab, conveniently low, of dirty sun-warmed marble, he heard the bare-footed friars of the order of St. Francis intoning their Christian vesper-hymn in a church that he imagined—but imagined quite erroneously [1] —to have once housed the cult of the Father of Olympus. It was then (he informs us in a famous passage) that "the idea of writing the decline and fall of the city first started to my mind." His plan, afterwards enlarged, was already sufficiently extensive. For the moment it covered the city and did not embrace the empire; but implicit in the design was the whole gigantic conception of past and present history, of the past that lives in the present, and of the present that endlessly and painfully continues to repeat the past. In the rhythm of that hoarse liturgical chant, he caught his earliest premonitions of a larger, subtler, more melodious, entirely pagan harmony.

　　Gibbon remained in Rome till the arrival of the New Year. Then, towards the end of January, he once again turned southward and, having jolted painfully over "the very worst roads in the universe . . . sometimes sunk in sloughs and sometimes racked and battered on the broken remains of the old Appian

---

[1] In his admirable short study of Gibbon, G. M. Young has pointed out that the church in which the friars were singing was built not on the site of the Temple of Jupiter, but on that of Juno.

way," he reached Naples, to find the city and its fabulous surroundings enveloped in the obscurity of a heavy winter fog. But
the clouds lifted; the waters of the bay reassumed their shifting
glassy brilliance; he was able to enjoy the spectacle of the slip-
shod, many-coloured city, "whose luxurious inhabitants seem to
dwell on the confines of paradise and hell-fire," and through "our
new envoy," that amiable virtuoso, Sir William Hamilton,
obtain an introduction to the presence of the youthful Bourbon
monarch. In the meantime, it had become clear that he must
think of returning to England; money was short; and he had discovered that, owing to the habitual incompetence and hopeless
extravagance of the elder Mr. Gibbon, the affairs of the estate at
Buriton were being seriously mismanaged. He regained Rome,
but there lingered as long as he decently could; and, when at last
he had broken the spell and reluctantly resumed his journey, by
comparison no place he visited seemed quite to fulfil his hopes.
The fertile regularity of the Lombard Plain he found soothing
and delightful; Verona was distinguished by its amphitheatre,
Vicenza by the grace of Palladio's classic buildings; but an air of
desolation brooded over Ferrara's empty, grass-grown streets: the
University of Padua was "a dying taper"; while, as for Venice, of
all the towns of Italy there was none in which he discovered so
little to admire as in the capital of the moribund republic. "A
momentary surprise" soon gave way to "satiety and disgust," as
he surveyed "old and in general ill-built houses, ruined pictures,
and stinking ditches, dignified with the pompous denomination
of canals, a fine bridge spoilt by two Rows of houses upon it, and
a large square decorated with the worst Architecture I ever yet
saw. . . ." Gibbon the historian was to turn a blind eye to the
qualities of the Byzantine genius. In Gibbon the traveller,
fortified by his impressions of Rome, the traces of Byzantium,
with which Venice is encrusted as with some delicate marine
deposit, would appear to have stirred feelings of impatience and
resentment that were less reasoned than instinctive.

Further disquieting news from Buriton hastened his journey
home. He halted, nevertheless, at Paris for "ten delicious days,"

and there, with mild satirical amusement, observed an old acquaintance in a new and surprising rôle. Suzanne Curchod had married—and married to great advantage; since, having finally abandoned all hopes of Gibbon, she had left Switzerland for Paris as the companion of a rich elderly widow, and in Paris had accepted the hand of a middle-aged financier, Jacques Necker, by whom she was afterwards to become the mother of that volcanic literary phenomenon, Madame de Staël-Holstein. At the beginning essentially a marriage of reason, it was at length to provide an outlet for the devoted loyalty and latent tenderness of Suzanne Curchod's nature. She grew to love and esteem her gifted, conscientious but low-spirited and unamusing husband; and by the time Gibbon arrived in Paris she was able to receive him with complete lack of emotion and dazzling self-assurance. Gibbon, on his side, was pleased and relieved, but also a little piqued. The Curchod (he told Holroyd) was "as handsome as ever and much genteeler." She seemed very fond of him, he was glad to note; her husband was civil and attentive as a husband should be, but displayed not the smallest flicker of matrimonial apprehension. "Could they insult me more cruelly? Ask me every evening to supper; go to bed, and leave me alone with his wife—what an impertinent security! It is making an old lover of mighty little consequence." And he consoled himself with one or two strokes of gently feline malice, remarking how, when he mentioned the fortune of another young person of Lausanne who had also married money, the wife of the mighty banker could not conceal her disdain. " 'What fortune?' said she, with an air of contempt—'not above twenty thousand Livres a year.' I smiled, and she caught herself immediately. 'What airs I give myself in despising twenty thousand Livres a year, who a year ago looked upon eight hundred as the summit of my wishes.' " At which, no doubt, they both of them laughed. But Suzanne, in the candle-light, after Necker had retired to bed, while Gibbon rapped his snuff-box and, with forefinger outstretched, discoursed upon his travels or described the various problems awaiting him as soon as he returned to England, was herself watching

EDWARD GIBBON
From a painting by Sir Joshua Reynolds

her old admirer, quietly sizing him up and deciding, without unkindness, that he lacked the solider virtues. It had been an inexpressible pleasure, she informed a friend "—not that I retain any sentiment for a man who I now see can scarcely be said to deserve it; but my woman's vanity had never triumphed more thoroughly or less improperly—I had him at my house every day; he has become gentle, adaptable, humble, decent to the point of complete propriety. . . . As a zealous admirer of riches, he pointed out to me for the first time the opulence of my own surroundings—till then, at least, such impression as they made on me had been merely disagreeable." Each account is a trifle malicious and slightly disingenuous: the ashes of their former love, from which would presently emerge a real and lasting friendship, were still capable of giving off a faintly acrid odour.

It was after an interval of two years and five months that Gibbon, who had driven straight from Dover, passing hurriedly "through the summer dust and solitude of London," once again presented himself at his father's house, on the 25th June, 1765. He had aged and matured considerably; his emancipation, he may have hoped, was now complete and final; but on his return he encountered further setbacks, and some years were to pass— years full of vexation and small discomforts—before he achieved the personal independence of which he had always dreamed. His egotism, however—for it would be foolish to pretend that he did not naturally look inwards—was qualified by a strong sense of the duties of family life; and when he saw the elder Mr. Gibbon ailing and despondent, and learned that the family estates, encumbered by a heavy mortgage, had long since ceased to pay their way, he did his best to sink the historian in the dutiful son and the industrious man of business. Motives both of piety and of self-preservation—with Gibbon a characteristic blend of interests—confirmed him in his conduct. He must honour his obligations towards his father; even more emphatically, he must save some remnants of the fortune on which the tranquillity and well-being of his future life depended. With Mr. Gibbon at the helm, the prospects of the family remained precarious; and his father's death, after a slow and painful illness, in November, 1770, was an event which although it occasioned him at the time deep and honest sorrow, he was able to accept in a spirit of philosophic resignation. He "submitted to the order of nature" and allowed his grief to be soothed by the "conscious satisfaction" that he had "discharged all the duties of filial piety."

The intervening years had been dull and slow-paced. They formed, indeed, the part of his life that (as he wrote afterwards) he remembered with least satisfaction and had passed with least enjoyment. Every spring, till 1770, he unwillingly dragged himself to the militia exercises; the summer at Buriton was enlivened by the regular appearance of his friend Deyverdun, with whom he engaged in various minor literary projects, including an annual review of British arts and manners, translated into French and entitled *Mémoires Littéraires de la Grande Bretagne;* when the winter months came round again, he fell back on London. Though neither embittered nor discontented, he was beginning to fret against the narrowness of the bounds by which his life was circumscribed. His grand design he still contemplated "at an awful distance"; the introductory chapters of a history of Switzerland, after three years of research and writing, had been at length abandoned; and *Critical Observations on the Sixth Aeneid,* published as a separate essay, received and, in fact, deserved very little notice. His father's death seemed to open a slightly wider view; but more difficult than the effort of resigning himself to Mr. Gibbon's death was his struggle to remedy the confusion his father had left behind. Luckily, he had a friend and ally. Dear Holroyd—soon to become Lord Sheffield—was both practical and patient; and, when letters arrived that he dare not read through, he contracted the habit of sending them unopened down to Sheffield Place. Nevertheless, he was acutely irritated. Lands must be sold; but the months dawdled by and they remained unsold, or a succession of dishonest purchasers went back upon their bargains. Very gradually, his prospects improved. By the autumn of 1772, he could report himself to

Holroyd as "happy . . . exquisitely happy, at feeling so many Mountains taken off my shoulders"; Buriton had been let; his stepmother, whom he loved, but did not wish to adopt as an inseparable life-companion, had retired to Bath, there to pass the remainder of her days in dignified obscurity; he could travel up to London and look round for a vacant house.

His choice alighted finally on Number Seven Bentinck Street, a small house by eighteenth-century standards, but elegant and comfortable, which he proceeded to equip in the height of contemporary taste. Thus, for the library, naturally the most important room, he selected "a fine shag flock paper, light blue with a gold border"; the bookcases were to be painted white and "ornamented with a light frize; neither Doric nor Dentulated" but chastely "Adamic." Six servants attended his needs; he kept a parrot and presently acquired a Pomeranian lapdog—"pretty, impertinent, fantastical, all that a young Lady of fashion ought to be"; from time to time he was able to welcome his friends at delightful little dinner-parties. He was elected, moreover, to several London clubs, White's, Brooks's, Boodle's; and, in 1774, he became a member of The Club itself. A year earlier, the same distinction had been conferred on Boswell; but between Gibbon, composed, urbane, gravely ceremonious, and Boswell, restless, talkative, volatile, hopelessly undignified, now cast down to the depths of despair, now heated with wine and flushed with enthusiasm, caught up in a mood of uncontrollable excitement, there was a lack of sympathy which soon developed, at least so far as Boswell was concerned, into furious antipathy. Gibbon, he declared, was an "ugly, affected, disgusting fellow" who poisoned every meeting. Nor against Johnson's thunders did Gibbon's measured periods resound to very much advantage. He prudently refrained from a trial of strength; and the protests on which he occasionally ventured were delivered *sotto voce*.

His sense of his own value, at this and later periods, was rarely self-assertive. In 1774, besides joining The Club thanks to the good offices of his cousin, Mr. Eliot, he slipped quietly into Parliament; but, although his first session was occupied by no less a question than the differences of the mother country and her refractory American colonies, and over the head of the new member swept the "profuse and philosophic fancy" of Burke, and "the argumentative vehemence of Fox, who, in the conduct of a party, approved himself equal to the conduct of an Empire," while Lord North, himself "a consummate master of debate," replied for the government or snatched an interval of sleep, upheld "on either hand by the majestic sense of Thurlow, and the skilful eloquence of Wedderburne," Gibbon listened and admired but refused to enter the field. It is not recorded that he ever spoke. Yet, just as his service with the Hampshire Yeomanry had been turned to useful purpose, so his mute attendance at the House of Commons was stimulating and instructive. He enjoyed the movement of a hard-fought debate; he appreciated the complex mechanism of a free assembly, and had "a near prospect of the characters, views and passions of the first men of the age." Lord North received his vote; when the time came, he might expect that his dutiful attention to the government cause would not go unrewarded. He cut, in short, a respectable but an unremarkable figure. It might have struck his acquaintances at Brooks's or Boodle's that Edward Gibbon—apart from the oddity of his appearance, which he exaggerated rather than disguised by the magnificent suits he wore—resembled half a hundred other middle-aged, moderately affluent men about London, with a pleasant house, a carriage and horses, a seat in Parliament and hopes, presently realised, of governmental pickings. He was comfortable, cultured, social. Yet working always within that, at first sight, somewhat flaccid organism was the tiny particle of singularity, the small hard scintilla of individual genius, that sets up the fruitful disturbance productive of works of art. He sat through debates; he attended dinner-parties; he even subscribed towards, and took a decorous share in, the social and scenic splendours of the Boodle's Masquerade, a gaudy perspective compact of "flying bridges, transparent temples and eighteen thousand lamps." In Bentinck Street, against the background of white-painted bookcases and pale blue gold-bordered wallpaper, he had begun an expedition which, till the summer of 1787, was to focus all his energy.

During the two years that elapsed between the death of his father and his establishment in London, he had made a preliminary examination of the ground that must be covered. As soon as he had a house to himself, he embarked on the actual work of writing, and composed and three times re-wrote the first chapter, twice patiently re-casting the second and third, before he was "tolerably satisfied" with the effect he had achieved, and the flow of composition became, paragraph by paragraph, more regular and rapid. We are told that, while composing, he walked to and fro across the library, and that the whole paragraph was complete—the necessary references, which he added later, having been jotted down on cards—when he finally regained his chair and resorted to pen and ink. Holroyd suspected that he was working too fast; but Gibbon reassured him; the whole fabric, he said, had undergone a long and elaborate process of correction and revision; his "diligence and accuracy," he afterwards told the world, were attested by his conscience. Thus he awaited the day of final publication without undue anxiety. During February, 1775, the first volume of *The History of the Decline and Fall of the Roman Empire* found its way into the bookshops and, from the booksellers, to "every table" and "almost every toilette." Cadell and Strahan had originally calculated on five hundred copies, but Cadell, with "prophetic taste," had increased this number to a thousand. The first edition to appear was immediately sold out, and two further editions were very soon exhausted. A great gust of fame seized on the modest author. His pride was immensely gratified; but it would be idle to pretend that he was either abashed or startled.

Besides, he had still far to go. For the next eleven years, though he never retired from the world and remained an attentive, if somewhat impassive, observer of the various revolutions of society and politics, the record of Gibbon's life is very largely the record of his work's development, as the original scheme gradually expanded through half a dozen volumes. Than the *Decline and Fall,* there is probably no book of equal size and scope more thoroughly imbued with the characteristic quality of a single man's intelligence. It is not that the historian makes arbitrary or unjustified incursions into the pages of his history; he has no reason to intrude himself, for, in fact, he is always there—not as a figure rising impertinently between the reader and his subject, but as an influence that colours every scene, moderates the verbal rhythm of each successive period, and links episode to episode in the same harmonious pattern. Naturally, such a feat of literary assimilation could only be achieved at the price, here and there, of a certain loss of sharpness. Detachment as complete as Gibbon's is not without its dangers. It is at a distance that we hear the tramp of iron-shod Roman legions: "the tremendous sound of the Gothic trumpet," reverberating through the streets of the silent unsuspecting capital, reaches us with a slightly muffled note, robbed of nothing of its dramatic dignity but of much of its primitive power. Gibbon's portrayal of the adventures of history is circumscribed by the limitations of Gibbon's temperament. Thus his heroes are urbane, accomplished, liberal-minded and occasionally a trifle pompous; his villains, either corrupt and feline, or outrageous in their barbaric offences against good feeling and propriety. Collectively, human beings are always a little absurd, corroded by those ruling passions that are the bane of human nature, rushing with deplorable precipitancy into foolish insurrections, or whipped into sudden rage by some unreasonable and untenable religious theory. His prejudices, moreover, extended both to human nature as a whole and to entire historic phases with which, owing to the peculiar constitution of his own mind, he happened not to sympathise. Its ability to cherish Gibbon would appear, in the last resort, to be the true standard of any age's culture. Yes, he would have been happy in the Age of the Antonines. There were characters he could recognise, a way of life that, although remote in time, was still in matters of the spirit distinctly comprehensible. Not so the Eastern Empire. Gibbon would have found no place in the swarming Byzantine world, among eunuchs and monks and furiously contending bishops. Hence his statement which, even by the light of common sense (apart from the additional light thrown by modern historical research) will not bear examination, that the Empire of the East "subsisted one thousand and fifty-eight years, in a state of premature and perpetual decay." Never has a decayed edifice been so long in falling, and seldom has an historic epoch been quite so grossly misinterpreted! Judged by Augustan standards, the civilisation of Byzantium was fragmentary and barbaric. But civilisation is a complex growth; human genius achieves fruition through many different channels; and there was only one line of achievement that Gibbon, in his own experience of life, had ever known or charted.

Such are the defects; the immense virtues of Gibbon's book need scarcely be underlined. Though he has been superseded, partially at least, as the authoritative historian of the decline of the Roman Empire, we must still salute him as its poet. Rhythmically sentence meets sentence, three separate sentences, between two full stops, frequently building up into one logical but allusive statement; and, with grave regular tread, paragraph follows paragraph to consolidate a chapter. Join the procession at almost any point, and you are immediately involved in the story, carried along by its development and submerged in the splendid music of solemn yet lively prose. For, though the surface of Gibbon's style is smooth, it is never dully uniform. It recalls one of those broad impetuous rivers, Rhine or Rhone or Garonne, whose massive glassy swells are continually erupting into small whirlpools, breaking into angry cross-currents that foam and vanish again. Every chapter has its incidents, its indignant or comic asides; but the main stream rolls evenly and swiftly forward, from the opening paragraph, whence Gibbon looks out across the vast ordered expanse of Roman Europe during the second century—an empire comprehending "the fairest part of the earth, and the most civilised portion of mankind," its frontiers "guarded by ancient renown and disciplined valour," its provinces united by the "gentle, but powerful influence of laws and manners"—to the sack of Constantinople and a last vision of Rome as it emerged, despoiled and almost unrecognisable, from the twilight of the Middle Ages.

Most gratifying of all the plaudits showered on his book was the generous approval extended by Hume and Robertson. He had his detractors too. Angry clergymen inveighed against the work's impiety; but few of their attacks were either well-informed or well-directed; and, though a pamphlet impugning his scholarship by a Mr. Davies of Oxford provoked Gibbon to compose a measured *Vindication* (published as a separate booklet in 1779), the clerical hubbub caused him little alarm and a good deal of amusement. Other critics took him to task on the ground of decency. Feminine virtue and religious faith were subjects on which Gibbon could seldom resist a jeer; and from irony he sometimes descended to the type of innuendo favoured by men of letters anxious to remind us that they are also men of the world. Gibbon's speculative salacity had a strongly bookish tinge. As disturbing is the tone of unctuous anticipation with which he approaches certain subjects, and the air of complacent detachment with which, now and then, he is inclined to look down upon his personages. "Nor does his humanity ever slumber [ran Porson's famous rebuke] unless when women are ravished or the Christians persecuted." Gibbon (Porson continued) wrote of Christianity like a man whom the Christian religion had personally injured. But he paid a high tribute to the historian's scholastic and literary merits; while the effect of his *Reply* to "the wretched Travis," one of the more ignorant of the critics who had questioned Gibbon's accuracy and whose defence of a spurious text had excited Porson's wrath, was to relegate that presumptuous scribbler to the ranks of immortal dunces.

Several portraits emerge from this auspicious period, illustrating both the pleasures of fame and its attendant perils. First, there is a slight self-portrait (contained in a letter to Holroyd) of the great man, on April 21, 1774, "writing at Boodle's, in a fine Velvet Coat, with ruffles of My Lady's chusing &c." Next, a glimpse of Gibbon with Johnson at an assembly of The Club. George Colman the Younger, then a boy, was present at the meeting. Having unwittingly provoked Johnson, he was set upon and castigated in the usual brutal manner, whereat Gibbon, no doubt in a spirit of contradiction, deigned to notice and console him, "condescending, once or twice, in the course of the evening, to talk with me." Johnson wore his rusty brown suit and black worsted stockings; Gibbon, flowered velvet, accompanied by a bag [1] and sword. As pronounced was the contrast between the style of speech that each of them adopted. "Johnson's style was grand, and Gibbon's elegant; the stateliness of the former was sometimes pedantick, and the polish of the latter was occasionally finical. Johnson march'd to kettle-drums and trumpets; Gibbon moved to flutes and hautboys; Johnson hew'd passages through the Alps, while Gibbon levell'd walks through parks and gardens." Johnson's eloquence proceeded with majestic impetuosity, regardless of his audience; Gibbon suited his conversation to the capacity of a shy and despondent youth. But it was done in his own way; "still his mannerism prevail'd;—still he tapp'd his snuff-box—still he smirk'd and smiled; and rounded his periods with the same air of good breeding, as if he were conversing with men—His mouth, mellifluous as Plato's, was a round hole, nearly in the centre of his visage."

Somewhat less happy in their effect are two succeeding sketches. Never averse from the applause of the *beau monde,* the historian attached particular importance to the praise of Horace Walpole. When it appeared in 1781, he had lent him a copy of his second volume, and Walpole returned it (as he told Mann) "with a most civil panegyric." Gibbon was pleased but still unsatisfied. He called on Walpole, expecting further applause; but the observations he now received were far less complimentary. Walpole allowed himself some petulant and slightly foolish animadversions upon the writer's subject. "Mr. Gibbon," he remarked, "I am sorry you should have pitched on so disgusting a subject as the Constantinopolitan history. There is so much of

---

[1] Bag wigs were a peculiarly French fashion and, when they were originally introduced to London, provoked the indignation of the populace, who were apt to amuse themselves by pulling the bags of inoffensive foreign visitors.

the Arians and Eunomians, and semi-Pelagians; and there is such a strange contrast between Roman and Gothic manners, and so little harmony between a Consul Sabinus and a Ricimer, Duke of the Palace, that though you have written the story as well as it could be written, I fear few will have patience to read it." Gibbon, not unnaturally, was shocked and mortified. "He coloured; all his round features squeezed themselves into sharp angles; he screwed up his button-mouth, and rapping his snuff-box, said, 'It has never been put together before'—so well, he meant to add—but gulped it. . . . I well knew his vanity, even about his ridiculous face and person, but thought he had too much sense to avow it so palpably."

More seriously disquieting was an incident that occurred in 1780, at a dinner given in Lincoln's Inn for the officers of the Northumberland Militia, who had been called down to London during the Gordon Riots. Gibbon at that time (the narrator informs us) was "not at all backward in availing himself of the deference universally shown to him. . . . His conversation was not, indeed, what Dr. Johnson would have called *talk*. There was no interchange of ideas, for no one had a chance of replying, so fugitive, so variable, was his mode of discoursing, which consisted of points, anecdotes, and epigrammatic thrusts, all more or less to the purpose, and all pleasantly said with a French air and manner which gave them great piquancy." Gibbon had just concluded "one of his best foreign anecdotes, in which he had introduced some of the fashionable levities of political doctrine then prevalent, and, with his customary tap on the lid of his snuff-box, was looking round to receive our tribute of applause, when a deep-toned but clear voice was heard from the bottom of the table, very calmly and civilly impugning the correctness of the narrative, and the propriety of the doctrines of which it had been made the vehicle." This voice proceeded from a tall, thin, rather ungainly-looking young man who, when Gibbon finally turned on him a surprised, disdainful stare, had relapsed into silence and was quietly eating some fruit. The historian undertook a reply; but the antagonist he had engaged was no less a personage

than William Pitt the Younger; and, after a brilliant and protracted debate, Gibbon was obliged to give ground, excused himself, left the room and was discovered by the solicitous narrator,
who had followed him, searching for his hat. Begged to rejoin
the company, he declined with emphasis, saying that he did not
doubt that the young gentleman who had interrupted him was
"extremely ingenious and agreeable, but I must acknowledge
that his style of conversation is not exactly what I am accustomed
to, so you must positively excuse me." And though Holroyd, who
was also present, did all that he could to supply a friendly pallia-
tive, he went off "in high dudgeon," the argument unfinished
and his discomfiture unavenged.

A significant and in some respects, it may be considered, a
slightly saddening story! Such blows to Gibbon's pride, however,
were luckily infrequent; the rewards he collected, on the other
hand, were numerous and dazzling. During 1776, he had received
a visit from his friends the Neckers—they were "vastly glad to
see one another," but Suzanne, he observed, was "no longer a
Beauty"; and during the spring of the year that followed, in
spite of plaintive protests uttered by Mrs. Gibbon, who feared
that her stepson and Madame Necker might once again become
entangled, or that he would be cast into the Bastille as the author
of an impious book, he himself visited Paris to enjoy the first
fruits of celebrity. On this occasion he had no snubs to endure
from a haughty British envoy, there was no need to fall back on
such mediocre acquaintances as Madame Bontemps. His reputation was established; the welcome that awaited him was spon-
taneous and abundant. Having set foot on foreign soil, he felt
his "mind expand with the unbounded prospect of the Continent" and five weeks passed after he had arrived in Paris, before
he could sit down at his table and attempt to give a coherent
description of "all that I have seen and tasted." Naturally he had
been much with the Neckers, whose reception of him "very far
surpassed my most sanguine expectations." Then, Horace Walpole had given him an introduction to Madame du Deffand, "an
agreeable young Lady of eighty-two years of age, who has con-

stant suppers and the best company in Paris"; and Madame du
Deffand had greeted him warmly and had written back to Walpole in eulogistic terms, declaring that he was *"véritablement un
homme d'esprit; tous le tons lui sont facils, il est aussi Français
ici qui MM. de Choiseul, de Beauvau, etc."* Later, she reported
that *"M. Gibbon a ici le plus grand succès, on se l'arrache . . ."*
Gibbon's own letters tell the same story of uninterrupted triumph. To his great satisfaction, he met and talked with Buffon;
he "dined *by accident* with Franklin," conversed with the Em-
peror of Austria, was presented at Court; and while his mornings
were occupied by visits to the public libraries, and his afternoons
by sightseeing, his evenings were disputed by a dozen fashionable
intimates, the Duc de Nivernois, the Princesse de Beauvau or
the Sardinian Ambassadress. His manner of living was pro-
portionately grandiose; his apartment was lined with damask and
two footmen, "in handsome liveries," hung behind his coach.
But, though I love the French from inclination and gratitude [he
wrote to inform his uneasy stepmother], I have by no means lost
my relish for my native country"; and the beginning of November, 1777, found him back at Bentinck Street, laid up with "a
very painful fit of the gout in both my feet." From the chair to
which it confined him he "jumped at once . . . into the warm-
est debates which I ever remember in my short parliamentary
life." Reports from America were "miserable"; his allegiance to
Lord North was on the point of wavering, and he doubted if he
could continue to give his "consent to exhaust still further the
finest country in the world in the prosecution of a war from
whence no reasonable man entertains any hopes of success.
It is better to be humbled than ruined." Information had
just reached London that, on October 17, General Burgoyne
and three thousand five hundred men had surrendered to the
Colonists at Saratoga. "Dreadful news indeed." . . . Nor did
the situation at all improve when tardy attempts at conciliation
were made by a bewildered government.

Yet, try as he would, Gibbon continued to observe public
affairs at a certain philosophic distance. Business thickened; the

French Ambassador left London and was pelted by the mob as he passed through Canterbury; war with France broke out again in June, 1778; French frigates threatened the safety of the East and West Indian fleets. Sittings grew longer and more and more excited; and "O Lord! O Lord!" (Gibbon murmured), "—I am quite tired of Parliament . . ." His book was still his real life; and he only wished (he remarked to his stepmother) that "all external circumstances," including the affairs of the Buriton estate, "were as smooth and satisfactory as the temper of my own mind." To heighten that peace of mind and considerably improve his financial circumstances, he was appointed in July, 1779, one of the Lords Commissioners of Trade and Plantations, a sinecure which added to his income between seven and eight hundred pounds yearly. The duties connected with this post were not exacting; days and weeks passed during which the demands of the Board of Trade did nothing to disturb the studious calm of Bentinck Street; a "perpetual virtual adjournment and . . . unbroken sitting vacation" (as it was afterwards unkindly and, Gibbon considered, even unfairly described) ensured the tranquillity of the historian and his fellow Lords Commissioners. During the summer of 1780, a demented Scottish enthusiast, Lord George Gordon, set London by the ears; Newgate was stormed; the houses of Papists were sacked and burned down. But, whereas Holroyd passed "all night in Holbourn among the flames, with the Northumberland Militia," saving Langdale's distillery and performing "very bold and able service," Gibbon recorded that "our part of the town" remained "as quiet as a Country Village." He did not visit the scene of the tumult; for "I am not apt, without duty or of necessity, to thrust myself into a Mob."

His second and third volumes appeared in the spring of 1781.[1]

---

[1] The story of how Gibbon presented the second instalment of the *Decline and Fall*, as he had presented the first, to the genial Duke of Gloucester, is well-known but too agreeable to be omitted. His Royal Highness "received the author with much good nature and affability, saying to him as he laid the quarto on the table, 'Another damn'd thick, square book! Always scribble, scribble, scribble! Eh? Mr. Gibbon?'"

Gibbon, at the time of this publication, had temporarily lost his seat in Parliament, owing to some differences with his cousin, the imperious Mr. Eliot; but, though he regarded the House of Commons as "a very agreeable Coffee-house," this was a deprivation that did not affect him greatly. His renewed attack on that "huge beast [the Roman Empire]," was received with less enthusiasm than had greeted the first assault—some readers went so far as to suggest that they were slightly disappointed—but the volumes "insensibly rose in sale and reputation." Meanwhile, as member for Lymington, Gibbon resumed his seat. His habit of thoughtful silence, however, remained unbroken; and, as a silent member and leisured pensioner of the benevolent Board of Trade, a hard-working writer, a copious talker and an assiduous diner-out, it is permissible to assume that he might have lingered on indefinitely, had Westminster not been swept by a gust of reforming zeal, had Burke [1] not risen in his seat to thunder against sinecures, and Gibbon and a variety of other less deserving gentlemen been thrust from their comfortable berths into unpensioned unemployment. Lord North's government collapsed late in March, 1782; and on May 4 Gibbon hastened to warn his stepmother that "the thunder-bolt has fallen, and I have received one of the circular letters from Lord Shelbourne to inform me that the board of trade will be suppressed and that his Majesty has no further occasion for my services." He had prepared (he added) for the catastrophe and could support it with firmness. "I enjoy health, friends, reputation, and a perpetual fund of domestic amusement . . ." By the way, did Mrs. Gibbon happen to be acquainted with "Lady Eliza Foster, a bewitching animal?" As to his gout—it had vanished, and he felt twenty-five.

For the summer months he had been lent a villa at Hampton Court. It was a counterpart of the "small pleasant house," which

---

[1] During the course of this debate, one member, protesting against the proposed abolition of the Board of Trade, ventured to point out that such works as the *Decline and Fall* were being produced beneath its ægis. Burke retorted that, although he reverenced the Board as an Academy of Belles Lettres, as a Board of Trade he considered it to be useless, idle and expensive. He compared it to a crow's nest full of imprisoned nightingales, and declared that he wished to release them, that they might sing more beautifully in freedom.

during the previous summer he had occupied at Brighton; but
here he had a key to the Royal Garden, "maintained for my
use but not at my expense"; the Thames, which he had once
dubbed an "amiable creature," flowed quietly beyond the trees;
he took short placid walks and made expeditions to the establishments of a few congenial neighbours. No, his sudden exclusion
from office did not much disturb him. It was clear, nevertheless,
that the way of living and the rate of expenditure to which he
had grown accustomed were somewhat in excess of his present
yearly income, and that a new scheme or new efforts were required to balance his budget. As he looked around and surveyed
his prospects, a plan materialised. After much thought and with
characteristic caution, he proceeded to give it definite shape in a
letter to Deyverdun.

Though they had been separated long and often, their friendship had never flagged. Deyverdun himself is a vague, elusive
figure, scholarly, polished, sociable—a friend, at all events, whom
Gibbon loved and cherished. The historian had learned something from Parliament—just as he had learned something from
his tedious servitude in the Hampshire Militia among drunken
country gentlemen. But its interest was now exhausted; and, if
the fascination of the London world was still as strong as ever,
he supposed that its better elements could be discovered and
appreciated in some smaller, foreign city. He was midway
through the fourth decade of a crowded industrious life; and in
this mood he wrote to Deyverdun, now settled at Lausanne,
where he had inherited from his aunt a house and property beside the lake, explaining his situation and touching lightly on
the idea that he might retire to Switzerland, *"ma seconde patrie,
non pas à Genève, triste séjour du travail et de la discorde, mais
aux bords du lac de Neufchatel, parmi les bons Savoyards de
Chamberry, ou sous le beau climat des Provinces Méridionales
de la France."* The proposal was unexpressed; but Deyverdun
was sufficiently delicate to grasp its import. He responded to
Gibbon's appeal, replied with a description of his house and its
surroundings—in which he had lately planted many excellent

fruit-trees—gave a sketch of his own temperament—". . . *vous comprenez bien que j'ai vieilli, excepté pour la sensibilité*"— and concluded with a suggestion that his friend should join him. An agreement was presently ratified; Deyverdun would provide the house, Gibbon bear the expense of their common household. For the time being, Gibbon intended that his stay in Switzerland should last about a year.

In fact, it was to last for ten years—and not once during the whole period did Gibbon repent of his choice. By September, 1783, all his effects at Bentinck Street, apart from his library, had been disposed of; and, as his post-chaise moved over Westminster Bridge, he looked back without regret across the masts, spires, roofs and belching chimney-pots of London—"*fumum et opes strepitumque Romae.*" Accompanying him were his valet, Caplin, and his lapdog, Muff. On September 17 he sailed from Dover, and on the 27th arrived safe and sound at Lausanne, where Deyverdun awaited him, eager to display his house. Like the garden and terrace, it proved even more agreeable than Gibbon had expected—unpretentious but commodious, with its back upon the city but beneath its frontage four acres of open ground which sloped towards the water. Each of the friends had his own apartments, and each had registered a solemn vow to respect the other's privacy. At the beginning of February Gibbon's books arrived from England and were arranged by him "in a room full as good as that in Bentinck Street, with this difference indeed, that instead of looking on a stone court, twelve feet square," it commanded, through three windows of plate glass, "an unbounded prospect of many a league of vineyard, of fields, of woods, of lake, and of mountains. . . ." The society at his disposal was interesting and varied, ranging from l'Abbé Raynal ("infidel" author of *l'Histoire philosophique des établissements et du commerce des Européens dans les deux Indes,* whose hand Dr. Johnson refused to shake, and who is also celebrated as an idolatrous votary of Sterne's Eliza) to the Neckers who, since the Director General's fall in 1781, had retired to the estate they had bought at Coppet. Mademoiselle Necker, "now about eighteen—wild, vain, but good-natured, and with a much larger provision of wit than beauty," was for Gibbon a personage deserving of special note, as the daughter of a woman whom, had circumstances been different and his own nature more impetuous, he might so well have married. He did not repine. Far pleasanter than the company of any single woman were the attentions paid by a coterie of solicitous feminine acquaintances, "(who, at least in France and this country, are undoubtedly superior to our prouder sex), of rational minds and elegant manners!" Rising early, he breakfasted alone, worked through the morning, and dined at two o'clock. Deyverdun, who was "somewhat of an Epicurean Philosopher," understood the management of a table, and a guest or two were frequently invited "to share our luxurious, but not extravagant repasts. The afternoons [Gibbon added] are . . . devoted to society, and I shall find it necessary to play at cards much oftener than in London; but I do not dislike that way of passing a couple of hours, and I shall not be ruined at Shilling whist." He could claim that he had always had an affection—certainly, a rather platonic affection—for the beauties of the landscape; but, thanks to Deyverdun, he was now learning to acquire "a taste for minute observation," so that he could dwell with pleasure upon "the shape and colour of the leaves, the various hues of the blossoms, and successive progress of vegetation," till the white acacia beneath his windows, which last autumn a brutal gardener had cut back too far, became the subject of solicitude and daily anxious glances. The terrace, a hundred yards long, which extended beyond the front of the house and led to "a close impenetrable shrubbery," provided a man of Gibbon's sedentary habits with all the exercise he needed. From that vantage point the London universe seemed immeasurably far away; the names of Pitt and Fox were "less interesting . . . than those of Cæsar and Pompey"; the old system had vanished, new names were emerging, and the country (he noted) was today governed "by a set of most respectable boys, who were at school half a dozen years ago." He had left England at a highly opportune moment. The plain, self-assured young man whom he had encountered at the Lincoln's Inn dinner-party, who had contradicted him so civilly and outmanœuvred him so calmly, had provided a foretaste of the new world of enthusiasts and patriots, where an attitude of ironic detachment had begun to lose its value.

Meanwhile, the historic edifice was slowly rising. Three storeys already were "exposed to the public eye," and there would be three more "before we reach the roofs and battlements." No man could accuse him of idleness; but many alterations and additions were yet required; and, during January, 1787, he formed the "extraordinary" and "meritorious" resolution of devoting the evenings, as well as the brief winter mornings, to the work of composition. All his materials were "collected and arranged; I can exactly compute, by the square foot, all that remains to be done. . . ." That summer he hoped to have finished and to be dining at Sheffield Place, his manuscript safely committed to the London printer. Nor was he wrong. "It was on the day, or rather night, of the 27th of June, 1787, between the hours of eleven and twelve, that I wrote the last lines of the last page, in a summer house in my garden. After laying down my pen, I took several turns in a *berceau,* or covered walk of acacias, which commands a prospect of the country, the lake, and the mountains." The air was cool, the sky clear; moonlight glittered across the lake; the whole prospect seemed to be enveloped in a profound, gigantic slumber. An immense elation filled his mind—"joy on recovery of my freedom . . . perhaps, the establishment of my fame." But a shade of melancholy soon descended. Beside the enormous journey he had accomplished through the past, and the distance into the future that he hoped his book might travel, the present seemed trifling, his own personal existence precarious and transitory; and, though he had gained his freedom, he reflected that he had said good-bye to an old and agreeable friend, an entity more real than himself, the book that had been his companion, in the many stages and revolutions of its development, for nearly seventeen years.

Then the manuscript was bound and a portion was read aloud. He planned to give it a personal escort on the next and last lap of its odyssey; but before he set out an incident is said to have occurred which, though the record is unauthenticated, and the story has been told in a somewhat different form,[1] suggests the exuberance of his emotions now that the book was finished. The "bewitching animal," Lady Elizabeth Foster, had visited him at Lausanne. Daughter of the notorious "Building Bishop," the prodigal Lord Bristol, granddaughter of that still more notorious personage, the Lord Hervey whom Pope had immortalised as "Sporus," Lady Elizabeth had all the charm of her brilliant unsteady line. She was the Duchess of Devonshire's greatest friend; she was also the Duke of Devonshire's mistress and the mother of his children. So intense was her fascination (Gibbon had once declared) that, were she to beckon him from the Woolsack, the Lord Chancellor himself would have no possible alternative but to rise and follow. Her delicate vixen-face certainly enchanted Gibbon; and it is said that, as they walked on the terrace, he dropped on his knees with a serious proposal of marriage; at which she bade him rise, and Gibbon, after a brief struggle, was obliged to admit that he could do no such thing— he had lately grown far too corpulent for the strenuous effort required. Servants were called from the house and, with some laughter and much heaving and tugging, his equilibrium, physical and emotional, was once again established.

If this tragi-comedy took place, it inflicted no permanent scar. He remained devoted to "the Eliza," and set off from Lausanne towards the end of July in a mood of lively expectation. He reached London on August 7, and from the "sultry and solitary metropolis" posted down to Sussex. There were the Sheffields to welcome him. By now he had come to regard them, together with Deyverdun and some of his closer friends at Lausanne, as constituting, in the most real and human sense, his family. He

---

[1] Madame de Genlis makes the heroine of this anecdote Madame de Crusaz, a voluminous novelist, authoress of a continuation of *Swiss Family Robinson*, whom Gibbon describes in a letter of January, 1787, as a "charming woman" and from whom he admits he had been "in some danger."

loved them all; but he had a particular affection for Maria Holroyd, "the tall and blooming Maria," who teased him familiarly and, either on her own account or as her father's amanuensis, wrote him long amusing letters. At their house, he revised and corrected his proofs; and, on April 27, 1788, their author's fifty-first birthday, the concluding volumes of the *Decline and Fall* were at last presented to the public. The double occasion was celebrated by "a cheerful literary dinner." His host was Cadell, the publisher, and Hayley (the untalented but good-natured poetaster who was afterwards, with unfortunate results, to become William Blake's patron) had prepared for declamation some effusive *Occasional Stanzas*. But even more gratifying was the tribute paid to his book before a larger, less eclectic audience. June saw the conclusion of the opening stages of the trial of Warren Hastings. "Sheridan surpassed himself," encouraged by a gathering of admirers, some of whom had offered fifty guineas to obtain a ticket, and, as he concluded, fell, apparently exhausted, into Edmund Burke's arms. The sweep of his oratory was tremendous; and, dilating on the enormity of Warren Hastings's misdeeds, he declared that they were without parallel "in ancient or modern history, in the correct periods of Tacitus or the luminous page of Gibbon." A splendid encomium; but Gibbon (the story goes) was so impressed by the compliment that he wished to underline it and, leaning towards his nearest neighbour, affected temporary deafness and inquired what the speaker said. "Something about your voluminous pages," crossly whispered back his victim.

Thus the curtain fell on "the august scene" at Westminster Hall, to be re-hoisted at irregular intervals till 1795. Gibbon, meanwhile, delighted as he was with his laurels and amused by a succession of dinner-parties and visits, was beginning to hanker after the peace of Lausanne. He had not visited his stepmother, since he apprehended that, both for her nerves and for his own, "the tumultuous pleasure of an interview" might have disastrous consequences and make the pangs of separation doubly hard to bear. No doubt she was disappointed, but she bravely acquiesced;

and by the end of July he was re-united with Deyverdun, whom he discovered in poor health and equally indifferent spirits. It was clear that his faithful companion had not long to live. During the autumn, Gibbon was suddenly called from the garden to find Deyverdun senseless; he had been struck down by an apoplectic stroke; further strokes followed; and, a year later, "the habits of three-and-thirty years' friendship" were finally cut short. Yet Gibbon's solitude was relative. During his sixth decade, though neither his book nor Deyverdun was any longer with him, though there were times when (as he had already written to Holroyd) he was apt to agree "that the immortality of the soul is on some occasions a very comfortable doctrine," and he was conscious of the "browner shade" which colours the end of life, he took comfort from the example of Fontenelle, who had declared that, in his experience—and it had been varied and protracted—the closing years were of all the best and happiest. His mind was still active, his amusements many. In October, 1788, Charles James Fox, fresh from "the bloody tumult of the Westminster Election," came sauntering through Switzerland. Gibbon did not approve of his politics, and was somewhat flustered by the presence of the devoted Mrs. Armistead, "whose wit and beauty . . . are not sufficient to excuse the scandalous impropriety of shewing her to all Europe"; but he delighted in the energy of Fox's intelligence and in the sweetness and simplicity of his private character. They sat talking from ten in the morning till ten in the evening. "Our conversation never flagged a moment; and he seemed thoroughly pleased with the place and with his Company. We had little politicks; though he gave me, in a few words, such a character of Pitt, as one great man should give of another his rival; much of books, from my own, on which he flattered me very pleasantly, to Homer and the Arabian Nights; much about the country, my garden (which he understands far better than I do), and, upon the whole, I think he envies me, and would do so were he Minister."

Some years later—it was in the August of 1792—there fluttered down on him once again Lady Elizabeth Foster, accompanied this time by the Duchess of Devonshire, by the Duchess's mother, that energetic and high-minded woman, Lady Spencer, and her sister, Lady Duncannon (better known as Lady Bessborough), with two children, Lady Duncannon's daughter, six-year-old Caroline Ponsonby (one day to make her mark as Lady Caroline Lamb) and Caroline St. Jules, Lady Elizabeth's daughter by the Duke, whose paternity was generally known but not explicitly acknowledged. In the Duchess of Devonshire's journal,[1] written for the benefit of her son and daughter at home, Gibbon figures largely; he entertained them in the "beautiful little Pavillion on his Terrace where after tea we had musick and our little Russian Princess and her friend danc'd Russian dances"; and she observed that he was "very clever but remarkably ugly and wears a green jockey cap to keep the light from his Eyes when he walks in his garden." Caroline Ponsonby was "quite entertained with it and made him take it off and twist it about." In talking to the great writer, Caroline allowed herself, and he permitted her, every kind of freedom, told him that "his big face frightened the little puppy with whom she was playing," and, on another occasion, out of the kindness of her heart, "wanted one of the footmen who had been jumping her, to jump Mr. Gibbon, which was rather difficult as he is one of the biggest men you ever saw. . . ."

During the interval dividing these two visits, the reverberation of the events of 1789 had travelled across Europe. To Gibbon the French Revolution was an occurrence equally incomprehensible and terrible, an outbreak of "popular madness," striking directly at all that he knew and understood, driving his friends—among them the Neckers—into hurried ignominious exile, sweeping with dangerous rapidity towards the very walls of Lausanne. That he himself had been in one sense a revolutionary, that his influence had done something to undermine the social system whose fall and disappearance he so much regretted, was a point that Gibbon, like many of his associates in

---

[1] In the Castle Howard MSS. Extensive quotations appear in Miss Iris Leveson Gower's biography of the Duchess of Devonshire, *The Face without a Frown*.

French Encyclopædist circles, proved incapable of grasping. He was content to deplore the tumult and condemn the bloodshed; and, disgusted by the present, he turned to the immediate past, and, with Lord Sheffield's encouragement, began to compose the series of autobiographical essays which his friend afterwards wove into a single continuous memoir. He also contemplated a volume of English historical portraits, from the reign of Henry VIII to the period of George III.

The spell of "autumnal felicity" to which he aspired seemed not likely to escape him. Reviewing his career, he felt modestly satisfied; and, as we look back with him today, we are inclined to confirm his judgment. It is true that, by some standards, his was a colourless record. How little Gibbon knew of the world as Johnson, for example, understood it and Boswell had experienced it; how inconsiderable had been his adventures compared with those of Wilkes; beside Sterne, how sedate and orderly was the course his mind had travelled! In his life there had been a succession of painful crises: his younger days were, if not stormy, at least clouded and unsettled. But his difficulties had been patiently endured or cleverly circumvented; and, at the end, good had come from evil, success from misfortune, and peace of spirit from the agitations and feverish indecisions that had pursued him before the quality of his genius at length became apparent. Yes, he had triumphed. Mildly but firmly he could claim—a claim few human beings can ever make with certitude—that what he had set out to do, that he had accomplished. Nor in his private relationships, such as they had been, had he reason to reproach himself. Both in his private and his public character, he had practiced (he liked to think) "the profane virtues of sincerity and moderation"; and they had diffused through his existence a cool, unwavering light, by which he had walked steadily, composedly, carefully, away from the dangerous regions of youth out across the smooth plateau of temperate middle age.

It may strike us that there was much he had missed—the pains and pleasures of love, the ardours of faith, the exciting vicissitudes of an active adventurous life. On the one hand, he had

avoided parenthood, marriage, or any kind of emotional attachment that he had felt he could not control; on the other, he
had steered clear of the costly but often rewarding experiences
that sometimes fall to the share of those who live at random.
He had seldom been reckless, rarely passionate. Yet, after all,
the "profane virtues" to which he clung had served him not
unhandsomely; and, though in a lesser man the air of decorum
with which they clothed his existence might have seemed a trifle
commonplace, Gibbon's genius was able to turn them to a noble
and magniloquent end. Thus, of mere caution he made a sort
of delicate and thoughtful circumspection, and of common sense
a virtue that bordered the sublime. He was "polished"; but the
polish had a singular bloom and depth. He was "correct," in the
somewhat limited Augustan fashion; but his correctitude was
so fine and deliberate—the product of such intelligence and
thought and labour—that it has the effect often on a reader's
mind of some new and beguiling grace. He was successful; more
surprising—he must be considered, on the whole, an unusually
happy man. But, if the portrait has no deep shadows, and the
face itself is tranquil and the setting dignified, let us admit that
there is a touch of absurdity in the general impression it leaves.
Looming behind are the huge relics of the splendid historical
past; the foreground is occupied by a small unshapely figure, in
ruffles and bag-wig and flowered velvet coat, with forefinger outstretched as he prepares to rap upon his snuff-box, while from a
mouth grotesquely circular stream the long euphonious periods
of his measured monologue. Gibbon, in fact, represents one
aspect of eighteenth-century civilisation carried to an extreme
point—its scepticism, its urbanity, its self-sufficiency, with the
disadvantages entailed by a deliberately limited view.

Among the various traits of this human and sociable century
was an unwearied addiction to the arts of friendship; and it was
an errand of friendship that, for the last time, lured Gibbon
away from Lausanne and home again across the Channel. In
April, 1793, he learned of Lady Sheffield's death and, though
half Europe was then plunged in war, he resolved that duty

obliged him to rush to the widower's side. Leaving Lausanne on May 8, the day after his fifty-seventh birthday, he hurried through Frankfort and Brussels, passing within sound of the artillery at the siege of Mayence, and reached London, none the worse for his adventures, during the early days of June. Sheffield greeted him: the consolation he supplied was both welcome and effective; and presently he found time to pay a visit to his stepmother, still at Bath and "in mind and conversation . . . just the same as twenty years ago. She has spirits, legs and eyes, and talks of living till ninety." His own health he considered equally good; but his bulk had increased immoderately during the last ten or fifteen years; his circumference was now grotesquely large; and it had for some time been obvious to all who met him (though even by his *valet de chambre* Gibbon refused to allow any reference to the subject) that he must be suffering from a rupture or perhaps a tumour. The complaint was of long-standing; but he had repeatedly postponed the tiresome business of consulting a physician. At length, he was obliged to give way: the doctors looked dubious; and on November 11 he wrote to warn Lord Sheffield that an operation might be necessary. An operation was performed, and then a second, both endured by the patient with the utmost cheerfulness and *sangfroid*. At the end of the month, he was already up and about; he dined with Wedderburn, the Lord Chancellor, and travelled as far as Lord Auckland's house in Kent, to meet the Archbishop of Canterbury, an amiable cleric, "of whom he expressed an high opinion," and, on a later visit, his old antagonist, William Pitt, with whom he spent the whole day, returning to Sheffield Place in extreme good humour.

Never had his conversation been more spirited, his anecdotes more lively. But his friends noticed that he was tired; he remarked to Lord Sheffield that "it was a very bad sign *with him* when he could not eat his breakfast, which he had done at all times very heartily; and this seems to have been the strongest expression of apprehension that he was ever observed to utter." A further operation was now imperative. He set out for London,

closely followed by Sheffield, who found him, after a third or-
deal, apparently much relieved and full of hopes and plans, but
in a physical condition that was rather more disquieting. On
January 15 he saw company, among others the Sardinian Ambassadress, ate the wing of a chicken, drank three glasses of
Madeira, and announced that he "thought himself a good life
for ten, twelve, or perhaps twenty years." That night his condition grew worse and, when the doctor arrived next day at
eleven o'clock, it was clear that he was dying. His last articulate
words were to his valet, whom he asked to remain in the room.
His senses did not desert him, and, his servant having put a
question, he made a slight movement to show that he understood. He betrayed no sign of fear and lay back on the pillow,
with his eyes half closed. At about a quarter to one, of the 16th
January, 1794, Edward Gibbon of Buriton and Lausanne
quietly ceased to breathe. It was such a death as he would have
himself desired. He was buried at Fletching in Sussex, among his
friends the Holroyds.

LAURENCE STERNE

IN JANUARY, 1763, Boswell had yet to complete his twenty-third, Gibbon his twenty-sixth year. Laurence Sterne, however, had travelled by this time almost half a century; and, unlike theirs, his beginnings had not been favourable. Poverty in its gloomiest form had attended his early progress. Behind him stood no Buriton, no Auchinleck, but the succession of barrack-rooms and cheap lodgings through which Ensign Sterne was followed by his wife and family. Now and then they were quartered on a more prosperous relative; for, though Roger Sterne was a poor and improvident soldier, he came of a hard-headed and successful line, being the grandson of a seventeenth-century prelate, bishop of Carlisle and afterwards Archbishop of York, whose descendants married wisely and enriched themselves considerably. But Roger, as a younger son, had his way to make in the world. At the age of sixteen, in 1708, he decided for a military life, joined the Thirty-fourth Regiment of Foot and was presently shipped to the Netherlands, where the regiment fought under Marlborough's command till the Peace of Utrecht.

Meanwhile he had contracted an unusually foolish marriage. Among other hangers-on who followed the Allied armies was a "noted Sutler," named Nuttle, encumbered with a stepdaughter by the name of Agnes Hebert, "widow of a captain of good family," whom he was anxious to dispose of. Since the Ensign was in debt to the Sutler, he would appear to have put forward the impulsive suggestion that he should settle his account by wedding Agnes; and the agreement was duly ratified on September 11, 1711. Such at least was the story told by their elder son, who did not love his mother but preserved all his life a sort of romantic veneration for his father's oddities. Laurence Sterne was born at Clonmel (where his mother had connections) on November 24, 1713, a few days after Mrs. Sterne reached London from Dunkirk. He was the second child, for he had been preceded by a sister in 1712, who grew up to be a beauty and died of a broken heart consequent on the merciless ill-treatment of her husband, a Mr. Weemans of Dublin, and was followed by "Joram—a pretty boy," carried away by the small-pox when he was four years old, Anne, Devijeher and Susan, who also dropped off early, as well as Catherine who survived to shame and annoy her brother. Laurence himself had been born in an exceedingly unlucky year. Peace entailed the disbandment of his father's regiment; Ensign Sterne "with many other brave officers" was cast "adrift into the wide world," and, as soon as Laurence could be moved, the Sternes took refuge at his grandmother's house at Elvington in Yorkshire, there to live the comfortless existence of deserving poor relations. Ten months passed before the regiment was again established, and the family re-embarked on their long and dismal odyssey.

"Perils and struggles" awaited them at every turn of the road. Twice they were nearly shipwrecked; children fell ill and died; Ensign Sterne never obtained advancement. But back in Ireland they were fortunate enough to stumble upon another rich relation, "a collateral descendant from Archbishop Sterne, who took us all to his castle," kindly entertained them for a twelvemonth, "and sent us to the regiment at Carrickfergus, loaded with kindnesses. . . ." It was during 1723 or 1724 that his father decided Laurence had reached an age when he should be educated in England, crossed the Irish Channel with him and placed him at a grammar school near Halifax. Henceforward father and son can have met but seldom. From Carrickfergus the regiment was moved to Londonderry; from Londonderry it was ordered to assist in the defence of Gibraltar; and there Roger Sterne, who in the meantime may or may not have been promoted to Lieutenant, fought the duel that probably shortened his days but was certainly an appropriate summing up of his gallant impulsive career. For the duel was "about a goose." To whom the goose belonged, in what circumstances it appeared, if it was alive or dead, whether its quality or its price was questioned, or its ownership disputed, Sterne has not recorded, in the autobiographical notes that he jotted down for the amusement of his daughter Lydia. But it was a goose that began the quarrel, which terminated in an affair of honour between Ensign—or Lieutenant—Sterne and a certain Captain Philips. Swords were the weapons selected, and the officers fought indoors. They fought with energy, Captain Philips running his opponent through the body with so well-directed and impetuous a thrust that (according to later accounts) "he actually pinned him to the wall behind." The Ensign's behaviour in this predicament was highly characteristic; for, "with infinite presence of mind" and a becoming display of courtesy, he begged Philips to wipe off, "before removing his instrument," any fragments of plaster which stuck to his sword-point and which "it would be disagreeable to have introduced into his system." Thanks perhaps to that inspiration, he recovered from his wound; but his constitution had received a shock which it never quite surmounted, and at Jamaica, his next post, he sickened with "the country fever" which little by little reduced him to a state of childhood. He did not complain but "walked about continually"; then, one day, sat down in an arm-chair and gently breathed his last.

Roger Sterne died, lonely and erratic as he had lived, during the spring of 1731, when his son was seventeen. To his family he left nothing, either in goods or prospects; but from his father Laurence received a legacy which, if less substantial, was also far less perishable—the recollection of a character that (unlike most such memories, even those to which we may believe, or may pretend, that we are most piously united) did not diminish or grow vague, but continued to exist and to develop in the depths of imagination. The "little smart man" became an ancestral legend—"active to the last degree, in all exercises . . . patient of fatigue and disappointments, of which it pleased God to give him full measure . . . in temper somewhat rapid, and hasty—but of a kindly, sweet disposition, void of all design; and

so innocent in his own intentions that he suspected no one; so
that you might have cheated him ten times a day, if nine had
not been sufficient for your purpose." Afterwards it was to be
just his father's qualities—kindliness, guilelessness and humour,
a sort of inbred, instinctive dandyism of thought and movement,
exaggerated by a strain of individual oddity—that the novelist
would exalt on the wings of the written word and from which
he would constitute his personal code of feeling and imagining.
For his father's image he had, in fact, the deepest sort of piety;
but almost every æsthetic achievement that reaches its full fruition would appear to have been fertilised by an underlying
conflict; and in Sterne's life the element of conflict seems to have
been supplied by his attitude towards his mother. Nuttle's stepdaughter, now presumably much soured by the buffeting and
bruising she had undergone in her vagrant married life, was a
vulgar, tactless, grasping woman whom it would have been hard
to love. Laurence, if he ever attempted it, proved singularly
unsuccessful. All he asked was to be allowed to forget her. But
that, alas, was not a privilege she was prepared to grant him.

Yet he was of a sensitive disposition and a readily affectionate
turn. And just as we may think that, in Boswell's career, we can
distinguish the effects of his failure to focus on Lord Auchinleck
the unusually strong filial emotions with which nature had endowed him, so the more exaggerated aspect of Sterne's emotionalism—the cult of feverish sensibility he would presently
evolve—had, it may be, some connection with the remorse he
felt because he was both ashamed of and disliked his mother.
During the most impressionable period of youth he lived with
his father's relations, who made no effort to conceal—particularly when Mrs. Sterne appeared, needy and importunate, upon
their doorsteps—their wholehearted condemnation of poor
Roger's *mésalliance*. So Mrs. Sterne was packed quickly home to
Ireland, there to exist on the profits of a small embroidery school
she had started and her husband's military pension of twenty
pounds a year. But Roger's son, Laurence, they treated fairly
and generously. A Sterne cousin, the Squire of Elvington, as-

sumed his father's place, educated him at Halifax and sent him up to Cambridge, where he entered Jesus College—not as a Gentleman Commoner, but as a sizar—in 1733.

He was poor but unabashed, dependent but apparently not ungrateful. A good deal of constitutional ebullience—inherited perhaps from his mother's French and Irish blood; for, from parents we hate as from parents we love, we receive very often valuable and important legacies—sustained him through the difficult business of finding a place in the world. At Cambridge he seems to have been happy enough; his tutor, Dr. Caryl, "a very good kind of man," let him have his way and, recognising Sterne's singularity and that he had been "born to travel out of the common road, and to get aside from the highway path," did not "trouble him with trammels." Among his contemporaries, he acquired a close and constant friend in John Hall (who later took the name of John Hall-Stevenson), "an ingenious young gentleman," five years younger than himself and "in person very handsome," a languid and leisured dandy, with whom he read Rabelais under the shade of an ancient walnut, called the "Tree of Knowledge," in compliment to the study of good and evil that they pursued beneath its branches. But, whereas Hall-Stevenson was a youth of fortune, Sterne had not a shilling. The income his cousin allowed him was barely adequate; and, by the time he left the University, he had been obliged to borrow money. Moreover, his health was precarious; a sudden hæmorrhage, which aroused him one night during his last year at Cambridge, warned him of the disease that had already attacked his lungs.

Sterne (we are told) went down with the reputation of "an odd man, that had no harm in him; and who had parts if he could use them." As a great grandson of Archbishop Sterne it was natural that he should enter the church; and in March, 1737, having taken his degree some two months earlier, he was ordained by the Bishop of Lincoln (before whom he appeared with testimonials certifying "his exemplary life, good morals and virtuous qualities") and appointed curate of St. Ives, a country town in Huntingdon. Thus his career as a priest opened quietly and easily; the slumbers of the Church of England during the fourth decade of the eighteenth century were still profound and peaceful; and thanks to the torpid influence of that midland landscape where church bell answers church bell across miles of fen, and the damp plain stretches unbroken as far as the towers of Ely, humped against a glimmering sky on their abrupt, mysterious island, the atmosphere of Sterne's charge was, no doubt, doubly soporific. He remained in Huntingdon, however, less than two years; for though he had had a difference with his helpful cousin, caused, it would seem, by his debts at Cambridge, an equally helpful relation soon appeared in the person of his uncle, Dr. Jaques Sterne, Canon of York Minster and Archdeacon of Cleveland, the type of proud, grasping, worldly ecclesiastic, adding benefice to benefice and sinecure to sinecure, politician, diner-out and master of intrigue, who figures so largely in eighteenth-century life. With his uncle's help Sterne now "sat down quietly in the lap of the church; and if it was not yet covered with a fringed cushion," a contemporary account assures us that " 'twas not naked." From his curacy at St. Ives, he moved as fully fledged member of the priesthood to the living at Sutton-in-the-Forest, a village a few miles north of York, situated in a region that had once been a royal hunting-forest and still enclosed some shaggy remnants of heath and woodland. His headquarters he established in the city of York itself. Sterne's was pre-eminently a social genius; and, during his lifetime, the great English provincial centres, grouped round their vast mouldering cathedral churches, formed each a distinct metropolis, hives of clergy and the resort of country gentlemen, who thronged to the assizes and races, and whose wives and daughters found at the Assembly Rooms, where they danced indefatigably under crystal chandeliers, a not unsatisfying substitute for the gaieties of London. York, moreover, at this period has its own company of players, and there were regular performances at the playhouse of every type of drama. None of these advantages did Sterne neglect; the profession he had adopted, or to which he had resigned himself, had very little influence on

LAURENCE STERNE
A bust by Joseph Nollekens

the conduct of his private life; and, when the young parson fell
in love during 1739, he had already acquired a considerable local
renown for humour and debauchery.

With the consideration of Sterne in love, we plunge at once
into the main problem of his peculiar personal temperament.
He was aged twenty-five or twenty-six when he met and attached
himself to Elizabeth Lumley; but his behaviour during this
episode was so odd, so characteristic and so true to the pattern
followed by his subsequent philanderings, that we gain no impression, as we observe him, of inexperience or immaturity.
Indeed, his gyrations have a strangely instinctive air. Some inward compulsion seems to determine the curious amatory dance
that he weaves about his mistress; and, though he is continually
appealing to the deepest human emotions, there is something, if
not quite mechanical, yet startlingly inhuman, about the pos-
tures he adopts—fluttering in tremulous rounds, quivering suspended in rapt excitement, as do certain birds whose amatory
displays would appear to be designed no less to stimulate their
own erotic frenzy than to capture the attention and arouse the
senses of a casually encountered female. Miss Lumley was not a
native of York; but as a young woman possessed of a small independent fortune, the daughter of Robert Lumley, incumbent
of a rich North Country living, who had left her an orphan
some years earlier, she was accustomed to spend the winter
months in the shadow of the cathedral, at the lodgings she occupied with her maid in Little Alice Lane. A trifle younger than
Sterne, she was not remarkably attractive, but is reported to
have been lively, graceful and intelligent. She had at least sufficient charm to form the centre of one of those elaborate imaginative evolutions that for Sterne were the necessary accompaniment of believing that he had fallen in love. Above all
else, it was the surrounding atmosphere—what in French would
be called the *ambiance*—that he sought for, cherished and endeavoured to prolong, in every adventure that engaged him,
whether it was of love or lust. Imagination refined the senses;
but the senses inflamed the brain. Two years were occupied by

the parson's courtship; and of letters written during that period
a small sheaf has been preserved. They show us Sterne at his best
and worst; they reveal both the natural vivacity of his constitution and the debauches of feeling for feeling's sake into which
an exceptional sensibility always tended to betray him. The
effect is as high-strung as the expression is high-flown. Their
eloquence may strike us as extraordinarily artificial; yet the
choice of epithets and, even more markedly, the rhythm of the
sentences—so simple, so smooth yet so ingenious in their harmony—confirm Gibbon's definition of style as an image of the
writer's mind.

The ruling characteristics of that mind it would be hard to
pin down—speculative, restless, impatient of restraint, passionately enamoured of words and devoted to the pursuit of ideas,
but apt to pursue them rather for their appeal to the imagination
than for their claims upon the intellect. The occasion of the
correspondence was Miss Lumley's withdrawal from York, and
from the attentions of a man whom she admitted that she liked
but had declared she could not marry, to her sister's house in
Staffordshire. During her absence Sterne occupied her vacant
lodgings; and the society of her *confidante*, the talk of the maid
who served him, and the sight of the rooms and furniture to
which she was accustomed, acted as a powerful stimulus on his
already electric mood. At every turn, some fine needle-point of
regret or desire lacerated his sensibility. His loneliness, he declared, was intolerable; the sight of the table laid reduced him
to despair. "One solitary plate, one knife, one fork, one glass!—
I gave a thousand pensive penetrating looks at the chair thou
hadst so often graced, in those quiet and sentimental repasts—
then laid down my knife and fork, and took out my handkerchief, and clapped it across my face, and wept like a child."

Having once, for the purpose of literature, taken out his
handkerchief, at least so far as literature was concerned, he never
put it properly back again. But there is another detail to be
underlined in this wildly effusive passage. Here is the first re-

corded use by any English writer of a word on which Sterne was
to base a large part of his celebrity and which from his work was
to find its way into the vocabulary of every modern language:
"*Sentimental!*" Was the word of Sterne's coinage? Or did he
adopt it and, if so, from what source was it derived? The letter
to Elizabeth Lumley must have been written before 1741. Yet
eight years later, Lady Bradshaigh, writing to another great professor of eighteenth-century sentiment, Samuel Richardson, in-
quires of the novelist his definition of "the meaning of the word
sentimental, so much in vogue among the polite. . . . Everything clever and agreeable is comprehended in that word. . . ." [1]
Walks, parties, and characters might all be sentimental. Evidently, at that period, the expression had not begun to lose the
bloom of fashionable unfamiliarity; and one is at a loss to understand what can have been the progress of the adjective during
the intervening years. How did it travel from York (supposing
that it originated there) to the polite world where its occurrence puzzled Lady Bradshaigh? Did Sterne give it to Hall-
Stevenson, and did his friend, on some leisurely peregrination
from which, unlike Sterne's, his means did not debar him, cast
the seed in London? We shall watch its growth and flowering;
we shall observe Sterne, as a high-priest of sentimentality, helping to introduce a cult of lachrymose divagation that was to
sweep across the world; no plant, no animal parasite, introduced
from a foreign climate, has had a more surprising history. Meanwhile the origins of the term remain mysterious. We see it drop
from the tip of Sterne's excited pen, as in an atmosphere of
high-pitched feminine solicitude, compounded of the attentions
of Miss Lumley's *confidante* and of Fanny, the beloved's maid-
servant, who administered doses of hart's-horn when his grief
grew too oppressive, he dashes off page after page of melancholy
expostulation. A new word has fallen into the human conscious-

---

[1] Mrs. Barbauld: Richardson's Correspondence, Vol. IV, p. 282. The second instance recorded by the Oxford English Dictionary is in a letter from Horace Walpole to Mann of 1752.

ness, to denote the most rarefied extravagances of feeling of
which the Augustan Age was capable. Its development at a later
time was the development of Sterne himself.

Leaving the mystery of the word, we revert to the odd reality
of Sterne's protracted courtship. Miss Lumley eventually returned to York and, carried away perhaps by the sentimental
violence to which she had been exposed during the last few
months, announced that she was sick of a consumption and
had not long to live. Parenthetically, she added that she had left
to her "dear Laurey" all her little fortune. In the course of the
affecting scene that followed, her resistance finally collapsed;
Sterne, overwhelmed with gratitude, again proposed that she
should marry him; and their wedding was celebrated in York
Minster on March 30, 1741. No sooner were they married than
the Sternes removed to his parsonage at Sutton-in-the-Forest;
and there for the next twenty years the "Parson who once delighted in debauchery" (to quote his wife's cousin, the future
Mrs. Montagu) led the life, with some individual variations, of
a contemporary parish priest, who farmed and gardened and
dined at the squire's house, with an ill-paid curate to lighten the
labour of burying and christening. Thanks to Mrs. Sterne's small
fortune, the parsonage itself was furnished and repaired; peaches
and nectarines grew in the walled garden, apples on the espaliers,
fine blue plums in the orchard; seven cows grazed the parson's
fields, and a large company of geese picked their way across the
stubble. Another living presently increased his income; and in
combination with certain members of the local gentry Sterne
was able to arrange the enclosure of a large expanse of common-
land, by rights belonging to the village; for his sensibility, at the
best of times a little uneven, did not extend to the wrongs of
the labouring masses.

On his country neighbours the impression Sterne made was
singular and puzzling. A lean man dressed all in black, riding a
horse as lean as himself, he drew after him every eye as he went
jogging through a hamlet. The villagers, leaving their work or
their play, gazed after him till he had disappeared with stolid

disapproval, while the little boys assembled and ran beside him. All this, as he later informed the world, he bore composedly. In spite of his accesses of feverish emotionalism, the face that for the most part he showed to the world was humorous and cynical, the face of a man who was both well aware of, and perhaps capitalised, his oddity, with a sardonic smile wrinkling his hollow consumptive cheeks. It was thus that he appeared to his friends in the cathedral city. They knew him as the parson, who, besides preaching an occasional sermon in the cathedral, where his uncle's influence had procured him a prebend's stall, was at home in the theatre and among the coffee-houses and devoted his attention at different times, and in a good-natured desultory fashion, to the arts of painting and music. Of painting he was particularly fond; and there has survived the engraving of a picture executed in conjunction with his friend Thomas Bridges which shows Bridges as a mountebank, painted by Sterne, and Sterne as the quack's "macaroni" or clowning assistant, the second and livelier portrait being by Bridges' hand. With mephistophelean eyebrows, high-bridged sensual nose and large mouth turned up at the corners in a thin-lipped derisive grin, Sterne stands poised against a panorama of eighteenth-century York. A lively crowd of citizens fills the background of the picture—young women in long bodices, caps and kerchiefs, men in three-cornered hats and waisted, wide-skirted coats, bearded Jews (of whom York then possessed a considerable population), a blind beggar led by his dog and a musician who turns the handle of his hurdy-gurdy. The scene is placid and provincial, in a setting of ancient houses. But no cathedral city was ever the seat of entirely unruffled calm; and in 1747 a violent quarrel broke out between Sterne and his uncle, who up to this time had zealously encouraged his advancement and, in return, had made use of his services as a political pamphleteer, caused either by Sterne's refusal to continue "such dirty work," which he considered far beneath him, or, according to some accounts, by a dispute over the Doctor's "favourite mistress." Jaques Sterne, at all events, became an embittered enemy, denounced him as "ungrateful and unworthy" in a letter to the Archdeacon, embarrassed, annoyed and thwarted him by every means within his power, and even enlisted against his nephew the support of the Archbishop himself.

Had the battle been confined to minor questions of ecclesiastical preferment—the Commissaryship of the Peculiar Court of Pickering and Pocklington, and other similar posts that Sterne coveted and to which his uncle was now determined he should not attain—Sterne's reputation might have suffered comparatively little damage, and the buzz of angry clergymen have long ago subsided. Unfortunately, in his efforts to discredit Laurence, Jaques Sterne made unscrupulous use of an earlier family quarrel and revived the whole distressful story of his relations with his mother. It was not a story that deserved resurrection or public exploitation. None of the parties involved had behaved with very much nobility; but Laurence, at least, had determined that, though his feelings might not be affectionate, his behaviour should be decent; and when Mrs. Sterne, on learning that her son was married to an heiress, had hurried over from Ireland to demand her due, bringing with her Sterne's unmarried sister Catherine, he had first attempted to disabuse them and begged them to return home, then doled out such small sums as his means permitted—twenty guineas here and another thirty there—and had shouldered his obligation in a resigned, if not in a cheerful, spirit. Mrs. Sterne (even Dr. Sterne had to agree) was both "clamorous and rapacious." One of nature's poor relations, she continually demanded assistance but, as often as any scheme was devised for her benefit, proved impossible to satisfy. She arrived on a visit at her son's parsonage, considerably outstayed her welcome and departed grumbling, with the little present that, as she left the house, Mrs. Sterne the younger pressed into her palm. Catherine Sterne had a high opinion of her social dignity and flouted the suggestion that she should either join a nobleman's household or allow herself to be articled to the trade of mantua-maker. Having permitted plans to go forward and her sister-in-law to write on her behalf

to various acquaintances, she suddenly rejected these proposals
"with the utmost scorn, telling me [Sterne informed his uncle
in an indignant letter] I might send my own children to service
when I had any, but for her part, as she was the daughter of a
gentleman, *she would not disgrace* herself but would live as
such." Thus the situation had continued since 1742, Mrs. Sterne
complaining, the Doctor intervening, Laurence, with a more
or less good grace, contributing to his mother's support, "what
he could conveniently spare"; till, some eight years after her
arrival in England, Dr. Sterne determined to crush his nephew
by a single decisive stroke. Having committed the intolerable
pair to a public institution, he circulated the report that Sterne
had cast them off, and had refused to provide the ten pounds
that would have saved his mother from imprisonment.

For a man of feeling no position could have been more in-
vidious. What, no doubt, made the scandal particularly galling
was Sterne's recognition that the large and kindly attitude,
which as a general rule he professed towards his fellows, in this
special and important instance had failed completely to materialise. Where his mother was concerned, his feelings declined
to operate. He might have been fair, it was true; he had not
been over-generous. And, with angry and vulgar emphasis, he
reminded Dr. Sterne, in a letter of many pages justifying his
behaviour, that, while his wife was a person "whose birth and
education would ill enable her to struggle in the world" were
she deprived of the independent income he was endeavouring
to safeguard, his mother, "though it would give me pain enough
to report it upon any other occasion . . . was the daughter of
no other than a poor sutler who followed the camp in Flanders"
and had been "neither born nor bred to the expectation of a
fourth part of what the government allows her. . . ." Therefore, she should make the best of it and return to her embroidery
school. The subsequent history of the elder Mrs. Sterne—and
there is reason to believe that she died soon afterwards—still
remains obscure. She passed out of Sterne's existence, leaving a
permanent trace—perhaps a scar upon his conscience, certainly

an odour of scandal from which, even posthumously, he never quite escaped. In every cult of feeling such as Sterne professed there is an element of hypocrisy—since it ignores the intermittences of the human heart, the numerous "dead notes," so to speak, in the range of the emotional keyboard; and the peculiar vivacity and picturesqueness of Sterne's emotional life encouraged very often a kind of literary make-believe which assumed curious and, now and then, slightly repulsive forms.

In another relation, too, the character of the *âme bien née*— the well-bred spirit, exquisitely attuned to all the finer shades of sentiment—was somewhat difficult to support as he advanced on middle age. Two daughters had been born to the Sternes. The elder died in infancy; the second, like her sister named Lydia (a sentimental name of the period with romantic associations) grew up as an affectionate and interesting child. In common with many selfish men, Sterne was a devoted father. As a husband, nevertheless, he was by no means satisfactory. The excitement of passion and the charm of romantic companionship had very soon evaporated. Elizabeth Sterne proved a prickly and sharp-tongued woman, who displayed great energy in housekeeping but very little skill, and spent much time in the business of butter-making, only to sell her butter at a worse price than any of her neighbours. Moreover, during middle life she showed definite signs of mental instability; and after a nervous breakdown (brought on, according to local gossip, by discovering her husband in the embraces of her maid) it was necessary to place her for a time under the care of a mental specialist. Sterne's behaviour at this crisis was kindly and attentive; he humoured her belief that she was the Queen of Bohemia, and for her health's sake drove her out coursing in a "single horse-chair"; but to live with her on everyday married terms was not so easy. A savage caricature, signed "Pigrich F.," gives us at once the measure of Sterne's half-humorous disillusionment and some indication of the wry, crabbed and cantankerous side of Mrs. Sterne's character.

More or less peaceably, they agreed to take separate courses.

Sterne had all the vitality and feverish love of life that sometimes go with a consumptive constitution; and he found many
amusements both in York itself and the neighbouring countryside. For example, there were the frequent visits he paid to his
Cambridge friend, John Hall-Stevenson, now settled at Skelton
Castle, a few miles from the remote fishing-village of Saltburn-
on-Sea. At this distance, the squire of Skelton, dilettante author
of *Crazy Tales, Macaroni Fables, Fables for Grown Gentlemen,
Pastoral Puke,* and *Monkish Epitaphs,* cuts a sympathetic, if
somewhat dim and puzzling, figure. Good-looking, idle, wealthy,
aimless, he was the owner of a fine classical library, a diligent
amateur of erotic prose and verse, and the possessor of a certain
small original literary gift, which he expended in vague rhym-
ing on facetious and satiric themes. His house had been re-
named "Crazy Castle" by the master and his inmates; a view
of the building forms the frontispiece to *Crazy Tales* (which
open with an *Apology* and *Dedication,* from the author to himself, as being the person whose judgment he most respected);
and the volume contains some oddly persuasive doggerel stanzas,
describing the epicurean seclusion in which he lived and scribbled. Hall-Stevenson, it is said, had once had plans for re-build-
ing; but a friend, thought to have been Sterne, persuaded him
to give them up; nothing must rob Crazy Castle of its air of
romantic decrepitude. Through the engraved frame of the land-
scape-frontispiece, we look past the Athenian owl, perched on a
garden-urn, down to a large, ancient, half-ruined mansion,
which squats beneath the encircling hills in the embrace of a
stagnant moat:

> From whence, by steps with moss o'ergrown,
> You mount upon a terrace high,
> Where stands that heavy pile of stone,
> Irregular and all awry. . . .
>
> Over the Castle hangs a tow'r,
> Threat'ning destruction ev'ry hour,
> Where owls, and bats, and the jackdaw,

Their Vespers and their Sabbath keep,
All night scream horribly, and caw,
And snore all day, in horrid sleep.

Oft at the quarrels and the noise
Of scolding maids or idle boys,
Myriads of rooks rise up and fly,
Like legions of damn'd souls,
As black as coals,
That foul and darken all the sky.

Such were the surroundings in which Hall-Stevenson, inspired, as he liked to suppose, by a philosophic conviction of
the shadowiness and inconsequence of human life, and the vanity and vulgarity of human aspirations, wrote his drolatic verse-
tales, peered apprehensively from his bedroom window at the
movements of the weather-cock—for he was the most superstitious of valetudinarians, invariably retiring to bed at the approach of the east wind—or entertained a large convivial company of Yorkshire squires and clerics. On his travels he had
made the acquaintance of Wilkes and Dashwood; and the Monks
of Medmenham Abbey were paralleled by the Demoniacs of
Skelton Castle, a society which, although its ceremonial was less
elaborate and its rites, apparently, far less obscene, belonged to
the same queer family of eighteenth-century clubs, founded for
purposes of drinking and loose talking, with now and then
rather half-hearted suggestions of black magic and diabolism.
Similar clubs—The Sublime Beefsteaks, The Beggar's Benison,
The Wig Club—existed up and down the country, and in Edinburgh and Dublin. The ritual they followed was usually blasphemous and priapic; many of the objects that appeared on
their tables were designed to appal the squeamish; while conversation across the dinner table maintained a high, if possibly
rather monotonous, level of bawdy and bravado. Little has come
down to us of the Demoniac meetings. We know that each votary
had a ritual nickname, Sterne being "The Blackbird" in reference to his parsonic clothes; that Hall-Stevenson's cellar pro-

vided abundant burgundy; and that during the daytime the Demoniacs shot, fished, engaged in disputation or raced their chaises wildly along Saltburn sands, one wheel splashing and scudding through the waters of the North Sea. Sterne's indebtedness to Hall-Stevenson is fairly obvious—and not only to the stimulating, slightly demoralising influence of his friend's society and the conversation that raged at Demoniac dinners, but to the wide and eclectic range of literature he had gathered on his book-shelves. Here, in vellum-bound duodecimos or massive calf-clad folios, were those rare works of eccentric erudition or unorthodox speculation in which Sterne most delighted, from the more fantastic fathers of the early Church to sixteenth-century French divines who tempered the parade of scholastic learning with flights of licentious fancy. They encouraged the natural twist of his mind, and stocked his memory with a vast, variegated accumulation he could draw upon at leisure.

Meanwhile, Sterne's course was entering its middle term. So far he had little to show for the distance he had travelled; the career he followed in the Church had brought him modest rewards; the ardours of youth had melted away in an exceedingly humdrum marriage; he was the author of some anonymous pamphlets, written for his uncle, and of two sermons under his own name, printed at sixpence each. During odd moments he played the fiddle and drew and painted. But the evolution of genius is as unaccountable as its nature is mysterious; and, some time between his fortieth and forty-fifth birthdays, there occurred in Sterne a sudden precipitation of creative energy. Hitherto his attempts to write had been casual and undirected —a poem on the passage of the soul, published in the *Gentleman's Magazine,* and a meditation on the plurality of worlds, in which he imagined the ripe plums in one of his orchard trees to constitute a whole stellar universe, and the bloom that clouded its planets to be their human or vegetable life. The discovery that of his writing he might make something more than a diversion was very largely accidental. Among Sterne's friends was the Dean of York, Dr. Fountayne, an amiable and easy-going ecclesiastic who, some years earlier, had become embroiled in a long and acrimonious dispute with Dr. Topham, the ecclesiastical lawyer of the diocese, a man with an insatiable greed for diocesan perquisites, over various small posts (including the Commissary-ship of the Peculiar Court of Pickering and Pocklington, eventually snapped up by Sterne himself) of which Dr. Topham claimed that the Dean had thwarted him. Involved in this drama, originally on the side of Dr. Topham, subsequently on that of the Dean and his supporters, was the invalid Archbishop. Topham was at length defeated; the detailed narrative of his intrigues, and of how they were confounded, is both tortuous and uninteresting; we have a general impression of proud pursy faces, flushed a deep crimson against snowy wigs and bands, of lifted fingers, marking the periods of an endless argument, of voices now raised in sonorous indignation, now sunk in an insinuating parsonic murmur. Having failed to gain his ends by diplomacy, Dr. Topham resorted to strenuous pamphleteering. Fountayne replied; Topham again attacked; and Sterne, excited and amused by the resultant hubbub, dashed forward with an allegory to deal Topham his *coup de grâce*. He was surprised and annoyed when the first flash of his weapon produced among the combatants a sudden apprehensive silence, and even his own party advised tremulously that he would do better to hold his hand.

The *Political Romance,* published in York in 1759, was almost immediately suppressed. Unfortunately, besides accounting for Dr. Topham, it was considered to deal disrespectfully with that mighty institution on which all the parties concerned were dependent for their livelihood. The Church itself would suffer from an allegory that portrayed the affairs of the archbishopric of York in the imagery of a backward country parish, where Trim (or Topham) figured as the sexton, dog-whipper, mole-catcher and clock-winder combined, who coveted the parson's cast-off breeches, lusted after the reversion of the great pulpit-cloth and old velvet cushion, and grasped at the opportunity of acquiring the Good Warm Watch-Coat that for two hundred years had hung behind the vestry-door. An admirable satire—in the very worst of taste! Sterne was persuaded to allow the cathedral dignitaries to buy up and burn all the copies on the bookstalls. Meanwhile, he had discovered the delights of unfettered self-expression; he had had a glimpse of his own powers and felt stir within his memory the accumulations of four decades—from the doings and sayings of that "little smart man," his father, to the books he had read and the fantasies he had indulged in at Skelton Castle. It was with an extraordinary sense of freedom, an enormous gust for life, a dazzled, enchanted apprehension of the amplitude and richness of the field he was surveying, that he sat down and embarked, then and there, on the writing of his second book.

Its composition proceeded at a remarkably rapid pace. There are some writers—certainly not many—who, as cats are reputed to do, give birth with satisfaction; and, though Sterne was a diligent artist and laboriously revised his work, his pleasure in writing usually preponderated over the pains and difficulties. Once he had begun, it was as if he were transcribing or remembering pages he had already written; and indeed there was little in the subject-matter of the book he had to fetch from outside, since it was the progress of his own mind and the history or legends of his own family he was recording upon paper. Thus Ensign Sterne, with no doubt many other hints and suggestions gathered from the past, lent shades of expression both to the narrator's father, the good-hearted, choleric, cross-grained retired Turkey-merchant, Mr. Walter Shandy, and to Uncle Toby, the retired soldier and fighter of mimic battles, who possessed that sweetness of temper and innocence of outlook for which the Ensign had been celebrated. Each of them is depicted with a minute fidelity that extends alike to their habits of thought and speech and to their smallest peculiarities of dress and movement. The minuteness of the author's descriptive method must be included among the strangest features of an often perplexing novel; and the suggestion was put forward not long ago that Sterne, mined by disease and haunted by the idea of death, was

consequently obsessed by the idea of time, and that the extreme
exactitude with which he records every gesture of his personages
—every posture they assume, every shade of expression by which
they betray their feelings—was a symptom of the preoccupation
that never left him. His characters are, so to speak, all of them
beating time; their movements denote the pulsation of hurrying
seconds; at his back Sterne heard always the rush of the time-
stream, carrying himself and his personages towards extinction,
and made haste to pin down the impression made by one instant
before it blurred into the next. The theory is ingenious, but
leaves out of account certain more obvious aspects of Sterne's
development. In the first place, the novelist was also a painter
and a draughtsman; his visual imagination was preternaturally
acute; and it is clear that he *saw* every human being whom he
described with a vivid, almost hallucinatory distinctness. Few
writers have been more fascinated by their own creations. The
ordinary novelist sets to work with a rudimentary conception of
how his characters should think and act, and a notion, equally
rudimentary, of how they should appear. For Sterne, on the
other hand, appearances were as essential an expression of personality as the mind or soul itself; the inward and the outward
were part of the same fabric; "superficial" and "fundamental"
were merely relative terms, with little bearing on the problem
of the human ego. Truth was revealed on the surface, as well as
below the surface. And it is with the surface that Sterne begins,
noting the changes of feeling and meaning that play across a
face, the tragic or comic significance condensed in the precise
disposition of hand, foot or knee. The quality of Mr. Shandy's
despair when he learns that the man-midwife has disfigured his
son's nose is conveyed by an exact description of the manner in
which he falls face downwards upon his bed:

> "The moment my father got up into his chamber, he threw
> himself prostrate across his bed in the wildest disorder imag-
> inable, but at the same time in the most lamentable attitude
> of a man borne down with sorrows, that ever the eye of pity

dropped a tear for.—The palm of his right hand, as he fell upon the bed, receiving his forehead, and covering the greatest part of both his eyes, gently sunk down with his head (his elbow giving way backwards) till his nose touched the quilt;—his left arm hung insensibly over the side of the bed, his knuckles reclining upon the handle of the chamber-pot, which peeped out beyond the valance;—his right leg (his left being drawn up towards his body) hung half over the side of the bed, the edge of it pressing upon his shin-bone.—He felt it not. A fixed, inflexible sorrow took possession of every line of his face.—He sighed once,—heaved his breast often,—but uttered not a word."

Observe—such are the qualifications of parental grief—that Mr. Shandy does not tumble headlong, so much as let himself collapse, with a certain meditative gentleness, to the prostrate position in which he is surveyed by Uncle Toby. He is distraught, yet not so distraught as to wish to be positively uncomfortable. An examination of Sterne's manuscripts shows the pains he took, not only to improve the verbal rhythm of every period, but also to increase the precision of every visual image. He worked always towards a greater sharpness of outline or a more vivid *chiaroscuro,* partly because (as I have already suggested) he had been trained to draw before he learned to write; partly because his view of character and his method of characterisation gave special emphasis to the outward evidence of inward happenings. The *psyche,* he insists, is no recluse, locked up out of sight in some inaccessible corner of the body; it appears continually, flows like an electric current through nerves and muscles, is manifest in the movements we make and even the clothes we wear. From an almost invisible centre (which vaguely we may apprehend but certainly cannot define) it throws out a constant vibration of changing impulses.

That these impulses are various and bewildering is a matter of common experience. Why then, says the novelist, try to portray human beings, or describe human life, in fixed or classical terms? Sterne is one of the first of literary impressionists; and when he came to create a hero and depict a family, he refused to resort to any of the commonplaces of official portraiture. *La vida es sueño*—existence is a dream; and Sterne, with little of the profound seriousness, at least in his attitude towards his own personality, that characterised Gibbon, and none of the exquisite moral scruples that tormented Boswell, let himself drift among the impressions and emotions, always vivid yet often dream-like in their inconsequence, that floated through his fancy. His plan, therefore, was to have no plan; his construction was to be circumscribed by no general outline but should grow out of his temperament as the mood directed, and owe its unity less to symmetry of design than to harmony of atmosphere. When he wrote of literature, he was often accustomed to think in terms of music; and Chapter Twenty-five of the original Volume Four, after a reference to "that necessary equipoise and balance (whether of good or bad) betwixt chapter and chapter, from whence the just proportions and harmony of the whole work results," includes a characteristic statement that, at least in this novelist's opinion, "to write a book, is for all the world like humming a song;—be but in tune with yourself . . . 'tis no matter how high or how low you take it."

Thus his novel was an astonishing combination of the precise and the disorderly. Into it he cast pell-mell the most incongruous and startling elements—scraps of his family legend; a portrait of himself as the eccentric Parson Yorick and of Hall-Stevenson as Eugenius; a savage caricature of an old enemy, Dr. Burton, the learned antiquary and gynæcologist, portrayed as Dr. Slop; philosophical disquisitions, and Rabelaisian anecdotes of the kind he may have gathered at Skelton Castle, from the "lounging books" and volumes of "facetious tales" Hall-Stevenson collected. Reading Sterne, sooner or later we are bound to think of Joyce; and, though the parallel should not be laboured, it is worth examining. Both novelists were of Irish blood; both suffered from chronic ill-health and were deeply versed in music; both were avid readers, devoted to curious learning; and, on each side, there is the background of a shabby-genteel youth, dominated by an ineffective but impressive father. Sterne's passion for words, and the virtuosity he displayed in their management, was as conspicuous as that of Joyce. . . . There the resemblance ends. No comparison can be made between Joyce's puritanism—surprising as were the shapes to which it sometimes fled for refuge—and Sterne's libertinism, tempered though it often was by intellectual delicacy. Joyce wrote at a snail's pace, building up his gigantic opus in stealthy solitude; Sterne composed in a transport of feverish excitement. And, notwithstanding a set-back said to have occurred when he read aloud part of the manuscript to his friends, the Crofts, at Stillington, and a number of his listeners fell quietly asleep, he had none of the hideous misgivings that usually impede the progress of the inexperienced artist. The book was a "picture of himself," he said; it was the reflection of a temperament and history he could not and would not change.

Besides the delight of self-discovery, Sterne experienced during the latter part of 1759 another type of stimulus. He had fallen in love—certainly not for the first time since his marriage but, it would seem, far more seriously than on any earlier occasion. Catherine Fourmantelle had come to York with her mother, to sing at the Assembly Rooms. She was young, considered beautiful and thought to be well conducted. Sterne was presented to her after one of her first appearances, and she was immediately involved in all the labyrinthine intricacies of a "sentimental" courtship. He wrote to her again and again, in progressively passionate terms. She was "dear Kitty," his "dear, dear Kitty." He adored her to distraction, he said, and would adore her to eternity. It was not long before he had proposed that, were God ever to "open a door" by removing Mrs. Sterne (of whom, about this time, he had written to Hall-Stevenson in expressive dog-Latin that he was *"fatigatus et aegrotus . . . plus quam unquam"*), Miss Catherine Fourmantelle should become his wife. Meanwhile he continued to press on her little gifts of honey, sweetmeats, sermons and Spanish wine. She found her way into the book he was writing, where her pseudonym occurs and re-curs, with an indefinably musical ring, as "my dear, dear Jenny," representative of all that was tender and feminine in the influ-ences that governed his existence, who was neither wife nor mistress, neither friend nor child, but for whom his feelings had a bloom and glow that partook of many different characters.

Miss Fourmantelle, for her part, would seem to have been pleased and flattered. Sterne she described as "a kind and gen-erous friend"; and the friendship of a celebrity, to a young woman cast adrift on a strange town to earn her living, is always doubly grateful. During the last days of 1759 the booksellers of York were displaying in their windows a volume, published by the famous London firm of Dodsley and entitled *The Life and Opinions of Tristram Shandy, Gentleman,* embellished with personal and local references and savage contemporary like-nesses that every citizen could recognise. In two days the book-seller had sold two hundred copies. The novel was simulta-neously on sale in London; but Sterne, though well-pleased with the local renown he gained and with the eulogistic notices printed by various papers, remained for a time almost unaware of the *furore* he was causing. Catherine Fourmantelle continued to distract his heart, Mrs. Sterne's nervous malady was still an expensive nuisance; when, one March morning, he happened to encounter his friend Stephen Croft who was setting out for London, and Croft suggested casually that Sterne should join him in the expedition, he himself paying expenses so long as the adventure lasted. Sterne hesitated, agreed, darted off instantly to pack a best pair of breeches. A few days later, he had arrived in London and hurried round, before breakfast, to call on Dods-ley. He learned that his book was enormously successful and that the public demanded more. Having rushed his London publisher into an advantageous contract, sold him a volume of collected sermons and promised that a new volume of *Tristram Shandy* should be written every year, he returned "skipping" with elation and poured out the story of the wealth he had acquired to Croft behind the breakfast-table.

Six hundred and thirty pounds was his immediate profit; and on this windfall he moved his lodgings from Chapel Street, Mayfair, to St. Alban's Street, Pall Mall, where for three months he lived in a waking dream of literary and social triumph. The whole metropolis was electrified by the news of Yorick's arrival. Invitations came ten at a time, visitors by dozens; Ladies of the Bedchamber crowded up his staircase. Chesterfield received him kindly; old Lord Bathurst, the friend of Pope and Swift, declared that *Tristram Shandy* had given him a new interest in existence; Bishop Warburton, somewhat apprehensive at the rumour that the next volume of the novel would contain a picture of himself, presented him with a purse of guineas and an armful of classic literature, selected (the Bishop explained) to help him "improve his style"; David Garrick paid him handsome compliments; and Lord Ossory commissioned Reynolds to paint his portrait. Sterne appeared for his first sitting, on March 20, already somewhat shaken. He had been in London less than three weeks; but the strain of incessant dinner-parties, to which favoured guests were usually bidden a fortnight in advance, though he did not cease to enjoy his success, had grown more and more exhausting; and, rather than sit upright, he sank sideways against a heap of cushions, one hand supporting his head, an extended finger rumpling his eyebrow and pushing his wig askew. But the expression is sharp and amused; and the folds of the new silk gown—replacing the rusty cassock he had worn at Sutton—are ample and magnificent. He may have been tired; he was by no means satiated. He had no false modesty in describing to Miss Fourmantelle how amply he had triumphed or reeling off the great names of his new acquaintances, who made of "Shandeism" a cult and of Yorick its high-priest. A dream, perhaps—but an absorbing dream. Certainly he meant to dream to the full now that the occasion offered. And during April he wrote to dear Kitty in York, suggesting she should join him.

She came at his summons, and installed herself in Soho. But between Soho and Pall Mall the distance is considerable; and

Sterne, caught up in engagements, now supping with the Duke of York (the royal personage who laughed at Boswell, and was later to accept from Captain Gibbon a copy of his thesis), now being lionised at Ranelagh and Vauxhall, where even the waiters whispered and pointed him out as he strolled arm-in-arm with fashionable companions down the long lamp-hung avenues, now being carried off to Windsor to watch the solemn investiture of new-fledged Garter-Knights and whirled home again to fresh pageants and balls and supper-parties, found it difficult to be as attentive as a few weeks earlier, when Yorick himself or a servant bearing his gifts was seldom off her doorstep. Whether she was still, or at any time had been, Sterne's mistress, it is now impossible to say. His objective in such relationships remains mysterious. Was the feeling he had entertained no more (as he presently told the world) than "that tender and delicious sentiment which ever mixes in friendship, where there is a difference of sex"? Were his emotions with regard to women in general (as was afterwards claimed by a French observer) so intense and yet so diffused that they were incapable of being concentrated on any single object? Whatever the solution of this and other problems, Miss Fourmantelle gradually recedes from his biography and then completely vanishes. He obtained for her an appointment to sing at Ranelagh. In a final note he laments that, although he has not had sight of her since Sunday, till Friday at two o'clock he cannot promise he will call: "Every minute of his day and to-morrow is pre-engaged, that I am as much a Prisoner as if I was in Jail—I beg, dear girl, you will believe I do not spend an hour where I wish—for I wish to be with you always. . . ." But there his protestations are cut short. The musical echo of Jenny's name continued to haunt his prose; but the echo is faint and the tone elusive. Left alone nearly a week in Meard Court, Soho, her pride may well have revolted at such an unfruitful servitude, and in the quarrel that ensued she may have angrily shaken free. Their desires can scarcely have coincided; through the mazes of self-interest they gradually wandered apart.

On Sterne, the effects of this breach (if a breach, indeed,

occurred) were entirely imperceptible. Except for the fatigue
he suffered, every circumstance combined to raise his spirits to
the very highest pitch; and, while London notabilities were still
scrambling to do him homage, he heard that he had been nomi-
nated to the living of Coxwold, a post more remunerative and
better-found than that of Sutton-in-the-Forest. There was nothing more he could wish, he declared. Rich—at least, in his own
estimation—recognised and flattered by those great personages
to whose applause no artist, even the most intransigeant, is ever
quite insensible, respected and acclaimed by fellow-artists as
authoritative as Garrick, Hogarth, Reynolds, he prepared after
three months for a triumphal return to York. A public convey-
ance had brought him to London at Stephen Croft's expense; it
was in his own carriage that, towards the end of May, 1760, the
writer travelled north again. Aglow with splendour and consequence, he rejoined his wife and daughter, whom he presently
transferred to his new parsonage at Coxwold, an old and rambling house, full of irregular, comfortable rooms, situated on
the edge of the moors, in a neighbourhood much healthier than
the marshy lands of Sutton. Besides, the house itself pleased him,
one of those massive agglomerations of ancient stone-work which
seem to grow out of the native soil in which they are solidly
rooted; and, having re-named it Shandy Hall or Shandy Castle,
he at once set to work on the third volume that would take him
back to London.

For two years London and Coxwold divided his time and
energy. Neither fame nor the back-wash of fame—the surge of
Grub-Street pamphlets and quickly run-up volumes, written in
imitation or criticism of *Tristram Shandy's* manner, that already,
before he left London, came tumbling from the printing-presses
—had yet dulled his imaginative enthusiasm or damped his
creative fire. A fire it was, raging at all times of day; sometimes
descending on him when he had hurried out and was half-way
through the village, so that he wheeled round and ran home-
ward before his excitement died; often blazing uninterruptedly
from morning until nightfall. Great confusion surrounded him

in the small ground-floor room he had selected as his study. Gouts of ink starred his manuscript, spattered on to the table and floor, and smeared his clothes and fingers. Seated in dressing-gown and slippers, he wrote without cessation; and in November, 1760, two further volumes were completed. Late in the year he went up to London to revise and correct his proofs. Once again he was exceedingly well received; but the new volumes, when they appeared, were voted somewhat less amusing than the old, and the attentions of critics and pamphleteers were even more exasperating. Undismayed, he pocketed his guineas and, as soon as he was reinstated at Coxwold, fell back into his story. Between June and November, he composed a fresh instalment, and for the third time took the road south—but in a state that showed the physical effect of the toil he had undergone.

Much has been written—with as yet little result—of the pathology of genius. To what extent can we attribute the activities of the brain to the diseases of the body? Are there certain morbid conditions—the disease from which Sterne suffered being evidently one, syphilis in its suppressed stages perhaps another—that intensify and accelerate the growth of a creative gift? The tendency to snatch at life, to sweep together greedily, and even ruthlessly, all the sensations and impressions daily existence offers, is said to be characteristic of the consumptive temperament; and such a tendency is reflected in the construction of Sterne's prose. At its most eloquent—and Sterne's eloquence at its best has the supreme virtue of absolute simplicity—the impression it produces is often oddly breathless. The system of punctuation he adopted is individual and, here and there (it may strike a reader), highly disconcerting. Each dash—and there are occasionally as many as twenty dashes to the page—seems to represent a gasp or a hurrying heart-beat; and, though the minute delicacy of Sterne's observation need not be attributed to his anxiety to run ahead of time, his method of delivery has an air of feverish haste that, combined with the extravagance of the author's improvisations, is dazzling but bewildering. By the winter of 1761, the pace at which Sterne wrote, and the expense of vitality writing entailed, had begun to tell upon his organism. It may be that he felt a little less sure of himself than during previous visits. The lampoons and the piracies had increased in number; the sales of the last instalment had been slightly disappointing; Sterne's behaviour in company was rather more unguarded. And Johnson, who met him at the house of Sir Joshua Reynolds and gravely took him to task for his abuse of the English language, was obliged, when Sterne extracted a pornographic drawing from his pocket and showed it to the company, to lumber out of the room in elephantine disapproval.

He had reached London in indifferent health. A severe hæmorrhage suddenly reminded him of his experience at Cambridge. Death, a long-legged spectre, appeared abruptly at his elbow. He gave himself up for lost, yet resolved to flee. A state of war, however, still existed between France and England; but English ministers were determined that a man of talent should not die for want of their exertions; it seemed improbable that our humane enemies would refuse to lend their aid; and, though he could not procure a passport, Sterne was provided by Pitt with letters to various members of the French government. Desperately yet light-heartedly, leaving behind him a provisional testament "in case I should die abroad" and a letter to his wife in which he assured her they would never meet again, Laurence Sterne during mid-January, 1762, set sail across the Channel.

The Novelist

His first rush from death had carried Sterne as far as Paris. He arrived, in mid-January, 1762, feverish and broken down after an exhausting journey, and was at once assured by the local doctors that he had not long to live. They did not count on the remarkable vitality of their patient's constitution. Within a few days he was up and visiting the French theatres (where he admired Clairon and Dumesnil, though he considered that the French stage could provide nothing "which gives the nerves so smart a blow" as the great tragic personages portrayed by Garrick) and, within a few weeks, had stepped to the centre of the Parisian literary world, which recognised in him a wondrous and genial eccentric, representative of all those extraordinary English qualities that the restless taste of the period had then begun to value. He was as strange a phenomenon as Shakespeare, as eloquent and affecting, and far more polished! Sterne, with his usual versatility, seems very soon to have picked up the somewhat difficult knack of Gallic conversation; and, ranging freely to and fro in a society which included the Duc d'Orléans on the one hand, and farmers-general and famous actresses upon the other, with Encyclopædist *salons* as a convenient midway point, he put behind him the last vestiges of his parsonic and provincial youth.

Even the clerical gown, in which Reynolds had painted him, was temporarily discarded; and Carmontelle's water-colour, executed at the command of the Duc d'Orléans, shows him standing on the terrace of the Palais Royal, his back turned towards the Invalides, clad in the complete apparatus of the contemporary *homme du monde*. Lace ruffles cover his exiguous wrists; one spidery hand is thrust deep into his breeches pocket; his thin body is enclosed in a black full-skirted coat. His right elbow supported on a brocaded arm-chair, he leans or lounges forward, alert and sharp-nosed, a faint smile contracting his parchment cheek and forming a long satiric wrinkle, furrowed from nose to chin. He looks easy, amused, reflective and (unlike the Sterne who appears in Reynolds' portrait) not at all satanic. The influence of French society on Sterne's character had been stirring and yet mollifying. At the age that he had now reached, though talents may still be improved, the temperament in which they are rooted very seldom changes; but no intelligent man could explore such a society and remain completely unaffected. For Sterne had arrived in Paris during one of the brightest and happiest moments of French or European culture. Paris was still the clearing-house of European intellect. Here, gathered together within the confines of a single city, were Diderot and d'Alembert, d'Holbach, Crébillon, Marmontel, Morellet—Voltaire and Rousseau were powerful but distant figures—flanked by women as remarkable, each in her separate sphere, as Madame du Deffand, Madame Geoffrin and Mademoiselle de Lespinasse. It was a society that held a delicate balance between the pleasures of thinking and feeling. Rarely have men and women been more passionately addicted to thought, or more thoughtful in their passions; and Sterne, with his cult of emotion for the emotion's sake, his peculiarly deft mingling of sense and sentiment, his elaborate parades of feeling and sudden strident explosions of outrageous mockery, struck a note that reverberated on already responsive ears. Naturally, he "played up"; for he had much of the comedian's gift—shedding public tears over the victims of the great fire at St. Germain, dropping to his knees before Henri Quatre's equestrian statue, and puzzling and interesting the guests at the Baron d'Holbach's table (where he had acquired a devoted admirer in Jean Baptiste Suard) by a declaration that the Bible and Locke were the two models that had contributed most to the formation of his style. In the midst of learned argument and facetious anecdotage, he would arouse "new emotions [we are told] in tender hearts by his naïve and touching sensibility." Never had Suard beheld so buoyant yet so sensitive, so outspoken yet so courteous, so entirely odd and original a type of human character; and to the last days of his existence he never quite forgot him. A gesture would return, an image, a turn of phrase: he would see again the attenuated Englishman in his suit of becoming black, and hear him talk of the soul or Locke or the Christian faith, variegating his discourse with lightly improper allusions or glancing from pathos to irony in his usual erratic manner, showing always the same delighted readiness to surrender to a transient mood.

Of Sterne's friendship with Diderot, probably the most important of all his Parisian associations, little now remains on

record. They had met through the Baron d'Holbach and presumably, among other subjects, they must have talked at some
length of the beauties of English literature, since Sterne presented Diderot with a selection of English classics, Chaucer,
Pope, Locke and the Sermons of Tillotson, accompanied by as
much of *Shandy* as had yet been published. Voltaire he was
never to meet; but from afar the great old man extended to
Sterne's novel his paternal approbation, noting the acuteness
of its domestic portraiture, which he compared favourably with
"the paintings of Rembrandt and the sketches of Callot," and
acclaiming this author, side by side with Swift, as "the second
Rabelais of England." A useful passport to immortality, but
not perhaps a very accurate description of Sterne's essential
merit! Indeed, Sterne at this period, before the publication of
the *Sentimental Journey,* received from French admirers rather
more flattery than critical understanding. They admired the
delineation of his main characters; they appreciated the prodigious vivacity of the novelist's discursive style—*Des pensées
morales, fines, délicates, saillantes, solides, fortes, impies, hazar-
dées, téméraires; voilà ce que l'on trouve dans cet ouvrage. . . .
L'Auteur n'a ni plan, ni principes, ni système, il ne veut que
parler, et malheureusement on l'écoute avec plaisir;* but they
were disconcerted—maybe they were sometimes a little bored
—by the shapelessness of the work in its entirety, and by the
extravagant licence Sterne had allowed himself in pursuing his
disgressions. Sterne, however, was not a man who often troubled
to criticise his critics, provided, that is to say, they helped to increase his sales. What he enjoyed was celebrity and the privileges
it brought him—the sight of *Tristram Shandy* carefully opened
on a nobleman's *écritoire* in preparation for his visit, or lying
on a dressing-table among combs and pomatum-boxes. The Duc
d'Orléans certainly welcomed him, and might or might not read
him. He had the entry of the Palais Royal; and La Popelinière,
a princely figure in the world of finance, offered him the freedom
of his "music and table" for the remainder of his stay. Meanwhile his friends and family were kept acquainted with his

progress. It could not be said that, either as a husband or a father, he had failed to do his duty—sometimes, indeed, a little more than his duty—now that his literary reputation was extending throughout Europe; and when, in the April of 1762, he learned that Lydia's health was troublesome and doctors had advised she should be removed from England, he decided to cancel his own plans (which had involved returning home by leisurely stages during the early summer), persuade his wife and child to join him, and set out for the south of France.

In the furtherance of this scheme, he proved at once patient, practical and energetic. There were letters to be written to the Archbishop of York and to Lord Fauconberg, the patron of his Coxwold living, and long, long directions to be sent to Mrs. Sterne, advising in detail on the luggage she should come equipped with—negligées and a gown or two of English painted linen, a pound of Scotch snuff and her silver coffee-pot, watch-chains to serve as gifts to various helpful friends, a copper tea-kettle, pins and needles, "as also a strong bottle-skrew, for whatever Scrub we may hire as butler, coachman, &c., to uncork us our Frontiniac." Then, there were passports to be procured from the Duc de Choiseul; and it was while he was attending to this last requirement that over-exertion brought on a recurrence of his former malady, and he was attacked by fever which "ended the worst way it could . . . in a *défluxion poitrine,* as the French physicians call it," and he "lost in ten days all I had gain'd since I came here." But once more he rallied and, about the middle of July, a period of sweltering heat, accompanied by Mrs. and Miss Sterne, whose expensive equipage had rolled into Paris a few days earlier, he took the road south, in his own carriage, bound for Toulouse, which he intended to make his refuge during the autumn and winter months.

Their journey was uncomfortable and adventurous. From Lyons, where the chaise in which the Sternes were riding broke down, fell to pieces and was sold for scrap, they travelled by water to Avignon, there again transferred to a carriage and, with Sterne himself sometimes ahead and sometimes far behind, riding or walking or joining in peasant dances, stopping a country-woman to buy her figs, talking with a couple of Franciscan friars or with a drum-maker on his way to the fairs at Beaucaire and Tarascon, they presently dawdled into Toulouse about the middle of August, 1762. Sterne was to remain in the south for nearly two years, first in Toulouse, the inhabitant of a large, elegantly furnished house, "most deliciously placed at the extremity of the town," afterwards in Montpélier, Aix and Marseilles. During this period his health, in spite of some preliminary improvement, remained exceedingly precarious. He suffered from the searching cold of a Mediterranean winter, spat blood, shivered with ague, and was once "almost poisoned" by what the physicians of the neighbourhood styled a *bouillon rafraichissant*—" 'tis a cock flayed alive and boiled with poppy seeds, then pounded in a mortar, afterwards pass'd through a sieve. . . ." Such "scuffles with death," in which the long-legged spectre who had followed him from London seemed often as near as in England to getting the upper hand, left him pallid, emaciated, nervous yet never quite exhausted. His faculties were still clear, his eyes still sharp; he was still talkative, ribald, inquiring wherever he found himself; or with a bottle of Frontiniac at his elbow (as often as he was not dieting on ass's and cow's milk), and for prospect the "serpentine walks" of his Toulouse garden, worked away intermittently at the task of completing his book.

It was lack of money that, in the end, brought him home to London. And the decision to return had important domestic results; for Mrs. Sterne, who had found very much to her taste the mixed and lively social world that she and her daughter could enjoy in Toulouse, announced that her rheumatism obliged her to stay behind. Sterne acquiesced, with considerable private relief though some alarm at the prospect of maintaining henceforward two separate establishments. But, so long as he breathed, he refused to despair of the future; and in March, 1764, with a touch of real sorrow at leaving his "little slut," Lydia, and a seemly show of regret at parting from Mrs. Sterne, he set out again towards Paris on his way to London and York. In Paris, caught up in the crowd of travelling Englishmen who since the suspension of hostilities had begun to sweep across the Channel, he enjoyed a holiday from domestic tedium that lasted for two months. Wilkes was there, endeavouring with his usual success to make the best of both worlds, alternately the man of pleasure and the courageous, devoted victim of a despotic government; and Sterne joined him in "an odd party" (so Wilkes informed Churchill) to which various "goddesses of the theatre" had also been invited. Hume, the sleepy lion of a brilliant bevy of admirers, he met and argued with good-naturedly over the table of the British Ambassador, Lord Hertford. For the purposes of this argument, which occurred after Sterne had preached an affecting sermon in the chapel of the Embassy, he reassumed the rôle of parson and, among much laughter on both sides in which the company joined, gravely pretended to assert the truth of miracles. But perhaps he was more than half sincere. So little concerned with facts, so deeply absorbed in all those impressions, visions and imaginings that give our life its colour, he was certainly no sceptic of a logical or positive cast. The nature of the self was a mystery, his own continued existence a kind of miracle; and a new hæmorrhage presently reminded him that the miracle on which he relied might not often be repeated. Back in London at the beginning of June, he stayed long enough to sit for another portrait by Joshua Reynolds, then travelled north for York races and an interval of parish work. Finally, having refreshed himself by a trip to Scarborough, he was able to fix his attention on the business of writing a novel, and turned out the seventh and eighth volumes of *Tristram Shandy*, probably the most unequal that he had yet produced, in time for publication at the close of January, 1765.

His next task was to obtain a large body of subscribers for two further volumes of *The Sermons of Mr. Yorick*, that curious and, from a mystical point of view, not very consolatory compilation of religious essays in which the Second Person of the Trinity is but rarely represented, and the First and Third as

Abstract Benevolence or Deified Common Sense. Their appearance provided an excuse to return to London; and in London he dined out again so well and energetically that, as usual, his health suffered and he was obliged to retire to Bath. There, surrounded by a crowd of idle and admiring women, it was natural that he should fall back into a series of flirtations, of the half-passionate, half-platonic kind to which his peculiar sexual temperament, so lively yet so volatile and so unfocused, had always predisposed him. He may or may not have *made* love, but the proximity or possibility of love afforded a stimulus that his imagination needed. His heart was generally in a condition of pleasing unrest; and, while his time at Bath was spent in oscillating between such luminaries as "the charming widow *Moor*," "the gentle, elegant *Gore*, with her fine form and Grecian face," and "another widow, the interesting Mrs. Vesey, with her vocal and fifty other accomplishments," having returned to London he is discovered sending tender and somewhat equivocal propositions to Lady Percy, Lord Bute's daughter, the ill-behaved wife of the heir to the dukedom of Northumberland, whose "eyes and lips," he declared, had totally bewitched him.

These gossamer associations were attractive but thin-spun; and, when during the second week of October, 1765, Sterne embarked on the last and most famous and fruitful of his continental journeys, there was no bond, either of heart or head, to hold him back to England. He set out in exuberant spirits. . . . But all that deserves to be remembered of the expedition—high-lights of feeling and observation that the traveller brings home with him at last as his only real treasure-trove—remains imprisoned under crystal in the book he was soon to write. Besides the essence of his adventures as he himself conveyed them, any additional information research can supply seems clumsy and irrelevant. But it is worth noting that, after his meeting with the Piedmontese Lady who shared his bedroom at the "little decent kind of an inn" when he was held up by a fall of rock on the road "between St. Michael and Modane," he pressed forward through the terrors of the Alps, emerged with relief on the northern Italian plain, admired Turin, was well received at Milan (where he enjoyed an amatory brush with the celebrated Marchesa Fagniani), paid a brief visit to Florence and dined with Horace Mann, performed the usual round of Roman sightseeing, and basked, full of vitality and contentment, beneath the beaming sky of Naples. It was not until May that he again traversed the Alps—much improved (he told his friends), fat and sleek and handsome, and quite prepared for the rather hazardous business of meeting Mrs. Sterne, who was wandering at large with his daughter among the resorts of France. But the meeting, when it occurred, passed off not unpleasantly. The poor woman, he remarked, had been "very cordial, etc.," but begged to be allowed to remain in the land that suited her; and Sterne gave his permission and quietly went on his way. During the summer of 1766, he stepped down for the last time from the deck of the Channel packet, confident (he assured Hall-Stevenson) that he would live another ten years.

He returned, enriched and refreshed. The contribution of France and Italy to Sterne's development needs very little underlining. *Tristram Shandy* from first to last is an exceedingly uneven book, obscured by patches of fog, disfigured by the perverse oddities and deliberate eccentricities that have appealed always to certain aspects of the English temperament. It suggests the climate of Yorkshire and the humours of a provincial city. Soon Sterne's imagination was to assume a clearer, warmer and less uncertain colouring. Illness had given an added quality to his appreciation of the South—the beauty of southern landscapes in which by a very small stretch of fancy he could retrace the classical countryside of Claude and Poussin, with its dark myrtles, shaggy hills and vast, gold-glimmering, ethereal prospects, and the gaiety and sensual simplicity of Mediterranean manners. Life at Coxwold by comparison seemed bleak and anxious. His health had deteriorated since his return to England; Mrs. Sterne's demands for money were a continual nuisance; the plan to increase his acreage by the enclosure of Stillington Common made repeated, tormenting inroads upon his time and energy. In spite of these annoyances he yet contrived to work, and resumed the rather tangled narrative of Uncle Toby's love-making. By the end of the year, the ninth volume of his novel had been handed to the publisher.

In fact, the ninth was the last; but it did not conclude the story. To such a story there could be no end, since it had had no beginning; his reveries are not wound up but merely cut short; and the solution of Uncle Toby's problem remains perpetually unsettled. Perhaps Sterne now understood that he had embarked on an endless task; but, though there is a suggestion of fatigue about some of the later passages, and many of the travel notes that Sterne interpolated, presumably by way of padding, in Volumes VII, VIII and IX, are both facetious and irrelevant, his virtues proved as irrepressible as his accompanying literary vices. He is foolish, jaunty, over-whimsical; but his gift for simple and vivid imagery is constantly breaking through; and the travel-jottings, among much that is trivial and a good deal that is tedious, include the episodes of the poor, pensive ass which he had fed on macaroons at Lyons, and the mad girl, Maria (afterwards remembered in the *Sentimental Journey*), seated at the roadside, playing her evening tune. Uncle Toby and his soldier-servant are solid as never before. Displaying his customary grasp of detail, Sterne manages to invest the inventory of Uncle Toby's wardrobe, "his tarnished gold-laced hat and huge cockade of flimsy taffety," with an air of heroic significance that expresses the natural grandeur of a simple, unselfish man. Even Corporal Trim's improper stories have an oddly poetic side. Over the anecdote of the Young Beguine hovers the midday hush of the deserted Flemish farm-house; while the account of how the Corporal's brother Tom had married the Jew's widow at Lisbon (which terminates with an innuendo of a particularly salacious sort) is picked out by sudden glimpses of living and moving figures:

"Every servant in the family, from high to low, wished Tom success; and I can fancy, an' please your honour, I see him this moment with his white dimity waistcoat and breeches, and a hat a little o' one side, passing jollily along the street, swinging his stick. . . .

"When Tom . . . got to the shop, there was nobody in it but a poor negro girl, with a bunch of white feathers slightly tied to the end of a long cane, flapping away flies—not killing them.—' 'Tis a pretty picture!' said my Uncle Toby. . . ."

Memorable, too, are the long artful passages in which Sterne builds up an emotional effect with deliberate virtuosity; and just as Volume VI had contained the famous set-piece of Uncle Toby sleeping (so somniferous in its rhythm, in its imagery so suggestive of a group of allegorical statuary after the manner of Roubiliac), Volume IX introduces the exquisite invocation, the last that Sterne would ever compose, to his "dear Jenny," ghostly counterpart of Catherine Fourmantelle, now separated from him by many years, by age and alienation, perhaps by death itself. He is discussing the significance that posterity may or may not attach to Mrs. Shandy's sayings. But——

"I will not argue the matter. Time wastes too fast: every letter I trace tells me with what rapidity Life follows my pen; the days and hours of it more precious,—my dear Jenny,—than the rubies about thy neck, are flying over our heads like light clouds of a windy day, never to return more; everything presses on,—whilst thou art twisting that lock!—see! it grows gray; and every time I kiss thy hand to bid adieu, and every absence which follows it, are preludes to that eternal separation which we are shortly to make.—

"Heaven have mercy upon us both!"

So, as if a cold wind had swept across the page, the chapter ends abruptly. Gone for a moment are the old soldier and his servant and the amorous middle-aged widow who is planning Uncle Toby's downfall. Temporarily, his characters vanish; only the writer remains, confronted by the prospect, which grew more and more distinct, of his own approaching dissolution. His lungs (he had already told a friend) reminded him of a pair of badly mended bellows. There had been repeated hæmorrhages, further periods of complete physical exhaustion. Yet January, 1767, saw him back again in London, established in comfortable lodgings at 41 Old Bond Street, from which he hurried out to dinner and supper, renewed his admiration for Garrick and his acquaintance with the Duke of York, and made an appearance at Mrs. Cornelys's famous Carlisle House assemblies. Among his more recent friends was the celebrated Commodore James, distinguished for his expedition against the Bombay pirates, whom he had subdued in the service of the British East India Company. Reynolds's portrait of James shows an ugly but agreeable face; while Mrs. James, an alleged beauty, was both an "interesting" woman, in the eighteenth-century sense of the term and, even by Shandeian standards, highly sentimental. Sterne was soon the intimate of their house in Gerrard Street; and it was there, apparently not long after his return to London, that he encountered Elizabeth Draper, a young Anglo-Indian married woman, in whose career and supposed misfortunes the sympathetic and effusive Mrs. James took a very lively interest.

Mrs. Draper claimed to have been born on 5th April, 1744, and was therefore, at the time of her first meeting with Sterne, not quite twenty-three; but married at the age of fourteen to a man twenty years older than herself, Daniel Draper, now Secretary to the Government of Bombay, she was the mother of two children and had reached a point in the history of her married life when it was natural that she should look around her in search of fresh distractions. Her education had been frivolous, her existence with Mr. Draper neither stimulating nor romantic. By all accounts he was a mild-mannered and good-tempered man; but Elizabeth found him dull; and when her husband, having brought back his family to England in 1765, himself returned to his duties, leaving Elizabeth to arrange for the education of their children, she passed her time in a round of visits between the houses of various landed relations scattered through the country and the London establishment of her friends, the

Jameses. From them, and more particularly from Mrs. James, both her looks and her talents received their proper share of admiration. Nicknamed the *"belle Indian,"* she combined a charming face and a pathetic history. Soon she must say good-bye to England; and her numerous devotees continued to remind her how deep would be England's loss.

Such a tale of worth and suffering was bound to interest Sterne. Moreover, though (as he was once bold enough to admit) his first glance had shown him merely a plain and affected young woman, dressed in a fashionable but unbecoming manner, there was "a *something*" about her eyes and voice—a "bewitching sort of nameless excellence," calculated to appeal to any man of "sense, tenderness and feeling"—that Sterne and later admirers found inimitably persuasive. Her features were enclosed in a "perfect oval." As for the rest, "a statuary [according to one of the last of her adorers, that infatuated historian, the Abbé Raynal] who would have wished to represent Voluptuousness, would have taken her for his model; and she would equally have served for him who might have had a figure of Modesty to portray . . . Desire . . . followed her steps in silence." To the impression that she made on Sterne, something, no doubt, was added by her exotic origin. In the more imaginative type of love-affair, the figure that occupies the foreground is often much indebted to its immediate background; and haloing the personality of Elizabeth Draper were the sunsets of the Malabar Coast and the green palm-fronds of Anjengo. She belonged to a world not completely European, a world of bilious, blood-shot, grasping, hard-drinking men and of languid, frivolous, ignorant, short-lived women. Elizabeth, however, was of a more exuberant, cultivated and inquiring turn than the great majority of Anglo-Indian "nabobesses" whose upbringing and manner of life she found equally deplorable. Vaguely but persistently she longed for better things; and, in the company at the Jameses' house, which included several presentable and distinguished men, Sterne was the most distinguished and also, one may assume, by far the most beguiling.

In a very short time, he had written sending her his books —the sermons which arrived "all hot from the heart" and *Shandy,* about whose reception he was "more indifferent"—and had informed her that "I know not how it comes in—but I'm half in love with You . . . I never valued (or saw more good Qualities to value)—or thought more of one of Yr Sex than of You." They met frequently; and it was not long before Mrs. Draper was dining at 41 Old Bond Street alone with the author on "scallop'd oysters" or "Mackerel & fowl," attended by his sympathetic and understanding maid. In every life, just as there are shades of emotion that reappear, so there are situations that occur again and again; and these delightful dinner-parties had been foreshadowed some twenty-six years earlier by the "sentimental repasts" he had enjoyed with Miss Elizabeth Lumley. Then, too, they had had a *confidante*—the rôle that Mrs. James had now adopted; then, too, a sympathetic maid-servant had hovered solicitously around them. But the knowledge that no sensation, no situation, is ever quite new detracts nothing from its intensity. Behind Sterne lay more than three decades of tentative philandering, of tremulous approaches to the idea of passion. The new preoccupation, into which he gradually slipped, presently absorbed him to the exclusion of every other interest. The atmosphere of Little Alice Lane was revived at 41 Old Bond Street; the dead attraction towards Miss Lumley was reborn in a more powerful and much more absorbing guise. Sterne embarked on this latest adventure conscious that he might not live to see how the story ended.

Meanwhile, all was serenity, confidence and disinterested feeling. He called Elizabeth his "Bramine," himself her "Bramin"; they exchanged portraits by fashionable miniaturists, and Mrs. Draper presented her Bramin, some time during her stay in London, with "a gold stock buckle and buttons," to which he was soon to attach an almost talismanic value. But there was no pretence at privacy about their odd *liaison,* for both esteemed themselves superior to conventional prejudices—true "delicacy and propriety," Sterne was to declare when Mrs. Draper had

fallen ill and had announced that he must not visit her so long
as she remained in bed, had very little in common with such
"frigid doctrines"; and their friends were welcome to observe
how the attachment flourished. Observers could hardly mis-
interpret so pure a friendship. Mrs. Sterne, nevertheless, safely
in the depths of France, heard stories and caused Lydia to send
an inquiring message, possibly not cantankerous, yet decidedly
suspicious, to which Sterne wrote back in February, again
through Lydia, that he did "not wish to know who was the busy
fool who made your mother uneasy about Mrs. . . . —'tis true
I have a friendship for her, but not to infatuation—I believe I
have judgment enough to discern hers, and every woman's
faults." Some faults, it is true, he may have noticed earlier: during the opening weeks of their intimacy he may have been some
distance still from desperate infatuation. When a letter reached
London during the course of February, addressed to Mrs.
Draper by her husband, instructing her, firmly and plainly, to
return to her Indian duties, his last defences collapsed, reason
and moderation were finally overthrown, and Sterne was revealed as the despairing victim of an extravagant and hopeless
love.

To determine the part played by desire seems now an in-
soluble problem. In a letter written to Mrs. Draper after she had
left the country, describing the state of his health and an unfair
and improper diagnosis put forward by his doctors, Sterne declared categorically that he had told them that he had had "no
commerce whatever with the Sex—not even with my wife . . .
these 15 years . . ." [1] Was Elizabeth meant to accept this curious statement with certain reservations? And, if their relationship had been wholly platonic, would Sterne have ventured to
make the assertion at all? The question, it may be argued, remains relatively unimportant; for, whatever the forms that his
desire assumed, there seems very little doubt that the desire
existed, that Sterne's sentimentality had a predominantly sexual

---

[1] The whole of this passage is reproduced, almost word for word, in a letter
to Lord Spencer of 21st May.

tinge, just as his salacity, at its most unrestrained, was often suffused with a sentimental colouring. In Elizabeth Draper, it was both his good fortune and his tragedy—aided, as is almost every lover, by adventitious circumstance, by a need that he happened to feel in himself and romantic associations he himself supplied—to find a woman who stirred his imagination as it never had been stirred before. She gratified the imaginative concupiscence that was one of his strongest traits, and gave full scope to his large capacity for disinterested and tender emotion.

His feelings were now exposed to a peculiarly cruel test. Alleging that Mrs. Draper's "tender frame"—for she had "looked like a drooping lily" since she had first received Mr. Draper's command to return home—could not be expected to stand the shock of immediate transplantation, he begged that she would put off her departure at least another year, advised her to reason with her husband (who, "if he is the generous, humane man you describe him to be, . . . cannot but applaud your conduct"), offered, should Mr. Draper prove unkind, to pay her whole expenses and, supposing that her health was thought to need a course of foreign travel, to send her to France and Italy in charge of his wife and daughter. But Elizabeth, though not averse from enacting the rôle of matrimonial victim, was disinclined to forgo the advantages of a respectably married state; and with affecting resignation she decided to obey the summons. An East Indiaman was due to sail during the early part of April; Mrs. Draper's passage was booked; the last visits were made, the last gifts exchanged; finally, one day towards the end of March, he handed the Bramine into the chaise which was to carry her from London down to the ship at Deal, then, in agony of spirit, returned to his empty lodgings.

Perhaps he had not suspected how heavily the blow would fall. So long as Eliza remained in England, Sterne continued to write her feverishly affectionate letters, ordering an arm-chair for her cabin, purchasing her "ten handsome brass screws, to hang your necessaries upon," interviewing Zumps, the maker of musical instruments, as to the best method of tuning the pianoforte she was taking with her, and expressing tremulous anxiety when he learned that her sleeping-quarters had been freshly painted. Even now, he begged that she would consider the postponement of her journey. In a penultimate epistle he implored that, were Mr. Draper to die—and Mrs. Sterne, he added parenthetically, could not expect to live long—she would not think of giving herself to some wealthy nabob, "because I design to marry you myself. . . . 'Tis true, I am ninety-five in constitution . . . but what I want in youth, I will make up in wit and good humour.—Not Swift so loved his Stella, Scarron his Maintenon, or Waller his Sacharissa, as I will love and sing thee, my wife elect. . . . Tell me, in answer to this, that you approve and honour the proposal, and that you would (like the Spectator's mistress) have more joy in putting on an old man's slipper, than associating with the gay, the voluptuous, and the young.—Adieu, my Simplicia! Yours, Tristram."

Ten minutes after the letter had gone, he collapsed completely. ". . . This poor, fine-spun frame of Yorick's gave way, and I broke a vessel in my breast, and could not stop the loss of blood till four this morning." Then he had fallen asleep, only to be visited by a vision of Mrs. Draper, come to receive his "parting breath and blessing," and woke again "with the bosom of my shirt steeped in tears." Nevertheless he felt the principle of life, he assured her, still strong within him; he had high hopes that he would live to see her again; and, that the close sympathy they had once enjoyed might not be weakened or attenuated by the fact of separation, he began, after composing a "last farewell to Eliza" to go by "Mr. Wats who sails this day for Bombay," a *Journal to Eliza,* in which he proposed to keep a full and accurate record of all the visions and sensations with which her memory inspired him. He persevered from 12th or 13th April till 4th August, 1767 (when the arrival of Mrs. Sterne and Lydia distracted his attention), adding a tender postscript on 1st November, as soon as he had said good-bye to them and regained his independence. The result was an unusually interesting, if somewhat unpleasing, document. The writer opened with an

attempt at literary artifice: "This Journal wrote under the ficti-
tious names of Yorick & Draper—and sometimes of Bramin &
Bramine—but 'tis a Diary of the miserable feelings of a person
separated from a Lady for whose Society he languish'd—The
real Names—are foreigne—& the acc^t a copy from a french
Mans^t—in Mr. S——s hands . . ." Thenceforward he plunged
straight into a daily journal, undeterred either by considerations
of literary correctness or by the sense of modesty that usually
regulates such a display of passion. He is unashamedly, now and
then disturbingly or pathetically, explicit. No doubt, it is the
work of an extremely unhappy man; and with feelings of vexed
embarrassment we follow "poor sick-headed, sick-hearted Yorick," as he lies in bed (visited, however, by "40 friends, in the
Course of the Day"), totters out to dine with the Jameses, or
eats his chicken alone, washing down the meal with a sauce of
bitter tears. It is true that, in the search for diversion, he had
dragged himself as far as the Brawn's Head, there to carouse
with Hall-Stevenson and "the whole Pandemonium assembled";
but for that outburst he had paid "a severe reckoning all the
night"; and by the end of April he was too ill to leave his arm-
chair, passed his days in restless reverie, and the hours of darkness, as often as he snatched an interval of sleep, in dreams of
"things terrible & impossible—That Eliza is false to Yorick, or
Yorick is false to Eliza."

It is obvious that Sterne was completely sincere—that his
emotion, that is to say, was entirely genuine and the effect produced on his imagination exquisitely painful. But sincerity—
more especially when we are speaking of a literary artist—is
always qualified by a certain degree of unconscious self-decep-
tion; and, aware of the parallelism between his passion for Mrs.
Draper and the passion he had once entertained for Miss Elizabeth Lumley, he did not hesitate to ransack his ancient love-
letters and from the epistles he had formerly addressed to an
uninspiring wife to copy out a long passage for the benefit of a
beloved mistress: ". . . One solitary plate—one knife—one fork
—one glass!—O Eliza! 'twas painfully distressing.—I gave a

thousand pensive penetrating Looks at the Arm chair thou so
often graced on these quiet, sentimental Repasts—& sighed &
laid down my knife and fork,—& took out my handkerchief,
. . ." transcribing the paragraph sentence by sentence, and
almost word for word. As usual, his flight ended in a fit of
abundant weeping; during April and part of May, Sterne's energetic tear-glands rarely lacked employment; then the downpour
began to thin, though it was never quite suspended, and we
catch a glimpse of Yorick in a more familiar guise, driving in
the Park where a dashing acquaintance whom he had nicknamed
Sheba cantered up to his carriage to enquire how her Solomon
did, paying a brief call at Ranelagh Gardens, or supping at
Spencer House. The conclusion of May found him well enough
to return to Coxwold; and on the 22nd he left London and
Bond Street and travelled slowly northwards, breaking his journey at the palace of the amiable Bishop of York, to whom in
his family circle Sterne displayed the portrait of Eliza which he
carried next his heart, accompanying it with a "short but interesting Story of my friendship for the Original . . ." The epis-
copal family party was much affected; and Sterne was able to
record that he had been "kindly nursed and honoured"; after
which he once more set out towards his long-neglected living.

There he soon received the alarming intelligence that Mrs.
Sterne proposed to visit him. "This unexpected visit [he informed Eliza] is neither a visit of friendship or form—but 'tis
a visit, such as I know you will never make me—of pure Interest
—to pillage what they can from me." First, he was required to
sell a small estate and lay out the proceeds in joint annuities;
and to this he assented without much grumbling; but he dreaded
the prospect of being additionally plundered in a hundred small
particulars, "Linnens—for house use—Body use—printed Linnens for Gowns—Mazareens of Teas—Plate (all I have but
6 Silver Spoons)—In short I shall be pluck'd bare . . ." Meanwhile it was his consolation to lay plans for future felicity that
he still hoped might be realised: to stroll, when his health had
recovered, to a nearby romantic ruin, uprooting briars beside

the path and reflecting how often—"you swinging upon my arm"—at some happy, distant period he would perhaps retrace his footsteps: and to furnish at Shandy Hall "a sweet little apartment," diminutive but elegantly proportioned, with just space "to hang a dozen petticoats—gowns, &c.—& Shelves for as many Band-boxes," in a style worthy of the woman he considered his wife elect.

These dreams he turned over in solitude. Towards the end of June, he was sufficiently robust to pay a brief visit to Hall-Stevenson at Skelton, there pass Eliza's portrait round the Demoniac table and race his chaise along the mirror-smoothness of Saltburn Sands; but by 29th June he was back at Coxwold, surrounded by "all the simple clean plenty which a Valley can produce," venison, wild fowls, curds and strawberries and cream, yet pursued by the constant visionary apparition of the mistress-wife with whom he hoped one day to share it. Time plodded on slowly; desire and expectation haunted his days and nights; he walked "like a disturbed spirit" about his garden, or remained indoors, distempered and melancholy, observed only by his cat which sat quietly beside him, purring *pianissimo* "& looking up gravely from time to time in my face, as if she knew my situation."

It is not difficult to deride *The Journal to Eliza,* Sterne's extravagant sentimentality and effusive self-pity, which induced the lover to carry about with him against the beloved's return a collection of cambric handkerchiefs steeped in his heart's blood. But then, the book is to be regarded as a love-letter; and few letters of that kind, written with genuine passion, do much credit either to the niceness of the writer's taste or to the justice of his understanding. Admittedly, Sterne had lost his balance. Disease was working in him faster than he yet suspected; a long habit of evading passion—or of distilling from passion its sentimental essence, to be used like a heavy perfume, till drop by drop it evaporated on the common daily air—had at length broken down, with disastrous consequences to his health and sanity. But the balance, forfeited in one respect, was maintained

firmly in another. On 6th July he had informed the Jameses
that he was "now beginning to be truly busy at my Sentimental
Journey," and thenceforward *Journal* and *Journey* went steadily
hand in hand. Both were interrupted by the arrival, during the
early part of August, of Mrs. and Miss Sterne, Lydia, accomplished, affectionate, talkative, accompanied by her "rather
devilish" French dog, which he feared might break into the
pianissimo purrings of his sentimental cat, his wife full of plans
for her own financial future. But his apprehensions were un-
founded; the "restless unreasonable Wife whom [he told his
mistress] neither gentleness nor generosity can conquer," proved
far more amenable to reason than her husband had expected;
and, when the pair finally left his house on the first day of
November, Mrs. Sterne vowed that she would never give him
"another sorrowful or discontented hour"—and, what was no
less to the purpose, never return from France—while Lydia,
though a frivolous and self-indulgent girl, refused the small sum
with which he had presented her by way of pocket-money.

Released from the agitation they had caused him, he resumed
his travel-book. The work progressed rapidly; at the end of
November he had written the last page and lapsed into a state
of complete exhaustion, having "torn my whole frame into
pieces" (he informed a correspondent) by the violence of his
feelings. As usual, he rallied and, as usual, returned to London;
but *The Sentimental Journey* seemed to demand and to deserve
more meticulous revision than any of its predecessors; and February, 1768, was almost finished before two small octavo volumes
appeared in London and at once found their way across the
Channel to the Parisian literary public. The success of the work
(for which Sterne had already received an advance payment of
a thousand guineas) was extensive and immediate; Smollett's
hirelings might deliver some clumsy critical jabs, French readers
express surprise both at the "lowness" of Sterne's subject-matter
and the extreme oddity that characterised his relations with the
opposite sex; but here was a book in which, even more clearly
and brilliantly than in his novel and sermons, the intelligent

public of the age found its sensibility reflected, and recognised that peculiar blend of emotion and intelligence, of sympathy and understanding, suggestively summed up in the one word "sentimental."

His new book marked the climax of Sterne's literary development. *The Sentimental Journey* is the most readable of minor masterpieces, just as *Tristram Shandy*, taken as a whole, is probably one of the least readable of works to which critics of the past have decided to allot an important place upon our bookshelves. It was written with love, and (Sterne had assured his daughter) composed in a spirit of love, the design being "to teach us to love the world and our fellow creatures better than we do—so it runs most upon those gentle passions and affections, which aid so much to it." Of greater consequence than its moral pretensions (which we cannot discount but need not, perhaps, take very seriously) is the author's attitude towards himself and the world he was describing. Poets had already discovered that the mind was its "own place"; no prose writer of genius had yet suggested that the vagaries and adventures of the mind, outside the limits of poetry, rhetoric, drama, might provide their own literary justification. Or, if they had done so, they had not set to work with such complete shamelessness. Sterne is a traveller who laughs at guide-books, and the "objects of interest" to which writers of guide-books devote their space and energy. He is concerned solely with himself and with his personal response to the things that he observes. The only condition he demands is complete emotional receptivity:

> "What a large volume of adventures [he wrote] may be grasped within this little span of life, by him who interests his heart in everything, and who, having eyes to see what time and what chance are perpetually holding out to him as he journeyeth on his way, misses nothing he can *fairly* lay his hands on!"

The Sentimental Journey is, therefore, a text-book on feeling, an exposition of how, in any given set of circumstances, to

behave in a sentimental and civilised mode, and was presently
to be adopted as such by its admirers throughout Europe. But
what admirers and imitators could not borrow was Yorick's
special temperament, the odd mixture of detached interest and
passionate, effusive sympathy with which he turned his eyes upon
the world around him. Sterne's pathetic passages have a peculiar
vibrant quality; his erotic passages, too—so shocking to the
squeamish Victorian taste—are remarkably different from other
examples of modern erotic literature. There is the same detachment we are aware of when he is sentimental, the same careful
notation of movements and impulses, as if it were a piece of
music, not ordinary sexual dalliance between a man and a
woman, that the author were recording. Read, for instance, the
story of his visit to the glove-shop:

> "The beautiful *grisette* measured them one by one across
> my hand.—It would not alter the dimensions.—She begged I
> would try a single pair, which seemed to be the least.—She
> held it open;—my hand slipped into it at once. 'It will not
> do,' said I, shaking my head a little.—'No,' said she, doing
> the same thing.
>
> "There are certain combined looks of simple subtlety—
> where whim, and sense, and seriousness, and nonsense are so
> blended that all the languages of Babel set loose together
> could not express them;—they are communicated and caught
> so instantaneously that you can scarce say which party is the
> infector . . . It is enough in the present to say again, the
> gloves would not do; so folding our hands within our arms, we
> both loll'd upon the counter;—it was narrow, and there was
> just room for the parcel to lay between us."

The Traveller sees every object through the glass of his own
temperament, feels every moment in the setting of a particular
mood. He is low-minded, high-flown, sensual, compassionate—
all in as short a time as it takes to turn the page or let a sequence
of images cross the fancy. The charm of Sterne's method is its
constant changefulness. Yet through the changes runs a distinct,

if tenuous, thread of individual continuity. Shape merges into shape, but Yorick remains; and, though the world itself is presented as extraordinarily various in its human details and inexhaustibly entertaining, there, too, certain patterns perpetually turn up, certain aspirations that age, habit, suffering can never quite extinguish. Do not human beings continue to pine for freedom? A caged starling becomes the symbol of this thwarted longing:

> "I was interrupted . . . with a voice which I took to be of a child, which complained 'it could not get out'—I look'd up and down the passage . . . seeing neither man, woman, nor child. . . .
>
> "In my return back through the same passage, I heard the same words repeated twice over; and looking up, I saw it was a starling hung in a little cage;—'I can't get out—I can't get out,' said the starling."

And there are other impulses, equally strong, equally persistent, that confront the Traveller again and again through the course of his wanderings—impulses of passion and charity, of hope and pride, indestructible expressions of the human spirit, like the impulse that urged Candide to plant a garden. Thus, the book is the work of a humanist in the truest sense of the word, who makes his "true dimension" the capacity and mind of man, who loves life, welcomes experience, and has not yet lost all his faith in the infinite possibilities of common human nature. Sterne's own love of life was certainly a dominant trait. The writer who had been "torn to pieces" by the composition of the *Sentimental Journey,* the poor "sick-headed, sick-hearted" consumptive of the *Journal to Eliza,* presently rose from his sick-bed, put aside his journal and, accompanied by Hall-Stevenson, had come rolling back to London. There awaited him the customary round of visits and engagements, and, as soon as his book had appeared, even more than his usual share of flattery and attention. But the winter months were wet and cold; late in February he was attacked by influenza which, notwithstanding all his efforts and "something like revelation . . . [he wrote to Mrs. Montagu] which tells me I shall not dye—but live," proved impossible to shake off. Influenza turned to pleurisy; then on 15th March, in a tone that for the first time seems to suggest despair, he wrote a letter—almost, but not quite, a letter of farewell—to Mrs. James at Gerrard Street. He had been bled three times the previous Thursday, and blistered during Friday: "The physician says I am better—God knows, for I feel myself sadly wrong, and shall, if I recover, be a long while of gaining strength. . . . Dearest, kindest, gentlest, and best of women! may health, peace and happiness prove your handmaids.—If I die, cherish the remembrance of me, and forget the follies which you so often condemn'd. . . . Should my child, my Lydia, want a mother, may I hope you will (if she is left parentless) take her to your bosom?" There is no reference to Elizabeth Draper. Perhaps that delusive image had already begun to fade, as the distance between them lengthened and the approach of the long-legged phantom which had pursued him so patiently, so indefatigably, grew more and more perceptible. The last encounter occurred at four o'clock in the afternoon of 18th March, 1768, before only two indifferent witnesses. A large dinner-party of gentlemen, which included Hume and Garrick, the Duke of Roxburgh, and the notorious Lord March, the future Duke of Queensberry, sent an attendant round to Bond Street to inquire after their friend's health. "I went to Mr. Sterne's lodgings [the young man remembered]; the mistress opened the door. I inquired how he did? She told me to go up to the nurse. I went into the room, and he was just a dying. I waited ten minutes; but in five he said, '*Now it is come.*' He put up his hand, as if to stop a blow, and died in a minute."

JOHN WILKES

FROM small centres of agitation—so small that by a contemporary observer they are entirely unperceived—develop vast disturbances that sweep across a continent. Looking back, we are aware of warning signs, observe the men and women of the period as they go about their interests, unperturbed by a livid gleam on the sea or a faint rumbling from within the flanks of the extinct volcano, watch their confidence change to uneasiness, and uneasiness to a sudden bewildered appreciation of the danger they are facing. When Sterne returned to London during December, 1760, the old King had been dead for two months, and the young monarch, of whom little was known save that he was serious and well-intentioned, had taken his first tentative steps as a wielder of royal authority. On the whole, the impression was favourable. He knew everything (wrote Sterne), weighed everything maturely; "and then he is inflexible—this puts old stagers off their game." The old stagers, it appeared, were due for many surprises. The King's father, Frederick Prince of Wales, enthusiastic, generous, fickle and wrong-headed, had been the friend and pupil of Bolingbroke; and Bolingbroke's *Patriot King*, with its doctrine of the monarch who is above party limitations, was the manual on which the young prince had been educated by his mother. Was it not possible that George III would succeed in breaking down that close corporation of the great Whig families which had governed the country, almost without challenge, since the accession of his grandfather in 1715? Such was the end (according to some observers) that he appeared to have in view; "The King [Sterne noted] seems resolved to bring all things back to their original principles. . . . The present system being to remove that phalanx of great people, which stood between the throne and the subjects, and suffer them to have immediate access without the intervention of a cabal . . ." George had been bred for the rôle of a patriot prince, a philosopher-king who would make of the royal authority something real and sacred. It is unfortunate that the highest resolves and the noblest intentions should be obliged to work through the medium, often extremely dense, of an individual human character.

Neither a face nor a character can be ever completely reformed. The features of George III—the pink fresh skin already darkening into an apoplectic crimson, the pale blue prominent eyes, so soon to be underlined by heavy swollen pouches, the receding double chin and tall but sloping forehead—were those, down to the smallest detail, of his dominant German forebears. To them too—and more particularly to the unlucky Frederick— he owed the bad qualities by which his good points were cunningly circumscribed. Potentially at least, as his less tractable subjects very soon discovered, George III was the most dangerous type of autocrat, one who combined an exalted sense of his royal duty with an intense natural obstinacy, and who had all the determination of an extremely well-intentioned, with none of the flexibility of a cultivated and intelligent, man. When conscience spoke loudly, it was usually in his mother's voice. Her notorious admonition: "George, be a King!" was the counsel of a woman, herself exceedingly ambitious, whose husband during his lifetime had been deprived of any real power by the hatred of his parents and then cheated of the succession by his early and sudden death. Frederick Prince of Wales had died— perhaps from the effects of a chill, perhaps as the result of an accident at tennis—in 1751. George II had survived his elder son till 1760; and meanwhile the Princess Dowager had fallen more and more under the influence—it may be, at length, into the arms—of her husband's friend, a plausible courtier and grasping politician, the egregious Lord Bute. His unpopularity was equal to that of the Dowager Princess; and both stood, advising and urging, behind the youthful King, demanding that he should assert himself, that he should try his power before that power was wrested from him, preaching hatred of the great Whig families who closely encompassed the throne. Walpole had triumphed over Frederick, and had established a form of personal parliamentary government that reduced the royal power to a minimum. Now the ghost of Frederick haunted St. James's, pleading for redress and revenge.

The situation was in itself explosive. But history moves upon the pivot of individual passions; and, through a series of long hazards and curious chances, there emerged a human being qualified to take his place at the head of the opposite party and become a standard-bearer round whom they could rally as soon as the battle was joined. Yet John Wilkes might have seemed at the outset to have had few of the virtues that are usually expected of a tribune of the people. He was a frivolous character, neither hard-working nor unselfish, the dissipated child of wealthy parents, who had passed his youth with rich, thoughtless and depraved companions in amusements of the kind usually considered most enervating and unworthy. Nor, like many revolutionaries, was Wilkes by birth an aristocrat. His father was a successful tradesman, a prosperous distiller; and John, a second son, entered the world in St. John's Square, Clerkenwell, on October 17, 1727. An unusually ugly child, he was also tough, lusty and intelligent. Against the dim opulent background of his parents' household—the type of household we are familiar with in eighteenth-century conversation pieces, where the wigged merchant sits at table before a silver coffee-pot, while his strait-laced wife and daughters, attended by a Negro page, are grouped solemnly around him—John's temperament presently displayed itself in a succession of alarming sallies.

It was clear he had not been cut out for an exemplary civic life. But, although his mother was a devout Presbyterian and her influence seems to have counted for much in the Clerkenwell establishment, his father lived under the mild rule of the comatose Church of England and was generally a personage of a worldlier and kindlier sort. John was his favourite and, though presumably he was often shocked, he continued to treat him "on every occasion with tenderness and indulgence." Thus the young man grew up a rebel, but a good-natured rebel. There was nothing in the adult Wilkes of that deep-seated bitterness and ingrained hatred of society which are very often the by-product of an unhappy childhood. Two learned Presbyterians gave him his early schooling; and under their tuition, first at Hertford, then at Thame in Oxfordshire, and afterwards at Aylesbury, he "made the usual progress in the Greek and Roman languages." From Buckinghamshire he went direct to the University of Leyden, taking with him as bear-leader his master at Aylesbury, a certain Matthew Leeson, a solid and serious personage, suspected of Arian leanings. Master and pupil were soon at variance; and Wilkes first attached himself to another religious philosopher, nicknamed in the pleasant contemporary fashion "Immateriality" Baxter,[1] then entered the agnostic circle of the Baron d'Holbach. Personally the young man was distinguished by his remarkable ugliness, his vivacity and wild good humour—even in Holland, according to one companion, he "showed something of that daring profligacy, for which he was afterwards notorious"—and by his resolution to perfect himself as a scholar and man of the world. He returned home a finished product of the Augustan Grand Tour, only to learn that his parents in Clerkenwell, quite unconscious of the social and spiritual change through which he had been passing, were determined he should do them credit by marrying well and early. As his bride they produced Miss Mary Mead, thirty-two years old, neither amusing nor attractive, but the daughter and heiress of a wealthy drysalter. To please "an indulgent father," Wilkes consented. He was twenty at the time, gay, rakish and extravagant; almost from the outset the marriage was disastrous—he had stumbled, he said afterwards, as he entered the temple of Hymen. Polly Wilkes, the one constant passion of Wilkes's existence, was born in 1750, and husband and wife did not formally separate till 1754. Meanwhile with the help of his own allowance and Mrs. Wilkes's ample fortune, which included a

---

[1] See page 203.

country house and an estate in the neighbourhood of Aylesbury, he had emerged from the chrysalis of his commercial origins and had begun to allow his native genius the scope that it demanded.

Beside a strong desire to please, he had abundant personal charm. Maturity had done nothing to soften the effect of those curiously malformed features—a jaw that was crooked and prominent, squinting eyes set close together in an odd malevolent leer, a high bony forehead and a flat truncated nose. But good looks, he soon discovered, were an advantage he could dispense with; it took him, he declared, "only half an hour to talk away my face"; and once the face had been talked away— Wilkes talked with the ease of a man of the world but with the learning of a scholar—there were few, men or women, who, if he set out to capture their approval, could very long resist him. Women proved particularly sensitive to the rare combination he presented of physical exuberance and intellectual energy. In one respect at least Wilkes seems to have escaped the influence of the age in which he lived. He was a highly intelligent man, but neither a moralist nor a sentimentalist. Not for Wilkes were the exquisite struggles that accompany a sense of sin. All his life he remained passionately addicted to the pursuit of women; and there was no stage of his public life, even as a popular hero behind the walls of a London gaol, when patriotism and pleasure did not run in double harness. His public life, however, was a somewhat late development; and between his twentieth and thirtieth birthdays it was chiefly as a man of pleasure that he made his mark on the world. In this rôle he received much assistance and encouragement from the member for Aylesbury, the dissolute son of the Primate of England, a certain Thomas Potter; and there has been preserved a note, written by Potter during the year 1752, which neatly sets the tone of their friendship and contains a vivid reflection of the amusements in which they were both absorbed. Wilkes is urged to throw up dull domestic obligations and join Potter in a descent he planned on Bath—if, that is to say, "you prefer young women and whores to old women and wives, if you prefer toying away hours with little Sattin Back to the evening conferences of your Mother-in-Law . . . but above all if the Heavenly inspired passion called Lust have not deserted you."

It was by Potter, no doubt, that Wilkes was introduced to Dashwood and thus found his way into the society of the Monks of Medmenham. Too much has been written and, since the destruction of their records within living memory, too little is really known, of the practices and aims of the original Hell Fire Club, which held its meetings either in the Gothic solitude of Medmenham Abbey or deep in the chalk caverns under West Wycombe Park. The legend they have left behind is speciously picturesque; but the organisation, like many others of the same kind, from Hall-Stevenson's Demoniacs to the Irish Dalkey Kingdom, has a more illuminating and, historically, a more important aspect. A recrudescence of paganism, not unconnected with the fertility rites of the European middle-ages, these clubs provided an outlet for some of the violent and revolutionary impulses that had begun to ferment beneath the smooth surface of a so-called "age of reason." They represented a revolt against Christian ethics, the desire of the individual to explore dark labyrinths in his own nature from which conventional morality and the dictates of common sense alike debarred him. Debauchery is a key that has often been employed, though very seldom with success, in an attempt to make new discoveries on the mental and spiritual plane; mysteries and orgies are frequently hard to distinguish; and, whereas it would be unwise to attribute too solemn a significance to the extravagant mummeries enacted by the monks and nuns of Medmenham, we should yet regard them as the frivolous inheritors of an ancient and serious cult.

Certainly, they invoked the Devil and, on one occasion, according to rumour, they thought they had succeeded. But Sir Francis Dashwood, a dissipated, yet good-hearted and good-tempered man, had very little in common with the mysterious thirteenth person who presided over the caverns of mediæval warlocks and whose embraces, declared witches, were always icy-cold. Very human, and indeed very characteristic of the period, was the combination of traits that went to form his personality. An accomplished and industrious rake, he was devoted to his wife and is said to have cared for her during her last illness with the most affectionate solicitude. A hard-working if untalented statesman and politician, he was a great collector, a friend of poets, and a patron of painters and sculptors. The Dilettanti Society, which he had helped to found, united the love of wine with the pursuit of classic taste, and was responsible, through its members James Stuart and Nicholas Revett, for one of the first scholarly examinations of the antiquities of Athens. To this it should be added that Dashwood proved a firm friend to Benjamin Franklin and, with Franklin's help, was at pains to revise the Book of Common Prayer on advanced Deist principles. Something of every element in Dashwood's composition seems to have inspired him to establish beside the Thames his modern Abbey of Thelema.

The famous device: *"Fay ce que vouldras"* was inscribed above its entrance. But, once we have climbed the park-wall of Dashwood's abbey and, after admiring the gondola he had brought from Venice moored upon the Thames, have explored groves and alleys and serpentine walks, embellished with many decorative phallicisms and architectural improprieties, benches and statues strangely inscribed, significant obelisks and meaning grottos, mystery surrounds us as we enter the house itself. The members, we learn, wore white suits, while the Prior, Sir Francis, was distinguished by a red cap or bonnet turned up with rabbit fur. Women were present at most, if not all, of their meetings; and in the Chapel, to which no stranger was allowed to penetrate, were held ceremonies that resembled the Black Mass, at least in its more extravagant and less appalling details. Otherwise little has come down to us beside conjecture, by no means reliable and not always very interesting. The full list of those who were at various times members or guests of the Club has vanished with its minutes; but its inner circle, headed by Dashwood, included Lord Sandwich, a person as coarse, unscrupulous and unamiable as his friend was mild and tolerant, Bubb Doddington, that grotesque but cultured *parvenu,* the former favourite and butt of Frederick Prince of Wales, Potter and his protégé Wilkes (who, however, did not join, at any rate as a full member, till 1759), and three versifiers of some ability, Charles Churchill, Paul Whitehead and Robert Lloyd. Churchill, the best poet of the three, and at that period and later Wilkes's closest friend, was also, it is to be remarked, a parson of the Church of England, and in the rites of the Black Mass presumably officiated in the part of *mauvais prêtre,* the fallen cleric required by tradition to give the ceremony its meaning.

Though its political consequences were somewhat disastrous, Wilkes's connection with the Hell Fire Club was brief and unimportant. Thomas Potter had sponsored him in more reputable company; for it was through Potter that he received an introduction to William Pitt and to Pitt's brother-in-law, Earl Temple, the magnificent master of Stowe, head of a powerful political group who saw a serious threat to their ascendency in the accession of George III. Temple was such a patron as Wilkes had begun to need. The country gentleman of Buckinghamshire now aspired to political honours; appointed High Sheriff of the County in 1754, he had unsuccessfully contested Berwick during the same year, at the cost of four thousand pounds, and had been obliged to spend another seven thousand before he was elected as member for Aylesbury in 1757. Electioneering and high-living, complicated by transactions with City money-lenders, had left his finances in an exceedingly awkward plight; and he looked around for a lucrative appointment to help him recoup his fortunes. Had he succeeded in this ambition, the course of his life (it seems probable) might have developed very differently. He was not an unselfish man; nor had he, when he embarked on his career, a very deep sense of public obligation. Through an odd chance, the interests of Wilkes (originally his chief concern) were involved, as the drama proceeded, with those of Liberty, since the enemies of Liberty were also the enemies of Wilkes and Temple. Yet, there is no doubt, that,

once he had identified himself with the cause, the cause itself—
a high, if perhaps rather vague, sense of what it represented, and
the intense mental excitement of his dangerous and conspicuous
rôle—enflamed his imagination and possessed him and swept
him along. The natural recklessness that had completed his education as a debauchee and gambler made him a rebel prepared
to take any risk, an obstinate, vindictive opponent and a re-
sourceful and determined ally.

Certainly, before he delivered his final attack on the administration, Wilkes spared no pains to procure a position as its pensioner. The demands he made were in proportion to his idea
of his own capacities. The Embassy at Constantinople and the
Governorship of the new territory of Canada, where "his ambition was . . . to have reconciled the new subjects to the English, and to have shown the French the advantages of the mild
rule of laws over that of lawless power and despotism," in turn
were solicited for and in turn refused him. But, if he could not
negotiate or govern, at least he knew that he could write. Every
political faction required the assistance of talented pamphleteers. Bute had the services of Smollett, his fellow-Scotsman, and
had recently secured a claim on the support of Johnson; Wilkes,
with his aides-de-camp, Lloyd and Churchill, set up as journalist
of the Opposition, and paid back the partisans of the Court in
violence and scurrility. By way of counterblast to the *Briton,*
edited by Smollett, and the *Auditor,* which appeared under the
direction of Johnson's friend, Arthur Murphy, the *North Briton*
was established during June, 1762. It opened with a resounding
trumpet-blast: *"The liberty of the Press* is the birthright of a
Briton, and is justly esteemed the firmest bulwark of the liberties of this country." Wilkes and his assistants then proceeded
to turn that liberty to the utmost possible advantage, with overt
attacks on Bute and covert references to his position near the
Queen, unsparing attacks on the tribe of pensioned Scotsmen
who followed at Bute's heels, individual abuse of any public
figure, including Johnson and Hogarth, who could be suspected
of partiality for the present administration. Such invective was

not unparalleled in contemporary political life—fifty years later, the great tradition of personal invective was still preserved as a regular feature of English parliamentary government; but Wilkes's shafts were usually well-directed and had a cruelly cutting edge.

His diatribes were, of course, anonymous; and, during the same year that saw the establishment of the *North Briton,* through Temple's influence he was appointed to the Colonelcy of the Bucks Militia. In its uniform, as has already been recorded, Colonel Wilkes sat at the same dinner-table with Captain Gibbon and, no doubt not unmoved by Sir Thomas Worsley's claret, announced that in this period of public strife he intended, while the chance offered, to make his fortune. The *North Briton* had already created a stir; and, a few months later, the risks that he was running became apparent. Among his minor victims he numbered Lord Talbot, the Lord High Steward, whose horse, schooled to back out of the royal presence, had insisted at the Coronation ceremony on entering Westminster Hall in a reverse direction. The facile sarcasms of the *North Briton* touched the Lord Steward's pride. He demanded redress; and, though Wilkes had refused to admit any connection with the *North Briton* either as editor or author, after some angry correspondence he agreed to meet the offended functionary at an inn near Bagshot. There, according to his account of the affair dispatched to Temple, Wilkes "found Lord Talbot in an agony of passion. He said that I had injured, that I had insulted him, that he was not used to be injured or insulted. Did I, or did I not, write *The North Briton* of August 21st? . . . He would know; he insisted on a direct answer; here were his pistols. I replied that he would soon use them; that I desired to know by what right his lordship catechised me about a paper which did not bear my name; that I should never resolve him that question till he made out his right of putting it; and that if I could have entertained any other idea, I was too well-bred to have given his lordship . . . the trouble of coming to Bagshot. I observed that I was a private English gentleman, perfectly free and independent, which I held to be a character of the highest dignity; that I obeyed with pleasure a gracious sovereign, but would never submit to the arbitrary dictates of a fellow-subject, a Lord Steward of his household; my superior indeed in rank, fortune, and abilities, but my equal only in honour, courage and liberty."

Wilkes had previously declared that he would not fight till the following day, since he "was come from Medmenham Abbey, where the jovial monks of St. Francis had kept me up till four in the morning" and "that the world would therefore conclude I was drunk. . . ." But, on Talbot's blustering insistence, he agreed to put the matter to the test, as soon as he had had time to compose a letter giving directions, should he fall, for his daughter's education. Lord Talbot in the meantime "became half frantic; and made use of a thousand indecent expressions, that I should be hanged, damned, etc." His opponent, he declared, was "a wretch who sought his life"; to which Wilkes retorted, with considerable show of reason, that, whereas Lord Talbot fought him with the King's pardon in his pocket, he himself fought with a halter round his neck. But tempers calmed, and they presently left the inn and withdrew to a neighbouring garden, carrying ammunition and a pair of large horse-pistols. It was seven o'clock, and the moon shone very brightly. Shots were exchanged at a distance of eight yards; each gentleman missed; and Wilkes at once walked up to Lord Talbot and told him that he now avowed the paper; whereupon "his Lordship paid me the highest encomiums on my courage, and said he would declare everywhere that I was the noblest fellow God had ever made. He then desired we might now be good friends, and retire to the inn to drink a bottle of claret together; which he did with great good humour, and much laughter."

Trifling in itself, this incident seems to deserve a somewhat detailed record, since it illustrates both Wilkes's coolness in the face of physical danger and the vein of *bonhomie* that often endeared him to convinced opponents. Many adversaries admitted his charm; many acquaintances who did not share his principles continued to value his society. Had not the austere *devoted of interest to others*

Pitt remarked to Potter (as Potter reported to Wilkes) that he "found with great concern you was as wicked and as agreeable as ever"? But extreme altruism was not included among Wilkes's virtues; and even now, had the Court party pursued a cleverer line, it is possible that he might have discarded his weapons and quietly accepted office. Soon after the publication of the forty-fourth *North Briton*, during the early days of April, 1763, Bute, retreating from the storm of public detestation and suddenly panic-stricken by a glimpse of the dangers that appeared to lie ahead, resigned his post, to be succeeded by Lord Temple's brother, George Grenville, a plodding and industrious, but helplessly incompetent, statesman. Notwithstanding his relationship to Pitt and Temple, Grenville's administration reproduced many of the worst features of the old. Wilkes, imagining no doubt that the battle was won, had suspended the *North Briton* and taken a holiday in Paris; but, when he returned and paid a visit to his patron's London house, he found Temple and Pitt discussing, in terms of the highest indignation, an advance-copy of the King's speech, which the Prime Minister had sent them. Wilkes absorbed their criticisms, hurried home and, acting apparently on his own initiative, recast them in the *North Briton No. 45*. The result was an example of Wilkes's journalistic gift at its most acute and most envenomed—the most damaging and daring blow that he had yet been able to strike.

Its impact was carefully calculated. Wilkes began by dissociating himself from any intention of disloyalty towards the sovereign whose speech, he pointed out, "has always been considered by the legislature, and by the public at large, as the *speech of the Minister*. . . . This week has given to the public the most abandoned instance of ministerial effrontery ever attempted to be imposed on mankind. . . . I am in doubt whether the imposition is greater on the sovereign or on the nation. Every friend of his country must lament that a prince of so many great and amiable qualities . . . can be brought to give the sanction of his sacred name to the most odious measures, and to the most unjustifiable public declarations, from a throne ever renowned for truth, honour, and unsullied virtue." There followed a violent attack on the peace-treaty concluded by Bute, with particular reference to our alleged abandonment of the King of Prussia. Hitherto, Wilkes's campaign against the administration (now described as "a weak disjointed, incapable set . . . by whom the favourite still meditates to rule this kingdom with a rod of iron") had been one of intermittent, though savage, skirmishes. This was a frontal attack. It called, the ministers felt, for immediate retaliation. In its reference to the throne they thought they saw their opportunity. But they were frightened; and the retaliatory measures adopted by a frightened government are almost always foolish. The Attorney and Solicitor General were consulted, and gave it as their opinion that the paper might be considered "an infamous and seditious libel, tending to inflame the minds and alienate the affections of the people from his Majesty, and excite them to traitorous insurrections against his government." The administration now took a decision that in the history of weak governments has seldom failed to prove disastrous—they resolved that the time had come to act with firmness; and Lord Halifax, Secretary of State for the Home Department, issued a "general warrant," authorising the apprehension of the writers, printers and publishers of the *North Briton No. 45*. Only the printer was mentioned by name. Otherwise the terms of the warrant were comprehensive but anonymous. Armed with this imposing but, as it afterwards transpired, highly questionable document, two trusted King's Messengers walked out into the London streets.

The Patriot

IN a burst of candour equally creditable and characteristic, Wilkes once observed that he had become a patriot "by accident." But the accidents that befall us are usually those for which we are in some degree prepared; they correspond to a secret

propensity, and seem to have been evoked by the previous existence of some hidden strength or weakness; the drama that involved Wilkes during April, 1763, though possibly unexpected,
was certainly not unsought. Wilkes's nature needed excitement
and demanded exercise; and, as soon as he learned or began to
suspect that the publication of the *North Briton No. 45* had at
length stirred a sluggish government to precipitate and ill-
considered action, his love of adventure and gift of strategy were
called into immediate play. But the larger aspect of the situation
would appear to have dawned upon him by extremely gradual
stages. He saw the struggle as a fight between warring political
juntas; he still envisaged his own rôle as that of "Lord Temple's
man"; he looked forward to a conflict in which the ministerial
party would be worsted and his patrons, Temple and Pitt, would
gain the honour of a resounding parliamentary triumph. Fore-
warned that a general warrant would be issued against him, he
was quick to perceive that the issue of such warrants—which
named the imputed offence, in this instance the writing, printing and publication of an "infamous and seditious libel," but did
not name any or all of the persons by whom it was alleged to
have been committed—was not only hard to defend in law but
might well become the focus of a storm of popular fury, since it
could be represented as striking direct at the liberties of the
individual subject. He submitted his findings to Temple; and
Temple agreed that, if Wilkes were to be arrested, an application should at once be made for a writ of Habeas Corpus—not
to the Court of King's Bench, however, where Wilkes could
expect to meet with little sympathy, but to the Court of Common Pleas, the province of Pitt's supporter, Lord Chief Justice
Pratt. General warrants would be declared invalid: there would
result a complete and public humiliation of the ministerial
party.

The government agents were indiscreet, perhaps not incor-
ruptible. There is no doubt, at least, that both the King's Messengers, originally commissioned to lay hold of Wilkes, treated
him with a circumspect consideration strongly suggestive of

connivance. Having reached his house in Great George Street, Westminster, late on the evening of April 29, they failed to arrest him when he returned home under the apprehension (according to their subsequent account) that their victim was "in liquor." It is not improbable; but next morning he was at all events sufficiently recovered to leave the house as early as six o'clock in an extremely resolute mood—so resolute that he evaded one Messenger and brushed politely past the other, gained the loft where he kept his printing press, broke in with the help of a ladder borrowed from a local artisan, took an impression of the *North Briton No. 46* (which the printers in his pay had already set up), disposed of the forms and placidly walked home. There the less subservient of the two Messengers rather dubiously accosted him. Wilkes demanded to be shown the offensive warrant, informed the bearer haughtily that it was no concern of his, "advised him to be very civil," and assured him that if he attempted violence he would "put him to death in the instant," adding that, if the Messenger would follow him quietly into his house, he would proceed to give convincing proof of the document's complete and utter illegality. Intimidated by Wilkes's sword or fiercely forbidding spirit, the man acquiesced and was presently joined by other companions on duty, to be harangued by their prospective prisoner on the intolerable indignity to which he was subjected and the legal worthlessness of the warrant they were proposing to carry out. Soon the house was crowded with puzzled emissaries. To make the situation, from Wilkes's point of view, more delightfully ridiculous, he lived in the same street as the Secretary of State, Lord Halifax, and the confusion was increased by constant coming and going. Then through the bewildered crowd shouldered Charles Churchill, Wilkes's chief henchman and greatest friend, also due for arrest under the verbal instructions imparted to the Messengers. Wilkes saved the situation with his usual presence of mind, greeted Churchill as "Mr. Thomson" in loud, emphatic tones, and inquired, with renewed emphasis, whether it were not true that Mrs. Thomson was dining in the country. How the Messengers could have failed to recognise so well-known and so conspicuous a figure as the burly parson-poet, with his swollen bruiser's face, his blue coat, gold-laced waistcoat and gold-laced hat, is one of the many puzzling details of a confused and mysterious day. It may be that they stood in physical fear of two such determined foes. Churchill, at all events, was permitted to take the hint, agree that Mrs. Thomson needed country air, leave the house unmolested and hurry out of London. Meanwhile Wilkes continued to temporise, and the exasperation of the Secretaries, awaiting him only a few doors distant, grew more and more intolerable.

Every means had been employed, and Halifax had dispatched a personal invitation requesting Wilkes to call upon him—to which Wilkes replied civilly that he had not been introduced—when the Messengers announced that, as a last resort, they would be obliged to send for constables or summon the Foot Guards. Then their prisoner grandly gave way, but insisted that a chair should be called, and was transported along the street in dignified publicity towards Lord Halifax's front door. Even better was the next scene; for whereas the Secretaries of State had prepared a *coup de théâtre* and were discovered in "a great apartment fronting the Park," flanked by groups of minor officials and seated behind a long table equipped with large quantities of virgin paper, Wilkes declined to play the rôle that his antagonists expected. It was clear that he was vastly enjoying himself, and it was equally clear that none of the portentous preparations they had made in the very least abashed him. The awful solemnity of the occasion failed to affect his nerves; and now with airily theatrical insolence he refused to answer any of their questions, remarking that, so far as he was concerned, the paper on their table should remain unsullied, now he treated them to a bold display of patriotic indignation and inveighed against the cabal of ignorant and despotic Ministers whom it would be his privilege to impeach at the bar of the House of Commons. Lord Halifax tried courtesy, Lord Egremont brutality; Wilkes declined to retreat an inch. In one respect alone had the plans concerted with Temple as yet miscarried; not until the evening was it possible to procure from the Court of Common Pleas a writ of Habeas Corpus and, in the meantime, the Secretaries of State were able to strengthen their position. For the general under which he had been arrested, they substituted a warrant in which Wilkes was named; and, with this authority, they decided to commit him to the Tower of London.

Halifax had offered him a choice of prisons. But Wilkes retorted that, except from his friends, he was not in the habit of receiving favours; and, while he waited for an escort, he strolled cheerfully about the apartment, commenting on the canvases with which the walls were hung. Arrived at the Tower, he requested particularly that he might not be put into a room that had previously housed a Scotsman, since, as he explained, he was afraid of contracting the itch, and asked if he might not have the apartment once tenanted by Lord Egremont's father, who had been imprisoned during an earlier reign for his Jacobite activities. He remained in the Tower from Saturday till Tuesday; and, in his absence, the recriminatory methods adopted by the government became increasingly outrageous. Under the general warrant, their agents had already arrested—and in some instances dragged from their beds—a large number of peaceful citizens, many of whom had had not the smallest share in the printing or publication of *No. 45*. They now entered Wilkes's house, forced the drawers of his writing-desk and removed in a sack every document, public or private, that they could put their hands on. Temple, as Lord Lieutenant of the County, was instructed to remove Wilkes from the Colonelcy of the Buckinghamshire Militia and, having obeyed, was himself removed from his Lord Lieutenancy. This wild series of high-handed and ill-judged measures combined to produce just such an atmosphere of suspicion and public irritation as, to present their case effectively, Wilkes and Temple needed.

It was already as something of a popular hero that Wilkes appeared on Tuesday at the Court of Common Pleas, where the Treasury Solicitor had, on Monday, been commanded to pro-

duce him. He improved the occasion with the help of a vigorous
speech, detailing the wrongs he had suffered but remarking that
he trusted that "the consequences will teach Ministers of Arbitrary principles that the liberty of an English subject is not to
be sported away with impunity in this cruel and despotic manner." He had struck the right note, and the appreciation of his
hearers was noisily enthusiastic. Pratt, however, declined to give
an opinion on the case until the following Friday, when Wilkes
again appeared and again pointed the moral of his own imprisonment. The issue to be decided, he declared, was one that affected
the future of each individual subject, since it involved "the
liberty of all peers and gentlemen, and (what touches me more
sensibly) that of all the middling and inferior sort of people who
stand most in need of protection." The last phrases, though not
completely ingenuous—for Wilkes up to this moment had
shown little concern with, and had, in fact, little knowledge of,
"the middling and inferior sort of people" whose representatives
swelled the crowd at the Court of Common Pleas—were extraordinarily well calculated to catch the public ear. But in the
appreciative crowd, half hidden by a column, lurked one vindictive enemy, an elderly, thick-set man with a sketch-book and
a pencil—William Hogarth, who remembered the rough handling that he, like Samuel Johnson, had received in Wilkes's
paper. The caricature he produced was savage; but Hogarth
was too genuine an artist to be able to handle so striking a personage without some touches of involuntary appreciation. The
expression is cunning and the leer malevolent; nevertheless
there is a look of resolute, almost diabolical, energy about that
tall forehead (surmounted by a wig of which the curls resemble
horns), the crooked prognathous grin, and sharply squinting
eyes. Here is Wilkes, confident of victory, exulting in his triumph. His right elbow poised on his thigh, his left hand clapped
on his knee with arm akimbo, he leans forward rakish and
self-assured, attentive to the legal proceedings, but with one
swivel-eye cocked at the audience that fills the court-room. The
campaign he had planned was working out in its main outline,

if not in every detail, just as Wilkes and Temple had designed it should do; but Pratt, more cautious than they had hoped, refused to pronounce positively that general warrants were illegal and, in delivering judgment, declared merely that Wilkes was immune from arrest under his privilege as a member of the House of Commons—a privilege from which were excepted only treason, felony and breach of the peace. The prisoner was therefore at once discharged. Through the cheering crowds that carried him back to his house in Westminster swept for the first time the resonant battle-cry of "Wilkes and Liberty."

At this point, with a tactical victory to his credit, Wilkes might have decided to withdraw from operations. But he was excited by success and enraged by the seizure of his private correspondence; no sooner was he again at large than he wrote a peremptory letter to both Secretaries of State, observing that he found his house had been burgled, that he was informed that the stolen goods were in the possession of their Lordships, and that he must "therefore insist that you do forthwith return them." He also applied at Bow Street for a search-warrant, which, however, the sitting magistrate prudently refused to give. Such was his opening move, the gesture by which he made it clear to his adversaries that, so far as he and his supporters were concerned, the struggle would continue. He followed the challenge by an attack on a considerably wider front, arranging that all the forty-nine persons, including himself, who had been arrested and detained under the general warrant, should take legal action for wrongful arrest against the government agents before Lord Chief Justice Pratt in the Court of Common Pleas. The government employed elaborate delaying tactics; but one after another the various plaintiffs were awarded substantial damages, till Wilkes, at the end of the year, triumphed to the extent of a thousand pounds over Wood, the Under-Secretary. A more important result of these prosecutions was the judgment on the whole subject of general warrants they finally elicited. Pratt expressed the opinion that the issue of a general warrant had not been legal, later clinching his judgment by the remark that, were

higher jurisdiction to declare his opinion erroneous—in fact, it
was afterwards confirmed by a full bench of judges—"I submit
as will become me, and kiss the rod; but I must say, I shall always
consider it as a rod of iron for the chastisement of the people of
Great Britain." No more was heard of the legality of general
warrants. But other rods were being prepared, if not for the
chastisement of the people of Great Britain—"the middling and
inferior sort" who cheered every verdict as a brilliant popular
victory—at least for the correction and subjugation of their
self-appointed tribune.

Wilkes knew what he could expect from his enemies: he was
less certain, unfortunately, of the attitude of his so-called friends.
No settled policy governed the conduct of the Opposition; and
the motives of expediency that united the great Whig magnates
were extraordinarily divergent. They distrusted Wilkes and,
apart from its merits as a political toast, they had very little grasp
of the idea of Liberty. Pitt remained aloof, proud, lonely, un-
predictable. More than six months were to elapse between
Wilkes's release from the Tower and the reassembling of Parliament, when the ministerial party must be expected to renew
the contest; and during that period Wilkes had had time to
grow at first restive and suspicious, then exasperated and resentful. By July it was reported that he had begun to "complain
extremely" of his allies, and on the 20th of the month he abruptly departed from England, bound for Paris, a city that he
had always loved, where his daughter, the adored Polly, was
now receiving the benefits of a fashionable education. His departure was ill-advised; Wilkes's spirit, at its boldest during a
crisis or in any position where he confronted immediate danger,
was apt to weaken during intervals of enforced quiescence. But
more important than his departure were the occupations with
which he had whiled away the last few months in London; for,
beside reprinting in book-form all the back-numbers of the
North Briton, including *No. 45*—an unnecessarily provoca-
tive, and, from the strategic point of view, a somewhat point-
less gesture—he elected to print twelve copies of an indecent

parody of Pope's *Essay on Man* which had already been in circulation among his Medmenham acquaintances. Such *jeux d'esprit* were a sideline of the Monks' activities; but it seems unlikely that the verses had been written by Wilkes himself (whose share may have been limited to the array of facetious and scandalous annotations) and highly probable that they were the work of his old friend, Thomas Potter, whose libertine career was already ended. Wilkes printed a small edition merely to amuse his intimates—certainly he had no interest in creating a public scandal, and no thought that, if the *Essay on Woman*, with its blasphemous notes and its priapic title-page, were to fall into hands for which it was not intended, it might one day be turned against him as an extremely damaging weapon.

The government's spies were inquisitive and omnipresent. Snuffing around the purlieus of Wilkes's printing press, they presently found means of obtaining a fragment of the *Essay*, and after a while were able to worm their way into the confidence of a discontented workman. Prominent in this intrigue were William Faden, a government hack-journalist, and John Kidgell, the disreputable Chaplain of the notorious Lord March. Together they procured and forwarded to the Secretaries of State a complete copy of the *Essay;* the government pounced on this odd treasure-trove with the liveliest satisfaction, though their treatment of their hard-working spies was typically ungenerous; and word went about that, before the end of the year, Wilkes would be confounded and the entire Opposition reduced to silence. Somewhat casually their arch-opponent came strolling back from Paris; and a few days later, on November 15, Parliament reassembled. There were two claimants for immediate attention—Wilkes, determined to raise the question of parliamentary privilege; Grenville, who announced that he was the bearer of a royal message. According to parliamentary precedent, the question of privilege should have taken first place. But the administration, with the Speaker's assent, had decided otherwise; their supporters had had careful schooling in the part they were expected to play; and by a considerable majority the House ruled that the royal communication should be heard forthwith. Grenville thereupon read a message in which His Majesty requested that his faithful Commons would take into consideration the case of *No. 45;* a debate on the whole episode was at once begun; Lord North proposed a motion, stigmatising the offensive number as a "false, scandalous, and seditious libel" which manifestly tended "to excite to traitrous insurrections against His Majesty's Government"; and, in spite of Pitt's Olympian oratory, reverberating through a long series of hard-fought minor battles, the motion was finally carried by more than an hundred votes. Further to emphasise their extreme displeasure, the House ordered that the *North Briton* should be burned in public. When Wilkes at last rose to complain of the breach of privilege, only a few tired and indifferent members remained to hear him.

While this tragi-comedy was enacting in the House of Commons, the Upper Chamber was abandoned to scenes of uproarious farce. Lord Egremont had recently died after an apoplectic seizure, and the vacancy had been filled by the appointment of Lord Sandwich, a debauchee who, with Lord March as possible runner-up, had established an almost unchallenged record in contemporary dissipation. But it was Sandwich, former boon-companion of Wilkes and Churchill, and the victim of Wilkes's most famous *bon mot*,[1] whom the administration had deputed to lead the attack upon the *Essay*. This task he accomplished with a degree of unction that even his friends and supporters found a trifle disconcerting. Never before had he heard the Devil preach, murmured Dashwood, lately elevated to peerage under the title of Lord Le Despencer, as Sandwich embarked on the enjoyable business of reading the *Essay* aloud, pausing now and then to register his own emotions of disgust and incredulity and horrified astonishment. Presumably, he did his material credit; for in its printed form the *Essay on Woman* seems a remarkably tedious work; the flash of spirit with which the parody opens is

---

[1] "Wilkes, you will die of a pox or on the gallows." "That depends, my Lord, on whether I embrace your principles or your mistress."

very soon extinguished; and the effect after two or three couplets becomes uniformly turgid. But all that the *Essay* lacked in wit was made up for by the broad comedy of its public presentation. While Dashwood whispered audibly behind his hand about the Devil preaching, Lord Lyttelton begged that the reading might cease; at which their Lordships insisted vehemently that the recital should continue. As soon as Sandwich had reluctantly made an end, Dr. Warburton, Bishop of Gloucester and the celebrated editor of Pope's collected poems, whose name had been taken in vain by the annotator of the *Essay*, rose to deliver a speech of solemn personal protest. Somewhat unnecessarily for so virtuous a man, he called God to witness that he had not written the notes, and declared that he doubted whether "the hardiest inhabitants of Hell" could listen unperturbed to such atrocious blasphemies. Sandwich, washed down by Warburton, formed a draught that flew straight to the head of the impressionable House of Lords; and they concluded the sitting with a resolution condemning the *Essay* as a "most scandalous, obscene, and impious libel." The British public, nevertheless, can on occasions rise superior to the attacks of mass-hypocrisy with which both the Upper and Lower Houses of Parliament are from time to time afflicted; and during the next performance of the *Beggar's Opera*, when Macheath reached the line: "That Jemmy Twitcher should peach I own surprises me," the whole theatre was suddenly overcome by a tempest of amusement— Lord Sandwich remained "Jemmy Twitcher" to the end of his political life.

Moreover, the attempt to burn *The North Briton* before the Royal Exchange was frustrated by a riot, in which the officers of the law were manhandled and the coach of a presiding dignitary was reduced to match-wood. But Wilkes saw, and his supporters let him feel, that he had suffered a major reverse. Pitt and Temple were equally out of patience; and perhaps it was as well that at this unpleasant juncture, exposed to the reproaches of his friends and the derision of his enemies, he was able to take refuge in violent and dangerous action. Among

Wilkes's most envenomed adversaries in the House of Commons debate had been Samuel Martin, one-time Secretary of the Treasury, who had been denounced by the *North Briton* and now avenged himself on its supposed author with an unusually virulent speech. Wilkes's name he did not mention, but he described the writer responsible, whoever he might be, as "a cowardly rascal, a villain, and a scoundrel." Early next morning, Wilkes sent him a note, observing that, whereas Martin had complained yesterday before five hundred gentlemen that he had been stabbed in the dark, "I whisper in your ear that every passage in the *North Briton,* in which you have been named, or even alluded to, was written by your humble servant." Martin promptly replied, repeating his description of Wilkes's character and desiring that Wilkes would meet him "in Hyde Park immediately with a brace of pistols each to determine our difference." Three facts bearing on this challenge deserve incidental notice; it was learned that Martin had been carefully practising with pistols and target for several months past; Wilkes, since he was the challenged party, should have had the choice of weapons; and his opponent, as Wilkes afterwards discovered, had received in the years 1762 and 1763 no less than £41,000 from the Civil List under the heading of "secret and special service." But, on the receipt of Martin's letter, Wilkes and a second hurried to Hyde Park. They met Martin and his attendant, made with them a brief detour to escape some passers-by; then the duellists fired at a distance of fourteen paces. Both pistols missed; and they immediately fired again. Martin's bullet glanced off a button on Wilkes's coat and struck him in the groin. He collapsed; but, when Martin rushed up, Wilkes, lying on the ground, in agony and, as he believed, mortally wounded, recommended him not to delay his flight and promised that he himself would refuse to discuss the affair. Having reached home, he gave orders that Martin's challenge should be returned to him as incriminating evidence.

Even Horace Walpole, no friend to demagogy, considered that Wilkes had been the object of a deliberate plot against his life.

"THE BRUISER C. CHURCHILL"

A caricature by William Hogarth

But Wilkes himself, confused and perturbed by his recent parliamentary mishap, was relieved to be able to treat the whole incident as an affair "between gentlemen," from which he and his antagonist alike had emerged as men of honour. Martin (he wrote to Polly Wilkes when, after two days, the surgeon informed him he was recovering) "behaved very well. We are both perfectly satisfied with each other." He also told his daughter that she might depend on seeing him in Paris before Christmas. In London, while he remained abed, his situation almost every day seemed more and more precarious; and his disillusionment was completed when he learned that Pitt had decided definitely to throw him over. It was a choice between the man and the principle; and, if the principle was to be upheld, the author of the *Essay on Woman* at any cost must be abandoned. To mark the occasion Pitt appeared in the House during the debate that followed the government resolution "that the privilege of Parliament does not extend to the case of writing and publishing seditious libels," clad in all the funereal majesty of an expiring elder statesman, lean and ghastly, crippled but dauntless, his gestures emphasised rather than impeded by heavy flannel bandages. Privately, over the dinner-table with Wilkes and Potter, he had condescended to a smile at productions at least as indecorous as the infernal *Essay*—indeed, it is not unlikely that he had smiled at the *Essay* itself; but private amusements and the public cause were entirely different matters; and, as a champion of the public interest against "those doctrines and assertions by which a larger stride . . . towards arbitrary power is made," he renounced Wilkes with a thoroughness that admitted of no mistake. On the whole series of *North Britons* he poured out his scorn; they were "illiberal [he declared], unmanly, and detestable. . . . The King's subjects were one people. Whoever divided them was guilty of sedition. His Majesty's complaint was well-founded." . . . And, warming to his work, he added that the author of the alleged libel "did not deserve to be ranked among the human species—he was the blasphemer of his God and the libeller of his King"; he had "no connection," he repeated deliberately, "with any such writer"—then hobbled back into retirement, there to bide his time and brood over the rapid and reckless surrender by both Houses of their constitutional rights. Meanwhile the Government had carried the day; and his fellow-members demanded that Wilkes should appear before them. When he protested that he was still an invalid, they ordered that two doctors of their own choosing should visit him in Great George Street and report upon his progress.

Just as Wilkes's nature often responded to the smallest touch of generosity—for example, to the gentlemanly treatment that he thought he had received from Samuel Martin—so insolence and brutality he always repaid in kind. With something of the same cheerful effrontery that, a few months earlier, he had shown in his handling of the Secretaries of State, he refused to receive either of the two physicians whom the House of Commons had appointed, underlining his defiance in a succession of satirical letters. His house, he knew, was watched, his correspondence intercepted. But he was still more than a match for plodding government spies; and on Christmas Eve, 1764, he slipped quietly through the net that they had spread around Great George Street and, though his wound was as yet unhealed and he did himself serious harm by his rough and hurried journey, posted down to Dover and immediately crossed to France. He had intended (or so he afterwards suggested) to spend the holiday with his daughter and return to London in time to attend the parliamentary session of January 16; but on the 13th he wrote to the Speaker, explaining that he was ill and enclosing a certificate signed by a brace of obliging French physicians. His illness may have at first been genuine; but, according to his own admission, he had very soon recovered, and his reasons for keeping his room were largely diplomatic. The House of Commons, at all events, was neither impressed nor softened; on January 20 a sentence of expulsion was pronounced against him; and, during the last week of February, he was prosecuted for the printing of *No. 45* and the publication of the *Essay on*

Woman in the Court of King's Bench. The judge was his enemy, Mansfield; Wilkes's solicitor, Philipps, was not above suspicion; the jury that tried the case had been carefully hand-picked. As a matter of course they found the defendant guilty and a writ for his arrest was duly issued. On November 1, 1764, since he had not yet appeared at the Court of King's Bench, the cycle of retribution was at length completed and John Wilkes was formally pronounced an outlaw. He himself had decided that he could never return to England. For what might he expect? —perhaps life-imprisonment, even the public humiliation of standing in the pillory; at best, renewed persecution by his enemies and a continuance of that "coldness and neglect from friends" of which, while he remained in England, he had already had a foretaste.

Wilkes's nerves were luckily resilient. This "unfortunate gentleman," wrote a contemporary journalist, might now be regarded as irrevocably ruined. To his supporters, for some time past, he had been a grievous liability; by the opponents he had once worsted he could be finally written off. No one wished him to return, but his funds were running low; his way of life, which in middle age he was not likely to curtail, had always been extravagant; and, if he remained abroad, an existence of pensioned obscurity, so long as Temple continued to meet his demands, was the best that he could hope for. He flattered himself, he said, "with no foolish hopes, not even on the restoration of Mr. Pitt and the Whigs." He counted himself "an exile for life"; but "Nature has given me some philosophy"; and "the necessity of the case," he added, had helped him to perfect it. No, he was not distraught. At moments he might be depressed, but he was still far from desperation—and farther still from any idea of becoming an embittered recluse, or abandoning the free enjoyment of forthright natural pleasures. He was devoted to his daughter, and he knew that she loved him. Besides, there was love of a wilder and fleshlier kind (which he found no difficulty in squaring with his pure, unselfish love of Polly); and his vitality, gaiety and sensuality were as strong and keen as ever.

The politician might be discomfited, but he was always a man
of the world. And his contemporaries who had become accustomed to the spectacle of Mr. John Wilkes, patriotic orator and
impassioned tribune of the people, were now treated to glimpses
of the same personage in an entirely different character, wandering to and fro across France and Italy, now in a drawing-room,
now in an opera-house, now dining with fashionable acquaintances, now enjoying the exquisite, though costly, favours of an
Italian courtesan. Accompanied by James Boswell he climbed
Vesuvius; in the rôle of Voltairean sceptic he mingled with the
Neapolitans at the festival of their patron-saint and closely
scrutinized the alleged miraculous liquefaction of St. Januarius's
blood; as an experienced lover of women, he basked for many
months in the meridional embraces of Gertrude Corradini.

Later, when he attempted to write his autobiography, it was
with a glowing account of the latter episode that he began and
ended. His references to other happenings remain brief and
incidental. Plainly, in a life that had been full of mistresses, from
the doting wives of City aldermen to such celebrated *hetaerae*
as Boswell's Mrs. Rudd, Gertrude Corradini had held a special
place. Her physical splendour delighted him; he was stimulated,
now and then a little surprised, by her capacity for sensual pleasure, complicated and improved on by her "divine gift of lewd-
ness"; he was charmed by the strangely virginal air, the look of
youth and candour and mute receptive innocence, that enveloped her fiery temperament like some delicate gauzy veil. It
was true that she was extremely stupid, but profound stupidity
in the woman beloved may exert a potent spell; and, though
Corradini was neither unselfish nor undesigning, Wilkes, as an
impartial student of human nature, noted that owing to her lack
of intelligence "her whole life had been sacrificed to the interests
of others," and that the greedy and possessive creature was herself doomed to perpetual exploitation. Bred in Bologna, she had
received her education in Venice—"the only education fit for a
courtesan, born with little or no wit, the art of adorning grace-
fully her person, and a flexibility of the limbs worthy the wanton

nymphs so celebrated of Ionia." From Venice, where she had
danced on the stage and had been for some while the favourite
of the British Consul, a Mr. Udney, she had come to Paris in
search of a career when the unfortunate Mr. Udney threatened
to go bankrupt; and it was there she met Wilkes in 1764. Having
conquered after a brief obligatory siege, he installed her in "elegant lodgings in the Rue Neuve des bons Enfans, which commanded the garden of the Palais Royal." For several weeks he
was unusually happy, passing his time between his daughter's
convent, his mistress's lodgings, and a number of Parisian *salons,*
including that of Madame Geoffrin, to which he had the entry.
Then the Corradini fell ill and from her sick bed began to give
proof of yet another characteristic which, with sensuality, stupidity and avarice, formed the basis of her temperament. She
was unreasonably and fiercely jealous; and her jealousy involved
her lover in a succession of violent scenes.

With some relief, then, he heard that she thought of returning
home, since she had been warned by the physicians that her
health ought not to be exposed to another northern winter. He
agreed to join her in due course; but meanwhile he had arranged
to meet Churchill at Boulogne-sur-mer. Churchill was bringing
his own mistress and they intended together to visit the South of
France and Italy. They had promised themselves an enchanting
classical tour. To his old friend and trusted henchman Wilkes
had had for many years a deep and genuine attachment; he loved
his companionship; he respected his scholarship; he professed,
moreover, an intense regard for Churchill's poetic genius. Nor
was his admiration entirely misplaced; even today, when the
pungency of his topical satire has to a very large extent evaporated, *The Duellist, The Ghost, The Epistle to Hogarth,* and
the other poems with which the debauched and penniless young
parson bludgeoned his way to celebrity, still deserve examination. At their best, as in the well-known portrait of Hogarth—as
cruel a caricature as Hogarth's sketch of Wilkes—or in the
merciless (if somewhat hypocritical) denunciation of Lord Sandwich's midnight roisterings, Churchill's verse has a tumultuous

energy that sweeps the reader along. The invective strikes home in a succession of hammer-blows; Churchill's use of the English language is always fresh and lively—it produces something of the same effect as Hogarth's use of paint; and from the poems of the one, as from the pictures of the other, emerges a whole vision of eighteenth-century London—the streets with brimming kennels and smoking oil-lamps; rudely loquacious passers-by who delight in tormenting the timid foreigner or the foppish stranger; taverns and watch-houses and swarming cellar-kitchens, where Sandwich and his cronies would spend the last hours of an uproarious drunken night, bawling out catches to the amazement of assembled pick-pockets and harlots.

Wilkes met Churchill at Boulogne towards the end of October, 1764; but no sooner had he arrived than Churchill succumbed to typhus, or, as it was then called, a "putrid fever," and died in his companion's arms after an illness of five days. At a subsequent period Wilkes was to declare that no event had ever struck him "so deep to the heart. He had never before suffer'd the loss of any friend to whom he had been greatly attach'd"; and "on his return to Paris he pass'd the day and night alone in tears and agonies of despair." Grief was perhaps accentuated by a sense of personal solitude; he was both an exile and an outlaw; the path that lay ahead was dark and dangerous and, at any moment, might slope down into complete disaster. But once again philosophy came to his aid—and, reinforcing the lessons of philosophy, a conviction of his own value as an independent human being. A revelatory anecdote tells how Madame Geoffrin once remarked to Wilkes that pride was an extravagance that the poor should not allow themselves. *"Quand on n'a pas de chemise,"* she announced, *"il ne faut pas avoir de fierté." "Au contraire,"* retorted Wilkes, *"il faut en avoir afin d'avoir quelquechose."* It was pride, coupled with his temperamental buoyancy, derived from a well-balanced constitution, that helped to support Wilkes during the years of exile. Yet about his pride there was nothing of the rather arid self-love, tinged, now and then, with a strain of self-pity, that was to characterise many po-

litical outcasts of a later, unhappier age. Little by little he had
rallied from the shock of Churchill's death; "The thought he
had always entertained began to return upon him with new
force, that we ought to endeavour the rendering of our own
being as happy to all around us, and to ourselves, as it is in our
power"; and, when almost every post continued to bring letters
from the Corradini, who pleaded that he would join her as soon
as possible in her Italian retirement, he gave way, arranged for
Polly to return to England and himself prepared to leave Paris
and embark on the southward journey. But before leaving, he
composed and published a justificatory letter in which he submitted to the electors of Aylesbury a full explanation of his recent conduct.

This duty performed, he bowed to the summons of pleasure.
Like Gibbon, he found the landscape of the Alps "highly entertaining" and was impressed by the "immense level" of the
luxurious but monotonous Lombard plain. At Turin he halted
to see the Old Masters in the collection of his Sardinian Majesty;
and in that city, visiting the theatre, he was recognised from the
pit by an excitable London acquaintance, also on his way south
after a tour of the German courts. A sudden glimpse of the notorious demagogue threw Boswell into a delightful, disturbing
flurry of "romantic agitation." His ideas unfolded at their usual
breakneck speed and with their customary inconsequence; "I
considered [he noticed in his journal] he might have been dead
as well as Churchill, and methought I viewed him in the Elysian
fields." When he had recovered his poise, he at once wrote to
Wilkes inviting him to dinner, but couched his invitation in a
vein of mingled impertinence and flattery, remarking that, although as "an old Laird and a steady Royalist," James Boswell
could not make a public call on Wilkes, nevertheless he would
be glad to receive him at a private party, and proposing, when
all else failed—for Wilkes had disregarded Boswell's original
message—that they should meet as rival philosophers "and continue the conversation on the immortality of the Soul which you
had with my Countryman, Baxter, many years ago at Brussels."

It is not clear whether Wilkes was immediately vanquished; but later, at Naples, a real friendship developed between the two curious English tourists; together they scrambled up the slopes of Vesuvius, peered into the yellow sulphurous smoke that seethed within the crater, and withdrew hurriedly beneath a cloud of burning volcanic ashes. Boswell treated his "classical companion" to frequent and facetious letters in English and dog-Latin; and not till he had reached Rome, in the spring of 1765, did the "old lord of Scotland," as Wilkes had affectionately styled him, feel that the time had come to make a solemn stand against scepticism, republicanism and the other grievous errors, spiritual and political, with which his friend was tinctured. He continued the campaign in a lengthy epistle from Venice, invoking the distant influence of his mighty adviser and protector. "O John Wilkes [he implored], thou gay, learned, and ingenious private gentleman, thou passionate politician, thou thoughtless infidel, good without principle, and wicked without malevolence, let Johnson teach thee the road to rational virtue and noble felicity." The conjunction of which he had dreamed was one day to be realised; Wilkes, thanks to Boswell, would win over Johnson, by a display of that conversational charm and personal plausibility of which he alone possessed the secret; and Johnson would pay a generous tribute to Wilkes's qualities: "Jack has a great variety of talk, Jack is a scholar, and Jack has the manners of a gentleman. . . . I would do Jack a kindness, rather than not." But their meeting, perhaps somewhat to Boswell's surprise, failed to produce the slightest alteration either of Wilkes's public career or of his private character; and Johnson, though glad enough to dine in Wilkes's company, to accept a helping of fine veal with a squeeze of lemon or orange, and to join in making broad fun of the proverbial poverty of Scotsmen, showed an unaccountable reluctance to embark upon loftier themes.

We return to Wilkes in 1764, travelling by rapid stages from Turin, through Milan and Parma, to Bologna where the Corradini was awaiting him. Their reunion was rapturous; his mistress had lost nothing of her *"air de vierge,"* and retained all her delicate proficiency in the art of making love. Years later he remembered with amusement how her bedroom had been furnished. It was a large and lofty room; on the bare walls hung two wretched representations of the Virgin Mary; and "the virgin appear'd again at the head of the bed with the bambino, and had a little green silk curtain drawn before her from the time the Corradini yielded those matchless charms, those heavenly beauties, to the view, to the touch, to the embrace of a mortal lover, till she arose in the morning." The effect was the more diverting and the more idyllic since the bed and the windows were alike uncurtained, letting the sunlight stream boldly in—"a circumstance in so temperate a climate, most agreeable to Mr. Wilkes, because every sense was feasted in the most exquisite degree, and the visual ray [he concludes with a decorative literary flourish] had some times in contemplation the two noblest objects of the creation, the glory of the rising sun, and the perfect form of naked beauty."

From Bologna the lovers travelled to Florence, and from Florence, through landscapes extravagantly *"pittoresque,"* pausing to admire the cathedral of Siena, they made their way to Rome. There Wilkes met the Abbé Winckelman, who, besides giving him the benefit of his taste and knowledge on archæological expeditions, often visited him in his lodgings and would sit conversing complaisantly with the Corradini's mother, when the daughter and her English admirer, as they frequently found occasion to do, had slipped from the apartment. Next it was the turn of Naples. Though March had not yet begun, "the air was silky soft"; between Mola and Capua, the hedges were full of lily, narcissus, myrtle, iris; and Wilkes was charmed for the first time by the sight of orange groves, with their simultaneous burden of leaves and flowers and fruit. After six weeks passed in the city, he "hir'd a country house about a mile from Naples, on a hill call'd Vomero, which was very large and convenient." Naples lay humming below; on the left the cone of Vesuvius sleepily smoked or glowed; while straight ahead, across the gulf,

the "bold island of Caprea" rose from the sea-floor. Around the
house were vineyards; and the traveller was delighted to observe
that the vines did not, as in France, creep upon the ground but
were garlanded "in proud festoons" from tree to tree. He was
pleased by the fireflies, and amused by mosquito-nets, which
gave to mortal lovers the appearance of Mars and Venus trapped
in Vulcan's web. But notwithstanding this romantic background, the Corradini became less amenable and more cantankerous; her temper deteriorated and her demands increased;
till finally she declared she was with child and, while Wilkes was
on a short visit to a friend in Ischia, decamped to her native city,
accompanied by her mother and uncle, and carrying as much
small silver-ware as she could cram into her luggage. To Wilkes's
pride and passion it was an equally cruel blow. She expected him
to follow; but with praiseworthy resolution he refused to obey
the lure, sending her instead a friendly letter and the sum of one
hundred pounds; and when he left Naples, in order to avoid the
perilous experience of passing through Bologna, "lest the dear
enchantress shou'd again draw him within her powerful circle,
and melt down all his manhood to the god of love," he sailed on
"a wretched French Tartan" direct from the South of France.
His destination was Paris—news recently received from London
had made it imperative he should be within easy call; but he
found time to spend a dissipated holiday in Marseilles, and included Savoy in his itinerary and the shores of the Lake of
Leman. Geneva depressed and disgusted him; the tomb of
Calvin proved to be overgrown—most appropriately—with nettles, briars and thistles; but the neighbourhood was enlightened
by the presence of the "divine old man, born for the advancement of true philosophy and the public arts," still an electric
centre of wisdom and malice, a luminary whose radiations were
felt and feared in every capital of Europe. Very different was
Wilkes's visit to the patriarch's shrine from the pilgrimage made
by Boswell some few months earlier. The old philosopher and
the middle-aged rebel were in complete agreement; each ex-
emplified most of the qualities that the other valued—courage

and independence and wit and cynicism. Wilkes's stay at Ferney would seem to have been singularly unclouded; in that happy society he "passed some weeks, and the laugh of Voltaire banish'd all the serious ideas the Englishman nourish'd of love and the fair Italian."

By mid-summer, 1765, he was once again in Paris. The news from London continued favourable; for Grenville's government had at last collapsed, giving place to a Whig administration headed by Lord Rockingham. Wilkes's hopes rose immediately; but to understand his conduct during the years that followed it is necessary to recognise a fluctuation in his aims and point of view. He was no longer the rebel who had left Great George Street; some of his chief enemies had fallen; the new government included men whom he believed his allies; the moment had come to sign an honourable peace and retire into private life or into the shelter of some post, either at home or abroad, worthy of the services that he felt he had done the kingdom. He had deserved well—that was the assertion on which he based his appeals; general warrants had been declared illegal; he had demonstrated that a Secretary of State could not with impunity break into a private citizen's house and carry off his papers. A free pardon was all he asked for, accompanied by an embassy or perhaps a governorship. But it was more difficult to effect a compromise than he had at first imagined; Rockingham disappointed him, and the only tangible reward that he received was a meagre pension, doled out covertly and unofficially, of a thousand pounds a year. Then Rockingham himself fell; Pitt formed a ministry but, owing to ill-health, soon handed over control to the Duke of Grafton; and again his supposed friends gave him an evasive answer. Between his return to Paris in the summer of 1765 and his final return to London, early in the spring of 1768, Wilkes paid flying visits to England on no less than three occasions. Always the result was unsatisfying; the funds at his disposal were running extremely low; and the bankruptcy of Humphrey Cotes, who during his exile had been handling his financial business, made his position at the end of the year even

more uncomfortable. Besides, though he loved France, he was
sick of living abroad. What remedy could he expect? None of
his friends would help him; it was clear that he must help himself. Since he could no longer retreat, he must perforce attack;
and he determined to risk everything in a headlong frontal assault, by seeking election to the very body that had repudiated
and expelled him.

Thus the "patriot by accident" embarked on the second, decisive stage of his public career in a mood of desperation. During
October, 1767, he published in a London newspaper a statement
to the effect that Mr. John Wilkes would shortly return to England and stand as a parliamentary candidate in the general election of 1768. He crossed the Channel at the beginning of February. Even now he was prepared to accept terms if his opponents
offered them; before throwing down his final challenge, he
dispatched his footman to Buckingham House, with a personal
letter addressed to the King in which he asked for pardon; and
it was only when, after a week had passed, his letter remained
unanswered, that he announced his intention of standing for
the City of London, and issued a manifesto setting forth his
parliamentary aims, should he be elected, in vague but moderate
language. His choice of a constituency was significant; he had
been advised that he would do well to re-enter Parliament as
member for a safe pocket-borough in Lord Temple's gift; and,
had he done so, his position would have been relatively unas-
sailable, since the House of Commons (it was argued) would
have hesitated to infringe the sacred rights of property by disputing Lord Temple's privilege of controlling his electors' votes.
But, with the sole exception of Middlesex, the City was one of
the most genuinely democratic of the various seats he might have
chosen. Here, indeed, he must rely on something like popular
suffrage, not on the support of a Whig magnate, deep in the
political game. When Wilkes mounted the hustings, during the
latter days of March, 1768, he had at length achieved that personal and political independence which, at a previous stage of
his career, he had very often professed, but never quite sincerely.

From this juncture he could honestly claim (in the words of his son-in-law, Sir William Rough) [1] that "his measures were his own measures, not the measures of a party; his struggles were his own struggles; his triumphs his own triumphs. . . ." We may add that the decision he had taken was taken at his own risk. But danger had always attracted him; and it was an impulse bred of desperation that contributed to drive him on.

His first candidature proved unsuccessful. The financial magnates who ruled the City were as shy of this celebrated fire-eater as the territorial magnates who controlled the Whig party; and electors of "the middling and inferior sort," though vociferous, were not sufficiently numerous to carry their champion through. But he was undeterred and let it be known that, having failed in the City of London, he meant to stand for Middlesex. Here the electorate was predominantly popular; and besides the small tradesmen and prosperous artisans who filled the greater part of the Middlesex electors' roll, he had the support of certain large sections of the urban working-class—among others, the Spital-fields weavers and the London sailors—then aggrieved by falling wages and the threat of unemployment. Wilkes's canvassing methods were energetic; Temple, who had afforded some slight preliminary assistance, dissociated himself from the campaign in its dangerous latter stages; and the task of organisation fell on a small but active committee composed of Wilkes and his supporters, Sergeant Glynn and the Reverend John Horne. Glynn was legal adviser, Horne practical organiser; Wilkes supplied the quick wit, sharp tongue and air of genial bravado that made him the hero of many current stories. He would rather vote for the devil, observed one recalcitrant elector. "And if your friend is not standing?" replied Wilkes, with the same bland insolence he had already turned against Lords Egremont and Halifax. *45* became the distinguishing number now adopted by every loyal Wilkite and imposed by Wilkite crowds on every house-holder who hoped that his windows would remain unbroken.

---

[1] Sir William Rough was married to one of Wilkes's natural children. His only legitimate child, Polly, died unmarried.

None dared remove it but a half-demented visionary, Alexander Cruden, then deep in the compilation of his vast *Concordance,* who seems to have attached to the number some sinister cabalistic value and perambulated London with a sponge, devotedly removing the portentous symbol. Otherwise opposition kept at a prudent distance. On March 28, 1768, so huge a concourse filled Brentwood as almost to empty London; the rival candidates appeared late, after a rough and exhausting journey; Wilkes headed the poll by more than four hundred votes.

At once the excitement that had steadily mounted since Wilkes's return exploded in a deafening outburst of popular satisfaction. That night and the whole of the next day, the Wilkites held the streets. *No. 45* and Wilkes's blue cockade dominated London; no carriage could pass that did not bear the Wilkite number chalked upon its panels; stones crashed through the panes of every darkened window; an English Duke was obliged to make profession of the faith by drinking a public toast to "Wilkes and Liberty"; the Austrian Ambassador, patrician representative of the most despotic power in Europe, was hoisted from his coach and held suspended, while a bevy of enthusiasts inscribed *No. 45* in chalk upon his boot-soles. The tumult eventually died down—thanks, at least in some degree, to the efforts of Wilkes himself. For now, as during later crises, the paradoxical nature of Wilkes's success, and the contradictory strains that formed his character, were very much in evidence. By disposition he was a friend of order; his conception of liberty was essentially conservative; and though again and again there were to occur moments when the forces opposing him had evidently lost control and he might, had he wished, have called out the people in the grand manner of the revolutionists of 1789, he was careful, so far as he could, to keep the enthusiasm that he had evoked within constitutional limits. He had little taste for the part of Catiline; nor were the ideas that animated his conduct primarily subversive. Perhaps, had his political aims been in the first instance more genuinely altruistic, had he been less the opportunist and more the democrat, had he been a nobler, but also a rasher man, he might have plunged London in blood-shed and precipitated a revolt which would have brought the country gentlemen of England (like the Versailles troops of 1871) marching at the head of their tenants to subdue a rebellious city. But Wilkes's personal and political aims were closely interwoven; and the public motives with which Rough credited him were founded on a basis of intelligent self-interest. Thus his triumph, strangely enough, was a triumph of moderation. He used the people against the legislature—and, while doing so, secured the establishment of certain principles of justice and liberty in which, during the course of the struggle, he had come passionately to believe. Yet, by his example, he did much to preserve an autocratic and short-sighted government from some of the worst consequences of their own abounding folly.

London still resounded to his name and was scrawled and plastered with his symbol; from its centre in the Metropolis the Wilkite agitation had swept along the high-roads, as Boswell remarked on March 26, travelling down to Oxford to visit Johnson, and as Benjamin Franklin noted a few days later; but Wilkes deliberately absented himself and, in the rôle of unconcerned private gentleman, took the waters at Bath. There he was shunned wherever he appeared, but comported himself throughout his stay with the utmost reserve and dignity. In that well-dressed but wary figure, who would have recognised a *caput lupinum*, a man without legal privileges or hope of legal redress, classed by the mediæval statute with wolves and other dangerous vermin, then awaiting the heaviest sentence that his enemies dared impose? He had already announced that he would surrender at the Court of King's Bench on the opening of the new term; and, when the 20th April arrived, he duly kept his word, only to be informed by Lord Mansfield that, as an outlaw who had not yet been arrested, he had no legal existence that the Court could acknowledge. Not till a week had passed did the law condescend to take appropriate action. He was then properly committed to the King's Bench prison, but on his way to imprisonment had the disconcerting experience of being rescued by his followers, who surrounded the coach, unharnessed the horses, and trundled him with roars of triumph as far as an inn in Spitalfields, whence he escaped with considerable difficulty and hurried off late in the evening to claim his vacant cell. The release he sought was a legal release. As the patient victim of an unjust sentence, he could set the government a far more difficult problem than while he remained at large.

Moreover, the administration could probably be relied on to provide aggravating circumstances. This they presently did by throwing a cordon of Scottish troops around the King's Bench Prison. A skirmish soon broke out; stones were thrown; the troops fired into the crowd, killing six rioters; they followed up those who ran and, during the confusion, shot down an innocent young man whom they encountered in a cowshed. Lord Weymouth had previously written to the magistrates recommending firmness, and Lord Barrington, the Secretary of War, now wrote to congratulate the troops involved, assuring them that "His Majesty highly approves of the conduct of both the officers and the men," and promising them, in case of trouble, "every defence and protection." Thus brutality was complicated by idiocy; the government added to its record the "Massacre of St. George's Fields"; and the popular detestation of Scotsmen received a dramatic stimulus. Wilkes meanwhile appeared at the Court of King's Bench to hear Lord Mansfield pronounce judgment on his appeal against his outlawry. But Mansfield, a brilliant legal mind though a subservient and unscrupulous politician, had discovered an ingenious issue from the difficulties that surrounded him. Wilkes's outlawry was quashed on a trifling legal point—a judgment greeted, somewhat prematurely, with an outburst of rejoicing almost equal to the rejoicing that had greeted his election. It remained to sentence him for the offences of which he had already been found guilty—the publication of the *Essay on Woman* and the re-publication of *No. 45*. On June 18, his trial was wound up; he was to serve terms amounting to twenty-two months' imprisonment and to incur financial penalties totalling a thousand pounds.

JOHN WILKES IN 1763

An engraving by William Hogarth

For a man of even moderate means, during the eighteenth century life behind prison-walls was seldom very arduous; and Wilkes's year and ten months' imprisonment were almost exuberantly festive. Many of the cares that had haunted him immediately dropped from his shoulders; for a committee of admiring City gentlemen undertook the discharge of his private and public debts, and eventually paid out on his behalf some twenty thousand pounds. Nor were his supporters unmindful that a patriot, however devoted, might also be an epicure; and through the gates of the King's Bench Prison flowed an astonishing profusion of practical but luxurious tributes, game and hams and salmon and numerous hampers of wine, a butt of ale, live turtles, and forty-five hogsheads of American tobacco. The last two gifts came from across the Atlantic, where the colonists were beginning to pay a significant regard to the English patriot's sufferings. Other presents had been contributed by local Councils or by private clubs who wished to indicate their "indignation and abhorence" of the government's behaviour. His visitors were innumerable, many women among them, including the infatuated wife of one of his foremost civic allies. Persecution and imprisonment had given him an established place. During his earlier trials we see Wilkes's character in a state of evolution, responding to different emergencies, still partly fluid, capable, had circumstances warranted, of proceeding to develop along entirely different lines. From this juncture, its shape is definite, and, though the events of the next few years fill a large and important chapter in the constitutional history of England, they add comparatively little to our knowledge of Wilkes himself. He was now finally identified with the ideas he stood for; but as usual it fell to his opponents to lend a helping hand. Had the King's hatred of Wilkes been less passionately personal, the administration might not have embarked on the decisive step of expelling him from Parliament, and Wilkes could not then have raised the one tremendous issue that formed a convenient epitome of the whole of the Wilkite cause. Henceforward the problem was clear-cut, and Wilkes both in speech and writing presented it again and again, emphasising both its immense gravity and its extreme simplicity. Were free electors to be deprived of the right of sending to Parliament the representative whom they had chosen? Such a right was "coeval with our Constitution"; it was an essential part of "the original compact between the sovereign . . . and the subject. . . ." Yet the House, in retaliation for Wilkes's treatment of Lord Weymouth's letter, which was alleged to have precipitated the "Massacre of St. George's Fields" and which Wilkes had caused to be printed with appropriate observations, once more expelled him from their midst, on February 4, 1769.

The challenge was promptly taken up. During the months of February, March and April, Wilkes was thrice re-elected to sit for Middlesex and, as often, refused admittance by his fellow-members. On the last occasion the government, who despaired of finding any other candidate, had been reduced to putting up a certain Colonel Luttrell, a man whose reputation for profligacy far exceeded that of Wilkes and who was also renowned for drunkenness, dishonesty and brutal blackguardism. Yet, in spite of an attempted show of force which collapsed against the firm front maintained by Wilkes's supporters, the Colonel received less than three hundred votes and Wilkes was again elected by a large majority; whereupon the House of Commons, abandoning the last pretence of constitutional procedure, passed a motion that Colonel Luttrell "ought to have been returned," and, to the astonishment of the entire kingdom, installed him in Wilkes's stead. It was the fifth act of a tragi-comedy, declared Burke, "acted by His Majesty's servants . . . for the benefit of Mr. Wilkes and at the expense of the Constitution." From the point of view of the prisoner in King's Bench, the effects of royal obstinacy and parliamentary stupidity had much to recommend them; many observers, as Walpole remarked, though they had little affection for Wilkes, were beginning to regard the constitutional aspect of the question with considerable misgivings, and turned "to the study of those controversies that agitated this country a hundred years ago"; even Pitt, now metamorphosed as the Earl of Chatham, emerged from the shades to deliver a speech of solemn warning. The written debate was endless; Johnson, as government pensioner, supplied a specious and discernible pamphlet, entitled *The False Alarm;* but simultaneously there flashed across the sky, launched by an unknown hand, successive thunderbolts of diatribe bearing the name of "Junius"—the famous *"Letters"* which touched no one whom they failed to blast yet, as they annihilated, often conferred an air of satanic grandeur which many of their trivial victims certainly did not deserve.

Such testimonials were more valuable than the heartiest mob-applause. True to his policy of moderation, Wilkes made no attempt to exploit either his fourth expulsion from Parliament or his eventual release from the King's Bench Prison, which took place on April 17, 1770. During his imprisonment, in January, 1769, he had been elected an Alderman of the City of London; and, when he re-emerged, having discharged his score, it was in the rôle of City Magistrate that he elected to claim his revenge. Grafton had meanwhile fallen, only to be succeeded by Lord North, whose close and subservient collaboration with George III involved, among other direct results, a disgraceful and disastrous war and the loss of the American colonies. The reputation of the House of Commons had dropped to its lowest level; and over the question of the liberty of the press, with special reference to the right of London newspapers to print full reports of parliamentary proceedings, Wilkes was able to humiliate his old opponents, yet never for a moment transgress the strictest rules of magisterial decorum. The messengers of the House of Commons were arrested in the City; the Lord Mayor, summoned to appear before the Commons, was committed to the Tower. On both sides, resentment was furious; but there occurred no popular commotion to equal the riots of 1768; and during the years that lay ahead of him Wilkes was to show a peculiar aptitude for advancing by slow degrees, and for allowing his opponents to accept defeat by seeming, with an air of dignified deliberation, to submit to the inevitable.

The English grow fond of their enemies—first accustomed to
their existence, then attached to them as a part of the traditional
scheme of things. The Wilkite agitation had slowly subsided; in
1774, the year of the "Boston Tea Party," Wilkes was elected
Lord Mayor; in 1775 he at length returned to Parliament. The
King, if not reconciled to "that devil Wilkes," had now finally
made up his mind to letting the devil lie; and only a lingering
odour of brimstone clung to the Lord Mayor's robes. Thus he
appears in Pine's portrait which hangs in the Guildhall, a
companion-piece to a portrait by the same artist which decorates
the walls of the grateful House of Commons. Here is Wilkes on
his best behaviour, not subdued, but tranquillised and domesticated. No painter could hope to disguise his squint; but about
the vigorous face there is a look of sobriety which accords with
the furred collar of his robe and the massive chain of office. The
determination and the fire persist. Relatively little attention
has been paid to Wilkes's long and useful career from his re-
election in 1775 to his final retirement from public life in 1790;
yet during that period, notwithstanding the defection of some
of his supporters and the hostility incurred by his sharp tongue
and supercilious attitude in certain quarters of the City, the influence he exerted was uniformly liberal; and now we hear of
him busy with prison reform, now boldly advocating religious
toleration—had not Whitefield offered up public prayers for
him during his own adversity?—now championing the cause of
the American colonists, whose gifts of turtles and tobacco had
already expressed their admiration while he languished, a genial
martyr, in the dungeons of the King's Bench.

Looking back, he found that he had reasons for pride. General
warrants—the liberty of the press—the freedom of the electorate
—on each issue he had fought and on each he had carried the
day. Each battle represented a victory. And what victories could
be of greater consequence to the happiness and well-being of
individual British subjects? "The middle and inferior sort" had
had cause to thank him. Strange that the ardour he had brought
to their service had been kindled, at least in its remote origins,

by selfish personal motives, and that he had been not so much
an enthusiast who welcomed the struggle as an opportunist
swept into the controversy through a series of surprising hazards!
But if he reflected on the oddity of his progress, Wilkes was too
philosophic—perhaps too cynical—a character to quarrel with
its outcome. No touch of public humbug clouded his private
utterance. He preserved always his equanimity and air of ironic
poise; yet his cynicism was not untempered by the addition of
Christian virtues, in particular the twin virtues of Hope and
Charity. He was unacquainted with Faith, he had once remarked to his daughter; "but the other two good girls are my
favourites . . ."; and certainly during the course of a long life
he had needed their assistance. Thanks to Hope, he had come
cheerfully through a succession of bewildering trials; and it
was under the influence of her companion virtue that he now
accomplished a more meritorious and a far more difficult feat—
he outlived his success with dignity, and maintained his integrity
as a human being when the moment of triumph had passed. He
was still the scholar, the man of pleasure, the devoted father.
Learned editions of Catullus and Theophrastus appeared to
bear witness to his abiding love of books. His conversation had
the same energy and reckless gusto that, a quarter of a century
earlier, had startled Edward Gibbon.

Sometimes he ventured a smile at his own tumultuous record,
scolding an old woman in the street whose cracked voice revived
the ancient cry of "Wilkes and Liberty"; while for George III,
who, at last obliged to meet him face to face, was astonished at
the civility and gentlemanliness of the diabolical foe, he reserved
the candid admission that he *"never was a Wilkite."* Events were
gradually passing him by. During the summer months of 1780,
the London crowd—his "old pupils" of 1768—rose against
those same principles of religious toleration that he himself had
always strenuously defended; the Gordon Riots set London
aflame; and Wilkes, amid the "tremendous roar" of a drunken
and furious mob, when the kennels of Holborn ran with blazing alcohol from Langdale's sacked distillery, and houses and

prisons went up in a promiscuous bonfire, directed the guards who had been posted to defend the Bank of England. Nine years later reports of revolutionary happenings in France surprised and disconcerted him. Like Gibbon, he could discern no connection between his own activities and the bloody events that were then convulsing Paris—no link between the encouragement his example had given to the American colonists and an upheaval that owed much of its inspiration to the War of Independence. Men who have fallen behind are often supremely miserable; but the latter days of Wilkes's existence, divided among Polly, a homely but affectionate mistress and various natural offspring, were harmonious and unruffled. He lived on in a world that had begun to forget his story, an antiquated but energetic and good-humoured figure in white-powdered wig and dashing scarlet coat; and death, when it approached, came by slow and considerate stages. His last recorded words were a tribute to his "beloved and excellent daughter." He died on Tuesday, December 26, 1797; and at his request a single phrase was engraved upon his coffin:

"The remains of John Wilkes, a Friend to Liberty"

—an epitaph which, although at once briefer and more expressive than most sepulchral inscriptions of that or, indeed, of any other period, does little justice to the strange assemblage of sensual and spiritual traits marked so strongly and united so boldly in the features of the living man.

EPILOGUE

———— ◆ ————

A S JAMES BOSWELL during the spring days of 1768
rolled, gay and expectant, along the road to London, then
loud with the huzza-ing of Wilkite mobs, he devoted himself to
the elaboration of a "memorable fancy." He compared his mind
to a lodging-house, peopled by guests both invited and unin-
vited: "ladies of abandoned manners" who went rustling up the
staircase and whose noisy laughter reverberated from behind
bedroom doors; puritans prophesying damnation, to the owner's intense alarm; Catholic priests who had moved in and out
but had left some lingering traces of solemn religious splendour;
deists whose heterodox arguments increased the domestic hubbub. Henceforward, he determined, he would reform his household, expel the abandoned women and ranting false prophets,
and keep only such guests as were sober and well conducted. The
fancy has a peculiarly Boswellian cast; but it might be appropriated by any human being whose mind has remained open to the
exciting, disturbing influx of ideas and sensations. In some
respects, it might be enlarged on. Besides public apartments
crowded with daily callers, the mind includes dusky galleries
and capacious, cobwebbed store-rooms, filled with the portraits
of ancestors and the relics of past ages. By the householder they
may be rarely visited; but, though doors are bolted or doorways
walled up, the influence of mysterious inhabitants filters through
the building.

Whether we acknowledge or ignore them, Boswell, Gibbon,
Sterne, Wilkes are ancestors to whom every educated citizen of
the modern world is more or less indebted. In this volume, I
have attempted to refresh their portraits, to suggest similarities
and dissimilarities, and the relation that they bear to a wide
historical background. Each is the portrait of a man obsessed

by an idea—an aim, at first confused and elementary, which gained definition and acquired momentum thanks to the conflict waged between circumstance and the individual ego. Both accident and personal genius helped to make up the pattern: the result was a human being and a life-story, highly characteristic of an individual temperament yet expressive of certain general attributes of the age in which it flourished. To each portrait can be attached some distinguishing features of the latter eighteenth century. Wilkes typifies that passion for personal and political freedom which Englishmen had inherited from the preceding epoch and were to carry on triumphantly throughout the next; Gibbon, the ironic detachment with which classicism mined away at classicist foundations. Boswell, inquisitive and introspective, tormented by the desire *"savoir tout au fond,"* represents a new revolutionary mode in thinking and in literature. As for Sterne—it was his function to introduce the cult of sympathy and, whereas the Augustan Age had condescended austerely towards the weak and miserable, to discover in unhappiness and helplessness a positive moral charm, thus anticipating the age of Jacobin enthusiasts who for the sake of humanity would sign inhuman sentences, till the tyrannous reign of good intentions was at last replaced by the relatively mild despotism of a military dictator. During the lifetime of our protagonists, the harmonious civilisation they had enjoyed was gradually dissolving; the rule of the profane virtues was almost over; the virtues of the age that followed were far more ambitious but also far more deadly. Perhaps it is as well that human beings can distinguish the ultimate implications of their own ideas, or survive to witness the final evolution of the movements they have started; that, although the past is imposing and the future threatening, the present continues to hold us, and that present pains and present pleasures—the search for personal happiness and personal justification—provide most of the exercise and entertainment our restless spirits need.

LONDON
September, 1944.

Date Due